Merciless Deaths

An Asha Kade Private Detective Mystery Thriller

Tikiri Herath

REBEL DIVA ACADEMY

Merciless Deaths

Asha Kade Private Detective Mystery Thriller Series

www.TikiriHerath.com

Copyright ©2022 Tikiri Herath

Edition: 2022

Library & Archives Canada Cataloging in Publication

E-book ISBN: 978-1-989232-83-5

Paperback ISBN: 978-1-990234-41-5

Hardback ISBN: 978-1-989232-54-5

Audiobook ISBN: 978-1-989232-93-4

Large Print book ISBN: 978-1-989232-36-1

Author: Tikiri Herath

Publisher Imprint: Rebel Diva Academy Press

Copy Editor: Stephanie Parent

Back Cover Headshot: Aura McKay

Tikiri

A Gift For You

Thank you for picking up my latest novel. There's a gift for you for picking up this book!

HER DEADLY END is a 250-page twisty serial killer thriller about an unusual murder-suicide case that Tanya (Tetyana), Asha, and Katy accidentally stumble upon while vacationing in Paradise Cove.

It's a pulse-pounding, nerve-shredding mystery of a devious serial predator stalking a small seaside town in Washington State.

You'll learn about the characters in the Merciless murder mystery series which features private detectives, Asha Kade & Katy McCafferty, and those in the new Tanya Stone FBI K9 series which features Special Agent Tanya (Tetyana) & Max, her K9 German Shepherd.

Join the VIP Red Heeled Rebels Club and receive your exclusive gift. Click the link below to join.

HER DEADLY END: A gripping thriller with a twisty end
https://books.tikiriherath.com/ts-b0-mmm-herdeadlyend

There is no explicit sex, heavy cursing, or graphic violence in these books. There is, however, a closed circle of suspects, many twists and turns, fast-paced action, and nail-biting suspense.

NO DOG IS HARMED IN THESE BOOKS. EVER. But the villains always are.

The Red Heeled Rebels Universe

The Red Heeled Rebels universe of mystery thrillers, featuring your favorite kick-ass female characters:

Tanya Stone FBI K9 Mystery Thrillers
www.TikiriHerath.com/Thrillers
NEW FBI thriller series starring Tetyana from the Red Heeled Rebels as Special Agent Tanya Stone, and Max, as her loyal German Shepherd. These are serial killer thrillers set in Black Rock, a small upscale resort town on the coast of Washington state.
Her Deadly End
Her Cold Blood
Her Last Lie
Her Secret Crime
Her Dead Girl
Her Perfect Murder
Her Grisly Grave

Coming soon!

———◦———

Asha Kade Private Detective Murder Mysteries

www.TikiriHerath.com/Mysteries

Each book is a standalone murder mystery thriller, featuring the Red Heeled Rebels, Asha Kade and Katy McCafferty. Asha and Katy receive one million dollars for their favorite children's charity from a secret benefactor's estate every time they solve a cold case.

Merciless Legacy
Merciless Games
Merciless Crimes
Merciless Lies
Merciless Past
Merciless Deaths
One more to come.

———◦———

Red Heeled Rebels International Mystery & Crime - The Origin Story

www.TikiriHerath.com/RedHeeledRebels

The award-winning origin story of the Red Heeled Rebels characters. Learn how a rag-tag group of trafficked orphans from different places united to fight for their freedom and their lives, and became a found family.

The Girl Who Crossed the Line
The Girl Who Ran Away
The Girl Who Made Them Pay
The Girl Who Fought to Kill
The Girl Who Broke Free
The Girl Who Knew Their Names

The Girl Who Never Forgot
This series is now complete.

The Accidental Traveler
www.TikiriHerath.com
An anthology of personal short stories based on the author's sojourns around the world.

The Rebel Diva Nonfiction Series
www.TikiriHerath.com/Nonfiction
Your Rebel Dreams: 6 simple steps to take back control of your life in uncertain times.

Your Rebel Plans: 4 simple steps to getting unstuck and making progress today.

Your Rebel Life: Easy habit hacks to enhance happiness in the 10 key areas of your life.

Bust Your Fears: 3 simple tools to crush your anxieties and squash your stress.

Collaborations
The Boss Chick's Bodacious Destiny Nonfiction Bundle
Dark Shadows 2: Voodoo and Black Magic of New Orleans

Tikiri's novels are available around the world, on all Amazon stores everywhere. The nonfiction books are available on Apple, Kobo, Barnes & Noble, Indigo Chapters, and all good bookstores around the world.

All these books are also available in libraries everywhere. Just ask your friendly local librarian or your local bookstore to order a copy via Ingram Spark.

Happy reading.

MERCILESS DEATHS

A MERCILESS MURDER MYSTERY THRILLER

The Belly of the Beast

The young woman's anguished screams echoed loudly, reverberating off the thick steel walls.

The men ignored her.

They had a job to do. And their boss was watching.

"Stop it!" she cried, tears streaming down her face.

Her thighs and shoulders were bruised, and her long, disheveled blonde hair had fallen over her eyes.

She couldn't see much, but she couldn't push her hair off her face either, as her hands and feet had been bound by yellow marine cable. The rope cut deep into her flesh, creating raw, red marks around her wrists and ankles.

She could hear the waves slam against the outer hull of the vessel, and the constant swaying was making her nauseous. She struggled to get to her knees, but she was exhausted from the beating they'd given her only moments ago.

She was the one they were after. She knew they would kill her and dump her body into the ocean.

That was, before the men turned on her boyfriend.

The two thugs were now focused on the young man on the ground, their fat fists pounding his rail-thin body. One punch was so fierce he jerked up like a ragged puppet and landed with a dull thud on the hard floor.

Her boyfriend was an innocent man.

He was an artist who went mushroom picking in the woods, smoked weed on weekends, and graffiti-painted peace signs on the corporate buildings of downtown Seattle. The worst violence he'd experienced in his life—until now—was the day his puppy got hit by a car when he was seven years old.

"Let him go!" screamed the girl through her sobs. She turned to the third man in the room. "Why are you doing this to us?"

The third man was sitting in a chair by the spiral steel stairway, carefully positioned away from where the beatings were taking place.

In blue jeans and a golf shirt, he looked like a suburban dad—a typical middle-aged man you'd find yourself seated next to at a weekend football tournament. He observed the events like he was watching a game.

He hadn't said a word since he came into the room, but the girl knew he ran this macabre show.

Something glinted under the morbid yellow light on the floor by his chair.

It was a knife.

No.

It was a cleaver.

"He did nothing to you," shrieked the girl. "Tell them to stop! Please!"

The man in the chair merely raised an eyebrow.

"I told you, I don't remember it!" she cried.

One thug stopped his punching to wipe the sweat from his brow. "Stop screeching like a wildcat in heat." He shot an ugly smirk her way. "No one's gonna hear you down here, sugar."

The young woman kept her face pointed at the leader of the crew. "How many times do I have to tell you I don't remember any of it? Let us go! Please!"

"Try harder," the man replied, speaking for the first time since his arrival.

His voice was calm and low, but firm, like he was confident of his place as a respected man in his community. Someone others always listened to.

The woman broke into sobs, phlegm and tears rolling down her reddened cheeks.

"Enough." The man in the chair turned to his goons and put a hand up. "I think she got the message."

The thugs stopped kicking the man on the ground.

The girl's boyfriend moaned in pain. Trails of blood trickled down his face onto the hard surface under his shoulders, mixing with remnants of diesel and engine oil. His breath was harsh and raspy, and he was convulsing in pain.

He didn't look like he would survive this day.

But all three men's eyes were now on the girl.

"Do you remember it all now?" said the man in the chair, his voice as cold as the steel walls.

"No!"

"Try, if you want to live. Start from the top."

"Four, four, I think...," the girl stammered through her tears. "But I don't remem—"

"Will this help?" One thug raised his foot over the young man's head.

"No!" she yelled, her voice high-pitched, shrill. "Let me think!"

The men waited.

"Four... four.... six... nine...." She stumbled over her words, her voice cracking, her chest heaving. "I'm trying..."

The man in the chair looked bored, like the game he'd come to watch wasn't fun anymore.

He straightened up. "Remember, if it's wrong, it's not you, but others who will pay for it."

"Four, four, six, nine, zero, one, eight," blurted the girl.

She turned to the man in the chair, blinking away her tears.

"Can we go now?" she whispered. "Please."

He turned to his thugs.

"You know what to do," he said.

They nodded.

One goon swooped down to pick up the cleaver. He walked over to the young man on the floor, the deadly weapon raised high in the air, and towered over him.

The girl collapsed, like all her blood had been drained from her. She couldn't save her boyfriend now.

The thug swiped the cleaver down.

Outside those thick steel-hulled walls, no one heard her heart-wrenching screams.

New York

Chapter One

"Delivery for you, Asha!"

I looked up just in time to see the mail carrier wave from outside.

It was a cool Monday morning in April, and I'd been staring out the open window, my troubled mind elsewhere.

Outside, gentrified Harlem was bustling with people and traffic, hustling their way to work or school. Normal folk with normal lives.

There were days I wished I could be one of them.

"Thanks, Justin!" I yelled before the postal carrier disappeared around the corner.

I walked over to the front door. The package had fallen at the feet of our new street board. Katy, my bakery's finance manager, had placed it under the red canvas awning, just outside the door, that weekend.

The sign said: *Life is Short. Eat cake first. Welcome to the Red Heeled Rebels bakery.*

Katy had thought it was the perfect message to attract more walk-ins. My head chef, Luc, had thought it made his upscale cakes sound cheap.

I had stayed out of the debate, my mind swirling around the strange message left on my phone the day before.

It had been from Mary Hudson, an old friend I hadn't heard from in years.

She and her husband had retired to Portland and were living with their children and grandchildren. They were finally safe and sound, but her confusing message hinted at something terrible.

I'd called back five times since then, but no one had picked up the phone. That had been even more disquieting.

Her voice had been muffled and the number unlisted. I was no longer sure if it had even been my friend.

I stepped around Katy's board and picked up the brown package. "Hey!"

Win was running toward me along the sidewalk, dodging other pedestrians, a bright smile on her pretty face and her short black hair bobbing up and down.

Luc's wife, Win, was my resident computer expert who worked for a cyber security company in Manhattan. Or the White-Hat-Hacker-Babe, as she liked to call herself.

Her petite frame and casual dress meant most people mistook her for a teenager and sometimes didn't believe her Stanford education and higher-than-average IQ.

She stomped up to me, out of breath.

"Come to see Luc?" I said, straightening up with the package in my hand. "He's in the back."

"He said you got a weird call. Want me to trace the number?"

I nodded and opened the bakery's door for her.

Win skipped past me, her excitement to solve yet another of my puzzles palpable. She was always bright-eyed and bushy-tailed, even when I roped her into the most challenging investigations.

I closed the front door and followed her into my office.

I stepped behind my desk and laid the package on my lap, my mind still whirring. Win plopped on the chair across from me, picked up my phone without even asking, and started clicking away.

Normally, I wouldn't let anyone touch my cell, but this time, I let her do her thing. Win had hacked into the highest security networks in the country. My phone would be a breeze for her brilliant mind.

"Did a squirrel die in the chimney again?"

I looked up to see Katy walking into the office.

My best friend, Katy, always looked elegant in her hand-tailored, plus-sized dresses and her Irish red hair in a beautiful updo. She came to work every morning looking like she was headed to a fancy soirée instead of a bakery.

"Now you mention it, it stinks in here," mumbled Win, but her eyes remained glued to my phone.

Katy sniffed the air suspiciously. She was right. There was an odor coming from somewhere, but I had more important matters at hand.

I turned the package around with a frown. The postmark was from a local postal station, but there was no sender address.

That wasn't a good sign.

I placed the parcel on the table, plucked a pair of scissors from the drawer, and cut through the soft cardboard.

Katy peered over my desk as I opened the top flaps.

"A box in a box," she said, raising a brow.

I pulled the smaller packet from the cardboard package. The second box was wrapped in dark red paper, the kind you'd buy from a dollar store.

I ripped it open.

Katy clinched her nose with her fingers. "My goodness, what did you get?"

The stink was stronger now. It was the vomit-inducing smell of rotten flesh, and it was coming from the box.

I snipped through the smaller box and pulled the flaps down.

Win snapped her head my way.

"Eek!" she screamed, jumping out of her chair, dropping my phone on the desk.

"What in heaven's name!" cried Katy, stepping hurriedly toward the door, stumbling over her own feet.

I stared at my delivery.
Why would anyone mail me a dead rat?

Chapter Two

Something was stuck under the dead rodent's tail.

Holding my breath and using my scissors, I pried the business card out, trying not to disturb the remains. Win and Katy watched me nervously from a safe distance, hands over their noses.

I pulled the card out of the box and laid it on my desk, taking care to only touch it with the tips of the clippers. Then, I rooted around in the drawer for a pair of gloves.

While I owned the Red Heeled Rebels bakery, I had stopped baking cakes a long time ago, leaving that to my talented protégé, Luc. Very few people knew of my secret vocation as a private investigator.

The bakery provided an excellent façade for my moonlighting work. My second business had no name, no address, no phone line, and no bank account. Nothing that could be traced back to me.

The only clients I got were referred by a dead woman who seemed to pull my puppet strings from the grave.

Madame Bouchard had known me in my troubled youth. And she had known which buttons to push to make me do her bidding.

The day she died, she had made me promise to serve all her friends or family who called for help. In exchange for solving a case, her estate lawyer would transfer a million dollars in donations to our orphanages around the world.

How could anyone say no to an offer like that?

Even with her dying breath, she had manipulated me. But this time for a good cause, or so I liked to think.

Trying not to retch at the stench of the deceased animal, I put on the gloves and turned the card around.

"What does it say?" said Win.

It wasn't a business card, but a rectangle of thick paper on which someone had glued on cut-out letters from a magazine. I read it out loud.

"You're trapped. Like a rat."

"Who's it from?" asked Katy, frowning.

I flipped the card over and back again.

"No signature."

This wasn't the first time I'd received a sinister message.

It had started with an anonymous phone call a few months ago, followed by a nasty note stuck to the front door of the bakery. It had said; "I know who you are." Then came the ominous graffiti on the wall facing the back alleyway, threatening to burn us down.

The local police precinct knew me well. Not as a private detective, but as a small business owner who complained too much.

That paranoid bakery lady again.

As far as they were concerned, this was the annoying but innocuous work of bored street kids, a crazed loon, or a rival baker in town, none of whom would actually do harm.

Their plates were full of assaults, rapes, and murders. Serious crimes. My anonymous phone calls and poison pen letters got little traction with them.

I wished I could tell them about Madame Bouchard and the promise I'd made at her deathbed. I wished I could tell them about my work as an investigator, but that meant exposing our history.

Risking the lives of my found family was not something I was about to do.

Katy, Luc, Win, and everyone in my small but close-knit circle of friends had sought refuge in New York with one goal in mind. To get away from the horrors of our youths. We'd only hoped to start life fresh in a place where we didn't have to worry about goons chasing us, beating us, or trying to sell us.

Being trafficked survivors was never an easy thing. Every time I thought our nightmares were behind us, something arrived at our doorstep to remind me of the darkness in the world.

Like this dead rat.

I put the card back on my desk and searched for my phone, which Win had thrown down in her hurry to race out.

"It's time to make the cops take this seriously," I muttered to myself.

The mobile rang just as I picked it up, making me jump. I nearly dropped it on the dead rat.

I accepted the call and put the phone to my ear.

"Asha!" came a panicked voice.

It was Mary from Portland. Finally.

I put the phone on speaker mode. "Where are you?"

"Did you get my message?" There was a slight tremor in her voice.

"I've been calling you all morning," I said, stepping away from my desk and walking toward the door. The rotting smell of the rat was overpowering my office now.

I squeezed past Katy and Win into the bakery's empty reception area. They trailed behind me, flanking me on either side. I could feel their hot breath on my neck as they tried to listen in.

"So glad I got a hold of you," said Mary in a faint voice.

The sound of traffic rumbling came from her end, followed by a swoosh as a car raced by, then more rumblings.

Is she in the middle of a highway?

"Just got terrible news," said Mary before I could inquire. Her voice was high-pitched, like she was anxious, distracted. "Ever since the police said they couldn't do much, I've been pulling my hair out. I didn't know who to turn to."

"First things first," I said. "Are you in a safe place right now?"

"Hubby and me are fine," came Mary's voice, though her tone said otherwise.

"Where are you?"

"At a gas station off route five-oh-seven. Outside Tacoma. Oliver's filling up the car. We just left Seattle and are heading back to Oregon."

That partly explained why I hadn't been able to get a hold of her.

"What were you doing in Seattle?"

"Jane's my only cousin," said Mary, her voice shaking. "My only family left in the world. It's a terrible thing."

Next to me, Win rolled her eyes. I could imagine what was going through her mind.

These old fogies never get to the point.

Mary and Oliver Hudson had been lighthouse keepers off the coast of Oregon for decades. They had lived a remote existence most of their adult life, working for the Coast Guard or private island owners.

That was how I had met them.

With my friends, Tetyana and Katy's help, I had hunted a devious killer who had been terrorizing their lighthouse. It had been a traumatizing weekend we would all rather forget. Oliver and Mary had packed their bags and called it quits soon after that experience.

"What about your cousin in Seattle?" I asked, trying my best to remain patient. "Is she okay?"

"Jane's missing!" cried Mary. "Gone. Just like that!"

"How did that happen?"

"Went to town to go shopping last Saturday, but she never came home. Chris's in awful shape. I told him you would help him. You will, won't you?"

"Who's Chris?" I said, frowning.

"Her husband. Chris Grayson. He's at the end of his tether, especially after what happened to their daughter."

Win took a sharp breath in next to me.

This story was getting more convoluted by the second.

"What happened to their daughter?" asked Katy, leaning toward the phone.

"Poor girl. Barely eighteen. No one should bury their children. It was hard on Chris and Jane. They fell apart after that."

Something nagged at the back of my head. That surname. A story. A news piece from somewhere from a long time ago.

"How did your niece die?" I said, softening my voice.

"She ran away from home one night. They looked for her for years but never found her body. They buried an empty coffin, but Chris and Jane never recovered from the ordeal."

Chapter Three

M ary's voice cracked. "Now Jane's gone and vanished."

"What are the police saying?" I asked.

There was silence on the other end, so that for a moment I wondered if we'd lost the connection.

"Jane has a, er, reputation," came Mary's voice, hesitant, almost inaudible. "There were some signs..."

"What do you mean?" I said, my brow furrowed.

"Story around town is she started drinking heavily after Lily's funeral."

An edge had crept into Mary's voice.

"She started acting strange. Disappearing on weekends, sometimes calling Chris from a hotel room. She lost her daughter, for heaven's sake. That would drive anyone to drink. People were saying she was having an affair, but I don't believe it. She'd never do that."

Everyone believed their loved ones would never engage in wicked deeds. Even after they got exposed, the apologists were far more common than not.

As much as I cared for Mary, I wondered how much of what she was telling us was steeped more in emotion than facts.

"Have the police found any clues?" said Katy.

"They say they're under-resourced. It's infuriating. They told Chris to be prepared if she left him for her lover. I tell you, Jane's not that kind of woman. It's just mean-spirited gossip."

"Do you have *any* idea what's happened to her?" I said.

"Something terrible." Mary's voice was shaking again. "I feel it in my bones. Find her!"

Oliver's voice came from the background.

"Did she say she'll come?"

Mary turned away from the phone and mumbled something.

"Mary, please tell Oliver I'm not licensed in Washington State," I said, speaking loudly, hoping her husband could hear too. "But I'll find a private detective who can assist you over there."

A fumbling sound came, followed by Oliver's voice.

"Asha, we know you. We trust you. You helped us last time. Can't you at least come and see? Talk to Chris. He's desperate. He's already lost his daughter. This is killing him and it's killing Mary."

I sighed. I had a dead rat on my desk and threatening calls to deal with, but it was hard to say no to old friends.

"The police think Jane doesn't want to be found," said Oliver. "People do strange things when they lose their children, but she'd never walk out on her family."

Win, who had been busily tapping on her phone while I was talking, put a hand on my arm.

"Check this out," she said, showing me her screen. "Chris Grayson's the multimillionaire who holds ten patents in mobile engineering. He's a big deal in the tech world. I'd heard his name before."

"That's him," came Oliver's voice. "He did well for himself, but all the money in the world doesn't help bring a dead child or your wife back, does it?"

No one replied.

"There's one more thing you need to know," he added.

"Oh?" I said.

"Chris thinks someone's tracking his Internet activities, listening in on his calls, and even bugging his house..." He trailed off, sounding embarrassed. "He's become paranoid. Thinks there's a conspiracy against him."

Win perked up. "Someone hacked into his home?"

"Highly unlikely," said Oliver. "They live in a five-million-dollar float home in Hidden Cove. It's a gated community on a private lake with twenty-four-hour security alarms and guards. I doubt anyone has bugged his house or tapped his phone. He's just not himself these days. Thought you should know."

The phone crackled. Mary had taken over again.

"I used to play with Jane when we were kids, before my parents moved to Oregon. You don't abandon family when they're in trouble, right?"

"No, Mary," I replied in a soft voice.

"So, you'll come?"

After taking down Chris Grayson's contact details, I hung up, feeling like I'd just added another weight to my shoulders.

Win looked up from the news article she was reading.

"Tetyana's on FBI training near Seattle. She could help?"

"A missing woman who might be having an affair and has gone AWOL before?" I shook my head. "This is small potatoes. The FBI wouldn't lift a finger for something even the local police are downplaying."

Katy covered her nose as a wave of stink wafted from my office.

I frowned.

Did that poison pen letter and the dead rat have anything to do with Mary's call? Or was it just another loony threat to the bakery?

I shook my head to clear it.

The dead rat had been packaged and mailed well before Mary called.

I was about to go over and close the box over the animal when Win grabbed my arm.

"Check this out," she said. "Old article about the missing heiress. The daughter vanished on the same day and month as her mother, exactly two years apart."

Katy raised her brows. "Coincidence?"

I didn't believe in coincidences. There were too many red flags in this case, and we hadn't even started investigating it.

Win turned to me, her eyes shining.
"When do we fly out?"

Chapter Four

"**W**atch out!"

I pulled Katy away just in time.

The gray Honda Civic roared by us, its tires squealing on the asphalt.

Something rocketed out of the car's front window, smacked against my chest, and fell to the ground.

I jumped back, startled.

The Honda didn't stop.

Two drivers behind the car leaned on their horns, deafening us. A yellow cab screeched to a halt in the next lane, barely avoiding a collision with the rogue vehicle. An enraged face popped out of the taxi driver's window, followed by obscenities hurled into the air.

Katy raised a fist as the Honda revved down the busy street. "Jerk! You almost killed us!"

My heart was pounding, but my eyes were fixated on the car's license plate like laser beams. The taxi had slowed its getaway, and I only needed three seconds to memorize the numbers.

The Honda turned a fast right and disappeared around the corner of the bakery, almost hitting an elderly woman on the crosswalk.

More shouting. More swearing.

"What an idiot," spat Katy, turning an irate face toward me. "He could have flattened us like pancakes."

Katy and I had been standing on the curb in front of the bakery, waiting for our rideshare to take us to the airport. Win was in the kitchen saying goodbye to Luc, who wasn't too happy his wife had decided to take off to Seattle with such short notice.

I surveyed the scene.

There was no reason for a vehicle to jump the curb here unless they deliberately wanted to hit us. If I hadn't been keeping an eye up the street for our ride, Katy and I would have been crushed against the wall.

Katy kicked at something on the ground. "He threw his garbage at us, too. Seriously, New York drivers are the worst."

I looked down at the empty plastic bottle rolling near my feet. This was what had hit me in the chest.

"I'm filing a complaint with the city," huffed Katy. "They need to put a *Slow Down* sign in this corner."

I bent down and picked up the bottle. I was wrong. It wasn't empty.

I turned the crushed cannister in my hands. Instead of water, it held a crumpled piece of paper.

"Katy, do you have a pair of tweezers in your purse?"

She raised an eyebrow.

I held the bottle up.

"That wasn't just a bad city driver. I'd bet you anything this was the same guy who sent us the dead rat."

"Hey!" came a bright voice behind us.

We turned to see Win running down the steps with her backpack bouncing on her shoulders. "What's with all this shouting?"

"Some psycho tried to run us over just now," said Katy. "But Asha thinks it was—"

I nudged Katy with my elbow to silence her. David, my fiancé, who ran the martial arts dojo next to the bakery, was standing at the front doorway, his hands on his hips, and a frown on his face.

David leaped down the steps and marched toward us.

He gave me a concerned look. "What happened? Just got off a phone call when I heard the commotion."

I forced a bright smile. "New York drivers doing what New York drivers do. It'll be nice to get to the slower pace of the West Coast for a change."

"There's our car," said Win, waving at our rideshare which was crawling along the street checking addresses. As soon as it stopped by us, Win jumped in, bag and all.

"Seattle, here we come!" she squealed. "Get in, ladies."

David turned to me. "Sounded like a car crash."

"It's all good, hun," I said, giving him a peck on the cheek.

My man was always thinking of me. It was why I loved him so much.

He picked up my luggage and walked over to the back of the car.

"I really don't like you taking off like this," he said as he returned to take Katy's two suitcases. As usual, she'd packed for a month.

"It's only for a week and Seattle's just a short red-eye away." I gave a gentle rib on his waist. "Remember when we used to hop across continents with bad guys chasing us?"

David put his hands on my shoulders and pulled me close, his anxious eyes on mine.

"There's a reason we don't do that anymore, babe."

"You worry too much. This is a missing person's case. Jane Grayson has probably run off with her boyfriend and is hiding somewhere," I said, keeping my smile intact.

If David knew what I suspected, he would get a heart attack and do everything he could to convince me to stay home.

I got on my tiptoes and draped my arms around his shoulders.

"What if I promise not to chase after Saudi traffickers or Russian gun runners? Girl Guide's promise. Would that make you feel better?"

With a resigned sigh, he pulled me in for a kiss.

"Just be careful."

"Hey, you two lovebirds," came Win's voice from the car. "We're going to be late for our flight."

With a parting kiss, I joined my friends in the backseat of our rideshare.

"Do you have the tweezers?" I said as soon as our car rolled onto the road.

Katy was ready. "Here you go."

Win leaned over my shoulders to see better.

"Someone sent us a message," I said, gently extricating the paper from inside the water bottle.

I unfolded it and smoothened it on my lap.

The pencil marks were light, and the lettering almost faded, but the message was clear.

You're not welcome in Seattle. You'll regret it if you go.

"My gosh," said Katy as her eyes scanned the words.

"Whoa," said Win, pulling out her phone and snapping a picture. "Let me cross-reference this and see if I can find anything in the handwriting databases I have access to."

"That's a long shot," I said as I reread the note. "It's written in all plain capital letters. I'd bet you there are no fingerprints either."

"Now I wish I got the license plate number," said Katy, shaking her head. "All I saw was a bearded man with a hat, scarf, and dark shades."

"A good disguise," I said. "But I got the number."

I turned to Win to give her the plate number I'd memorized before it vanished into the jumble of thoughts swimming inside my head.

"Check it out in your databases, but something tells me that plate is fake, too."

Win was already clicking away on her phone, her face taut. "Don't worry, I will find him."

"Whoever threw this at us and tried to mow us down knew where we are going and why," I said, trying to think this through.

"Chris Grayson," said Katy, her frown deepening. "He thinks someone hacked him. If his Internet and phone connections have been compromised, anyone would have heard your call."

"Found it!"

Katy and I both turned to Win.

"That Honda was stolen two days ago," said Win, giving us a triumphant smile. "That was no accident. That dude wanted to run you over."

I gave her a wry look. That wasn't reassuring.

I sat back in my seat, clutching the mysterious note in my hands.

"This is not just a missing woman's case, girls," I said. "Whatever this is, it's worth killing for."

Seattle

Chapter Five

Katy shot a disapproval glance at Win. "I can't believe you drank all that alcohol."

We had just deplaned in Seattle and were heading toward the airport's arrival terminal.

"First time in first class. We need more clients like Chris Grayson," said Win, walking next to Katy along the narrow corridor. "When is the next time someone's going to give us free champagne and let me lie all the way down on a plane?"

"And make me take all those photos," grumbled Katy. "You're a sucker for Instagram likes, you know that?"

I followed my friends as they headed toward the main exit, my mind troubled.

It was past midnight in Seattle.

I was thankful Katy had booked our hotel and a rideshare because all I wanted was to crash on a soft bed and stop my brain ruminating with potential worst-case scenarios.

The only communication with my recluse multi-millionaire client had been a three-minute call. Chris Grayson had been so nervous about someone listening into our conversation, he'd told me to meet him at his home and tell no one I was coming, before hanging up abruptly.

His voice had been so shaky and faint, that for a moment I had thought I was talking to a septuagenarian. But Chris was a fifty-year-old man.

Fifteen minutes after that call, Katy had spotted the ten-thousand-dollar retainer in our bakery account.

I wondered about Chris. I preferred my clients to share details and be upfront with me.

If he hadn't been related to Mary and if Mary hadn't pleaded the way she did, I would have shut this case before it had even started.

Perhaps he'll open up once we meet him face-to-face.

But the stolen Honda that had almost bowled us over in New York was still fresh in my mind. I wondered if I had made a big mistake in bringing my friends on this trip.

Win was a trafficked survivor as well, but she had adjusted to her new life after her escape, going to college, getting scholarships, then finding a good corporate job before marrying my head chef, Luc.

Katy had fought the traffickers along with me in our youth, when our lives had been at stake. While the trauma of those days resurfaced from time to time, she had outgrown her victim story, and was now a happily married suburban mom who loved her job at the bakery.

Her husband, Peace, was my business attorney, a man who'd been a close friend since I was a little girl and whom I considered a blood brother. David, my fiancé, hadn't escaped the bruises of our brutal past either, but he dealt with his harsh childhood by focusing on teaching martial arts at the dojo next door to the bakery.

My own nightmares flared up often at night. I'd toss, turn, and whimper until David would hold me tight and we'd both fall asleep, our cheeks wet with tears from memories we'd rather forget.

The last thing I wanted was to drag Katy and Win back to a place where those nightmares could be revived.

"Ms. Asha Kade?"

A sleek black limo had pulled up next to me. I was in the passenger pickup area, just outside the airport terminal doors, following my friends, but my mind lost in my new case.

I peered into the car. "And you are?"

The driver bent down and smiled.

He was a well-built, thirty-something man in a sharp black suit and a chauffeur's cap. His partner in the passenger seat was also in a black suit, except he wore his hair in short, neat dreads.

"We're your ride tonight."

I bent down to scrutinize these two men.

"Randy Wilson, ma'am, and my partner Noah James," said the driver. "Mr. Grayson asked us to pick you up."

I frowned. "He didn't say anything about sending a car."

The second man pulled up a printed paper which contained my full name in large print and gave me a sheepish grin. "We even made a sign."

He had a singsong voice, one that reminded me of the tropical Caribbean islands.

"Mr. Grayson thought you'd be tired after your flight and wanted to get you to your hotel hassle free," he added, flashing a smile as bright as the sun.

Both looked like well-groomed staff a wealthy man would hire, but my spider senses were on full alert. I wanted to trust these friendly people, but my past had taught me to question everything.

I turned to see where Katy and Win had gone to. They were shuffling along the side of the building, heading toward the rideshare line.

The limo driver jumped out, walked around, and opened the back door.

"I'll take care of your luggage, ma'am," he said amiably, gesturing at the backseat.

"Hey, Asha! What are you doing?"

I spun around. Win was calling for me. I gestured for her and Katy to come over.

"Is *that* our ride?" hollered Win, stopping in her tracks.

The two men exchanged a confused glance. The driver raised his eyebrows as Win started running our way.

"We get to take a limo!" she squealed, making other passengers nearby turn around and give us envious looks.

Before I could say anything, she scooted inside the car.

A dark shadow crossed the second man's face. It was so fleeting I wondered if I'd imagined it.

The driver scrunched his forehead and turned to Katy, who was now stomping our way, her bags in tow, an exhausted expression on her face.

"Mr. Grayson said nothing about other passengers," said the driver, scratching his head.

"They're part of my team," I said. "We're staying at the same hotel."

"Mr. Grayson's not very communicative these days," he said, giving me a small smile as if he was too embarrassed to speak ill of his employer. "He told me and Noah to pick you up, but I guess there's space for everyone."

I stepped toward the back of the limo, pretending to check for messages on my phone, while I snapped a discreet photo of the license plate.

Just in case.

The second man jumped out of his seat and gave a polite bow to Katy as she approached the car.

"May I take your bags, miss?"

Katy relaxed her shoulders and let out a loud sigh.

"Thank you so much," she said, pushing her suitcases his way. "I'm dead tired."

"You'll be in your hotel room in no time, miss," he replied as he lugged her suitcases toward the back of the limo.

Without even looking at me, Katy stumbled inside and plopped in the backseat with another exhausted sigh.

I checked my phone, but there were no missed calls, emails, or texts from Chris Grayson. Or even Mary. I clicked on Grayson's number. It rang three times before going to voice mail.

The chauffeur walked toward me, digging into his pocket. He pulled his own cell and turned the screen my way.

"This might help, ma'am," he said in a polite voice. "My instructions from Mr. Grayson."

I squinted at the small screen.

Plane arriving at 23:55 PST. Take the lady to her hotel.

Chris Grayson had sent the message. But having a white hat hacker like Win for a friend meant I knew it would be easy to fabricate a text. Or even an email.

Anything was possible.

The chauffeur gave me a wonky smile. "I imagine a certified accountant like yourself would want to check all the details? I'm only happy to oblige."

Accountant?

Chris Grayson must not trust his own employees. He was more paranoid than I expected.

"Coming, Asha?" called out Katy from inside the bowels of the limo. "I'm dying for a shower."

"Can we go now?" That was Win.

My friends were of no help.

Is it just me?

I walked over to the back door and climbed inside.

Randy Wilson smiled and gave me a salute before shutting the door.

I wondered if I was going to regret this decision.

Chapter Six

"We can't live our whole lives paranoid, Asha," said Katy.

Win was lying on the seat across from us, her head snuggled against the plush leather, her eyes closed, a happy smile on her face.

She had already got Katy to snap a series of Instagram-worthy pictures of her posing inside the limo.

"Ooh, check that out, will you?" Katy jabbed me with her elbow and pointed at the mini-bar by the driver's seat in front. "Chilled champagne in a bucket. They know how to treat us right."

Win opened her eyes. "Did someone say champagne?"

"Help yourself, ladies," called Noah from up front. "I'd serve you myself if I were in the back. Hope you don't mind."

"Of course not," said Win, scuttling toward the front and reaching for the bottle and a glass flute.

"Don't you think she's had enough?" I whispered, turning to Katy.

"She's a grown woman," she scolded, slapping my arm. "She works hard every day for her company and for you. Let her have some fun."

I sat back with a sigh.

David always said I wasn't good at relaxing. Perhaps he was right. Maybe I needed to loosen up a bit. Maybe I needed a glass of champagne.

Something caught my eyes from the back of the vehicle. I twisted around and peered through the tinted windows. Two defused yellow lights were shining through the glass.

I shuffled over to the end of the seat and squinted.

It was a white van. One of those plain utility cargo vehicles. There was no decal or sign in the front. It was hard to see who was inside, though it was driving close to our bumper.

I scanned the front of the vehicle.

Oregon plates.

I watched as it kept following us, turning corners when we turned, revving up when we were going through an intersection.

Was it tailing us?

Or was I being so suspicious, I couldn't distinguish between regular traffic and something sinister? But it was well past midnight, and the streets were quiet. There was no reason for it to drive so close.

You're not welcome in Seattle. You'll regret it if you go.

I sat up as the ominous words from the note in the water bottle sprang to mind.

I had only shared that strange message with Katy and Win. I hadn't wanted to worry David or Peace, but there was someone else I could tell.

I plucked my phone out of my pocket and hammered a quick message.

Tetyana knew we were coming to Seattle, but she was on a two-day training program in an FBI field office in the outskirts of the city. We had planned to meet her on Monday at our hotel. Three days from now.

"Just landed," I typed quickly. "Client sent limo. Going to hotel. Chauffeur & assistant up front."

I paused, wondering how to best share that note without alarming her.

"Someone doesn't want us to solve the case. Got an anon msg in NY. On alert, but not serious."

I typed in the limo's license plate number. If these men weren't who they said they were, she'd have something to go by.

"See you at dinner on Monday. Can't wait. Lots of love."

After hitting send, I clicked on our hotel's address on my phone's GPS. I had been to Seattle once, but I didn't know the full layout of the city. The online map told me we were heading downtown, which was our destination.

The van behind us could be the airport hotel shuttle, traveling downtown, carrying a bunch of weary passengers.

But why would it have Oregon plates then?

The clinking of glass made me turn back around.

"Are you *working*?" said Katy, frowning my way.

She had scooted over to join Win and had poured herself a glass of champagne, too.

"Risk management," I replied.

"You're missing the party," said Win. "Poured one for you too."

Noah turned around and gave her a friendly thumbs-up. Win raised her glass to the man, then gulped her drink down in seconds.

Katy took a sip and sank into her seat.

"Aaah." She turned a tired smile my way. "First-class seats and a limo to the hotel. Can you find more clients like this?"

I joined my friends and took the glass Katy offered. I did need to relax more. I was about to take a sip when Win belched and rocked her head.

She put her hand to her temple, like her head was throbbing. After all that drinking on the red-eye here, I wouldn't have been surprised if she was getting a headache.

Win doubled over, her hands shaking. She dropped her empty glass to the floor and made gagging sounds.

"You okay, hun?" I said, leaning over, worried now.

"Sleepy," she said in a slurred voice, not looking up.

"No wonder. It's almost one in the morning," said Katy, checking her phone. "And you're sloshed."

"I feel sick," slurred Win, sliding down on her seat. Katy and I helped to get her feet up so she could lie down. Win closed her eyes.

My spider senses were back on full alert.

I nudged Katy with my foot and gave her a hard look.

"What?" she said.

I wanted to tell her not to take another sip of that drink, but I didn't want the men to hear, especially as Noah kept turning around every few minutes as if to check on us.

My gut was raising too many flags. Something was off.

Katy took another sip, then another. Just as I reached over to bump that glass from her hand, she leaned away from me and let out a satisfied sigh. Next to her, Win let out a snore.

Noah turned around again.

"You ladies must be exhausted," he said, flashing his sunny smile again.

"I'm not complaining about the service," said Katy, waving her half-empty glass at him. "You may have to pry me out of here when we get to the hotel, though."

The men chuckled up front.

I turned my head around. The diffused yellow lights from the van were still boring through the back window. It was so close now, I could hear the loud rumble of its diesel engine.

Who tailgates a limo?

We were driving at normal speeds, perhaps even slightly faster.

I scanned the streets. We were in downtown Seattle, but in a deserted business area with tall skyscrapers lining the road. I double-checked the map on my phone and turned to the front.

"Randy," I called out to the chauffeur. "Any reason to take the long way there?"

"Construction," he replied, without turning around. "Seattle uproots half the roads every month. It's a major pain."

"They do the same in New York," I said, keeping my voice casual.

A light snore made me turn to my friends.

They had fallen asleep, Win's head on Katy's lap and Katy's head lolling to the side against the leather seat. Her half-empty glass of champagne was still in her hand.

I leaned across and plucked the flute from her. Her hands fell limp onto her lap.

I shuffled toward the front and placed my full glass and her half-drunk one on the mini bar. Just as I was about to return to my seat, the limo came to a complete stop.

We had parked on the side of the road. But our hotel was still ten minutes away.

I looked around.

We were in the financial district. Tall business buildings towered around us. Everyone had gone home for the night and the lights had all been turned off.

I peeked outside.

We had parked in front of an imposing concrete building with a bronze sign on the facade.

Union Lake Bank. Est 1931.

"Hey Randy, what are we doing here?" I said. "This isn't our hotel."

Noah opened his door, mumbled something, and dashed toward the bank.

"Noah needs to hit a cash machine," replied Randy in a quiet voice. He had his face down, his hands moving quickly over his lap. "Hope you ladies don't mind stopping for a minute."

I was only a foot away from the front seats, so I craned my neck.

My heart leaped to my mouth.

The gleaming Glock in Randy's lap was unmistakable.

He was attaching a silencer to it.

Chapter Seven

My own Glock was tucked safely in the locked cabinet in David's office. Back in New York.

Bringing my weapon would have meant a thousand and one questions from airport security. Besides, I didn't have a license to carry in Washington. They would have confiscated it, if not charged me.

My suspicions were proving to be correct. There was much more to this case than a simple missing woman.

I kicked myself.

Why didn't I take that message in the bottle more seriously?

I slid back into my seat slowly, my brain swirling like a hurricane.

Think, girl, think.

I tried to recall the martial arts techniques David had taught me, the ones that worked best in narrow, confined spaces. Whatever I did next, the safety of my friends was paramount.

Then again, how much of an advantage would I have over a Glock with a silencer pointing at us?

I slid further in my seat, closer toward the back door. Just a few more feet and I'd be able to wake my friends and get us out of here.

"Freeze."

Randy's friendly face had vanished, and in its place was an ugly scowl.

I stared down the barrel of his gun.

"Put your hands up, lady."

A noise came from the outside. Noah was returning to the car, but he was heading to the rear of the vehicle. The back door clicked open, and he stepped inside the limo, two feet from me.

He had gloves on now, and in his right hand was a gun with a silencer. But his weapon wasn't pointed at me. He was aiming at Katy's sleeping head.

I stared at Noah, then at Randy up in front. These weren't small-time amateurs. They knew what they were doing.

"Who are you?" I said, my voice hardening.

"You stay real quiet and do as we say," replied Noah.

I could still see the headlights of the cargo van behind us, parked right next to our bumper.

What's going on?

"We don't have time," growled Randy.

I turned to him, my hands still in the air. "What do you want with a team of boring accountants?"

"Like my buddy said, keep your mouth shut and follow instructions," he replied in a quiet voice.

He hadn't corrected me when I said *accountants*. Did this mean he didn't know who we really were? If that was true, we had one advantage over them.

My heart was pounding and my limbs were numb, but my brain whirled, trying to figure out an escape plan.

I would have to grapple with Noah who was blocking our only way out and make sure none of us got shot during the getaway. That was an impossible task. Katy and Win were still fast asleep.

My eyes flickered to the open champagne bottle in the bucket. Was that alcohol laced with drugs?

"I don't know who you are," I said, turning to Randy, "and I don't want to know. Why don't you let me and my friends go and you do your thing? We'll forget this ever happened."

"Wish it were that easy."

"You're not Chris Grayson's men," I said, glowering. "You're just street thugs."

"Careful," said Randy, his voice dangerously low. "Careful who you go insulting."

"Okay, who are you?"

Silence.

"And who's in that van behind us?"

Noah guffawed. "Normal people freak out and pray for their lives. You're all talk back, girl. What's wrong with you accountants?"

Randy turned to his partner.

"Enough yapping. Get them inside."

"I'm not carrying them," said Noah.

"Wake them up then," replied Randy, irritated now. "Make them walk."

I doubted their real names were Randy Wilson or Noah James. But an even bigger worry was crawling through my brain. Neither man had had any qualms showing their faces to us.

That wasn't a good sign.

What did they gain by holding us at gunpoint? Was my new client a member of organized crime? Were these men his goons? Why hire us as private investigators only to abduct us?

"Who's paying you to do this?" I said, as Noah tapped Katy on the shoulder with his weapon.

"You asking to get shot?" growled Randy.

"Let my friends go. Leave them out of this. They're innocent."

Noah chuckled.

"We thought you'd come alone," he said, his smile widening, goading me on. "Should have thought of that before you invited your pals."

"Let me talk to Grayson," I said, reaching over to pick up my phone.

"Move one inch and I shoot you dead."

I turned to see Randy's steely eyes boring into mine. He wasn't joking. This was a man who would follow through with that threat.

"There's a reason you have silencers on. You don't want anyone to know you're here," I said.

The man's cool eyes gave nothing away.

"Why kidnap us? Is it money? Tell me how much you want and let's negotiate."

"Enough!" snapped Randy. "Wake your friends or I'll put a bullet through their heads."

I leaned over and touched Katy's knees.

"Katy?" I said, shaking her.

She stirred but didn't wake.

I raised my voice.

"Katy!"

She blinked and slowly opened her eyes. She turned to me, her brow furrowed. That was when she noticed Noah. Her eyes widened as she saw the gun inches from her head.

Her face turned white. She opened her mouth, but nothing came out. She turned to me and we locked eyes. The gravity of our situation had finally sunk in.

I shook my head. I had no explanation for her except I should have been more careful. I should have trusted my gut.

I leaned toward Win.

"Wake up. Win, honey, get up."

"Hey," said Katy in a trembling voice, shaking Win by the shoulders. "Get up, sweetie."

I cursed under my breath.

Where's my Glock when I need it?

Win woke up, her movements sluggish.

"Are we there already?" she said in a weak voice, rubbing her eyes.

"Phones first," said Noah, snapping his fingers.

Win stared at him and his weapon, her mouth open, her face clouded in confusion.

Before I could reply, Noah leaned in and grabbed my phone from the backseat.

"You too," he said to Katy and Win. "Hand your phones over and no one gets shot. At least, not for now."

Katy fumbled in her purse and plucked hers out. Then she took Win's phone from her hand and gave them both to Noah.

Win just stared incomprehensibly, as if she couldn't talk.

The champagne had been spiked. I was sure now.

I was glad Katy had only drunk half a glass and me none. We would need all our wits about us to escape these gangsters.

Randy leaned through the seats in front, the barrel of his gun aimed at my head.

"When I say when," he said in a low voice, "I want you three to follow my buddy into the building. No talking. If you even think of running, I'll shoot that one in the face."

A chill went through me as he turned his weapon on Win.

Chapter Eight

I made a fast decision.

We were better off outside than in this cramped space with two gun barrels inches from our heads.

I reached over and pulled Win by the arm.

"Hun, we need to get out now. Can you stand?"

She gave me a mute look but allowed me to pry her out of her seat.

It was a raggedy crew that disembarked from the limo.

Win could barely walk. She kept blinking rapidly and making gagging sounds. Katy shuffled alongside me, woozy, though the only alcohol she'd had was the half glass of champagne moments ago.

Holding Win up by one arm and telling Katy to hang on to my shoulder, I guided my friends toward the pavement.

The white van was parked behind the limo, its engine running and those ominous yellow lights still on. Its windows were tinted almost black, but I spotted a shadow moving inside.

A shudder of terror rolled through me. If I had to conjure the perfect serial killer vehicle, this would be it.

But Randy and Noah weren't pushing us toward it. They didn't even glance at the van.

"Get the girls inside," said Randy to Noah. "I'll go help Russ."

Russ?

"Move it," said Noah, pushing the barrel of his gun to Win's head. She lurched forward. I caught her just in time.

They were smarter than I thought. I was the only one alert and able to put up a fight, and both men had carefully kept their distance from me, their weapons pointed at Win or Katy.

That rendered me powerless, and they knew that.

"March!" said Noah, pressing his weapon against Win's temple. "Faster."

Win winced from the pressure.

I swallowed hard, trying to control a storm of fury broiling inside of me.

You hurt her, and I'll tear your eyes out of those sockets.

I wanted nothing more than to jump on Noah and put him in a chokehold, but I knew better.

"She's drugged, for heaven's sake," I growled. "We're doing what you asked. Let her walk at her own pace."

"We don't have all night," he grumbled, but he didn't push Win anymore.

We were halfway toward the Union Lake Bank's main entrance now.

I looked up at the glass and concrete monoliths surrounding us. It was easy to feel small and vulnerable among these towering giants. In this dark and lonely street, they looked like a mob of monsters, their beady eyes watching us, waiting to swallow us whole.

How do I get us out of this?

"Exactly why are we going to a bank?" I said.

Noah didn't reply.

I scanned the street, praying to see someone. *Anyone.* But there was not a soul in sight, not even a janitorial vehicle or a security truck.

The driver of the van had stepped out and was conferring with Randy near the back. That must be Russ. The two men were putting on gloves.

The van's back doors were wide open, like they were preparing to haul something out or put something in. I looked over at the limo. Tetyana had the plate number, but I was now sure it was forged.

That was when I caught a movement from the corner of my eye.

I turned my head.

My heart leaped.

A squad car!

It was driving at low speed along the crossroads that cut through the banker's street. The police vehicle's blue reflective decal was visible even from where we were.

It was all or nothing.

Pulling Win with me, I lunged backward. I whirled around and staggered along the road toward it, yelling at the top of my lungs.

"Hey! Help! Help us!"

From behind me, Noah swore. The men by the van looked up and glared, but went back to their chat.

The squad car kept driving by and soon disappeared behind the next block. I stared at the empty road, my heart pounding.

How did they not notice a bunch of people by the bank at this hour?

I stayed rooted to my spot, holding on to Win tightly, waiting for the police car to turn around, lights flashing, sirens blaring.

But nothing.

They didn't see us.

My heart fell.

Noah laughed a hollow laugh. I turned toward him. He was pointing his gun squarely at Katy.

"You just chose which friend of yours is gonna die tonight."

My blood chilled.

Katy had her arms in the air and was staring at me. I'd already made one mistake and had got away with it. I couldn't risk another fatal one.

I pushed Win behind me and stepped toward Noah. "If you want to kill someone tonight, you can take me, but leave my friends out of this. Let them go. That's all I ask."

He chuckled again. "Oh, man, you got this so wrong."

"Stop diddling around!" shouted Randy from the van.

Noah screwed his eyes tight.

His weapon was aimed at Katy, but his eyes were on me.

If Katy had had her full senses, this would have been the perfect moment to kick that gun out of his hands and bring him down. But my friend just stared, swaying on her feet.

"Stop playing stupid games," snarled Noah. "Get inside the building. You and your friends. Now!"

With my arm around Win's shoulders, I stepped toward the bank's main doors. Katy followed behind me while our captor kept close to her, his gun at her head.

My hopes rose as we got to the main entrance.

This wasn't a warehouse in the outskirts of town. Or a remote cabin in the woods.

This was a city bank with a security system in place. They had to have cameras, motion sensors, trip alarms, and well-trained and armed security personnel, all watching the building twenty-four-seven.

We slipped under the iron awning in front of the main entrance. As if by magic, the double glass doors slid open.

"Get in!"

I felt a rough hand on my back. Win and I stumbled inside, followed by Katy.

We stepped into the bank's foyer and walked through the second set of sliding doors, which opened as if operated by invisible hands.

Did they have an accomplice inside the building?

Except for our footsteps on the cold marble floor, it was deadly quiet. Only the security lights were on inside. There were no signs of personnel.

Noah pushed us toward the enormous brass reception desk, which was now empty. Behind that was the bank hall with rows of wooden counters, unoccupied and darkened by the shadows.

The three of us waited by the desk, with Noah watching over us.

I turned around as the doors closed behind us. Outside, Randy and the van's driver were struggling to pull something heavy out of the van.

While I watched, they hauled out a long black bag, both men bent awkwardly.

I peered through the glass doors, my imagination running wild. Under the dim streetlights, it looked large enough to hide an adult human body.

A body bag?
I gave my head a shake.
It was an ordinary construction bag.
Suddenly, I realized what the men were planning to do.
That bag contained equipment to cut into the vaults.
This was a heist.

Chapter Nine

"Basement three," barked Randy.

Russ, the van driver, punched a button at the bottom of the numerical pad. The machinery whirred quietly as it descended.

We were crammed in the service elevator. Heavy plastic liners hung on three sides of the lift to protect its shiny steel walls.

No one spoke.

Russ and Randy stood by the door, their backs to us. The bag they'd hauled across the marble floor lay in between them, at their feet.

Randy was ramrod straight, one eye on his phone and another on the elevator screen, which counted floor numbers as we went down at a dizzying speed. In his right hand was his weapon with the silencer.

Russ stood slumped at the other side of the door. He was a heavyset, short man in a pair of denim jeans and a crumpled blue shirt. From the back, he looked like the typical outdoor worker you'd meet at a corner tavern on any weekend, except he was carrying a kid's backpack, complete with a purple unicorn motif.

Russ was the only man with a black ski mask that covered everything except for his eyes.

Noah was in the back of the elevator with us, one hand gripping Katy's arm so tightly her skin had turned white around his fingers.

The gun to her head was a clear message. If I was going to outsmart them, I would have to think hard.

From chauffeurs to kidnappers to bank robbers. Just when I thought I'd figured these men out, they surprised me.

I held Win close, my eyes darting back-and-forth, looking for clues to their next step. My brain buzzed, trying to come up with an escape plan that wouldn't involve us getting killed.

Where are the bank's security guards? Are they in on this too?

Within seconds, the elevator came to a stop. The doors clattered opened and the two men up front bent down to pick up the bag.

Noah pushed Katy out after them. Win and I stumbled out of the elevator, following the crowd.

We were in an underground concrete bunker.

A quick scan told me there was nowhere to run. A security camera was pointed at the elevator, and another was positioned on the ceiling to get a clear view of the corridor. But I was no longer sure if they were operating or if anyone was watching.

The men were too confident in their movements. While they had yelled at us to hurry, they had calmed down once we were all inside the building.

I took stock.

Even if I could find a way for us to get back in the elevator, Katy and Win were incapacitated, one by an unknown drug, and the other by a barrel of a gun.

Noah turned toward a panel on the wall near the elevator and turned on a switch. It was like he had known it had been there all along. I blinked as a row of bright fluorescent lights flickered above us. Win rubbed her eyes.

While the main hall upstairs was an immense open space, everything was tight down here. Unlike the intricately decorated high ceilings on the first floor, Randy's head almost touched the bare concrete slab above us.

I wished I knew what their motives were. That would help me plot a getaway, negotiate, or trick them. Right now, I felt like I was flying a seven-four-seven in the middle of a thunderstorm, blindfolded, with a hijacker on board.

Randy and Russ hauled the black bag along the bleak and narrow passageway, while Noah pushed us along after them.

I thought the corridor would never end when we came to a small round foyer. Facing us were three enormous metallic doors, each large enough to drive a car through.

The bank vaults.

Win gripped my arm and closed her eyes, too scared to contemplate what was happening. Katy gave me a frightened look, her face drained of all color. I nodded, but my heart was palpitating and my palms sweating. I had to stay strong for them.

Russ walked to the third door to our right, tapped it, and said something in a low voice to Randy. Randy stepped up to the massive door and scrutinized the combination lock.

Ever since we got to the vaults, the men's energy had shifted. They didn't speak, but I felt it. Their faces were taut and their movements jerky. Russ was breathing fast and shallow, like he had just run a mile. Randy scowled and Noah's grip on Katy tightened.

I tried to figure out their game. There was no way we would be able to stay here this long if one of these men didn't work for the bank or their security team.

I turned to Noah, who was watching Randy work the lock.

"Why are we here?"

He didn't reply.

"Why do you need us to rob a bank?" I said, keeping my voice level.

"Shut up, bitch," spat Noah, turning a sullen face to me, startling Katy. He turned back to watching his partner, the lines on his forehead deepening.

Randy pulled out a piece of paper from his pocket and put his hand on the combination lock. As we watched, he turned the lock to the right, then left, and on, until we heard the click.

The vault was unlocked.

The tension heightened even more.

They were in a hurry now.

Russ reached the large gear lever on the door and turned it, but it didn't budge.

"The other way, you idiot," snapped Randy.

How could three men with hostages break into a modern bank in the middle of a city with no one seeing or hearing what was going on?

I prayed under my breath for guards or the police to arrive at any moment.

Russ turned the wheel, panting as he did.

Another click.

"Done," he said, as he reached for the steel handle and pulled on it.

Together, Randy and Russ heaved. The heavyset steel door opened inch by inch. Once open, Russ turned on a switch and the inside lit up.

We stared.

The vault was a long, narrow, claustrophobic room with safety deposit boxes stacked from the floor to the ceiling. Everything, including the steel walls and the safety boxes, glistened like they had been polished to a blinding shine.

Russ pulled out a handkerchief and wiped his eyes. Noah stood stiffly next to us, his gun still at Katy's head, but his gaze on Randy, as if expecting something.

With a signal for Noah to wait, Randy swiveled around and stepped inside.

"What are you waiting for?" said Randy's impatient voice, echoing inside the vault.

After hesitating a few seconds, Russ crossed the threshold.

They had left the long bag lying by the doorway. I had been so sure it had carried equipment to allow them to break in. What was inside?

Through the narrow opening, I could see Randy and Russ walk down the length of the vault.

We all strained to listen. No one breathed. I wasn't sure what to expect. The sound of drilling? A dynamite blast?

That was when I heard the moan.

I snapped around, frowning. That wasn't Win. It wasn't Katy either.

The low, anguished moan came again.
My heart raced as I located it.
It had come from the bag lying on the floor by the door.

Chapter Ten

There's a person inside that bag!

Noah hadn't flinched. He hadn't even seemed to notice, intensely focused on his teammates' activities inside the vault.

Who is in that body bag? Why did they bring them here?

Randy and Russ's furious whispers had risen to a heated squabble, muffled by the thick walls.

But I caught the gist of it. They were throwing numbers out, contradicting each other, and accusing the other of not having done the job they had promised to do.

I kept one ear on their argument while my eyes stayed steadfast on the bag. I could make out the faint outline of a human shape, curled up, and lying on their side. It wasn't a big person.

Was it a child? A petite woman?

I watched carefully, expecting to see movement or hear another moan, but the bag lay silently in a crumpled heap.

Were they dead?

I had suspected something ominous all along. The way the men carried the bag and its shape had given hints to what it was, but I had dismissed it as a wild idea, my imagination working overtime. But my instincts had been right.

Noah was leaning in, his face tight like he didn't like what he was hearing inside the vault.

He let go of Katy's arm and reached into his pants pocket to pull his phone out. He let out an annoyed *tsk* after glancing at the screen.

Was their time limit up? Was an alarm going to be triggered? Would security come if they stayed longer? Whatever it was, he was feeling the stress.

Perfect.

I turned to him. "Seems like your buddies are a little lost. Need some help? We, accountants, are good with numbers."

Noah snapped his head my way, his beady eyes narrowing. With a dismissive jeer, he turned back toward the open vault door.

I tried again. "Can you tell me who's inside the bag?"

No answer.

"This looks like something the mafia would do. Do you guys work for them?"

Noah snarled something incomprehensible, but kept his eyes dead ahead. He shuffled his feet and a nervous twitch came on his face.

Good.

I needed his attention diffused.

"Is it Chris Grayson?" I continued my prodding. "Or is he the local mafia boss? Wish I'd known before, because I would have asked for a bigger retainer."

My smile was met with a low growl, but I was undeterred.

"Why drag us in here, Noah? What benefit do we have for your operation? Seems like a dumb idea to bring a bunch of civilians off the street to watch you break into a bank."

Silence.

His face was twitching faster. He still held the muzzle of his gun aimed at Katy's head, but his mind was elsewhere.

I took a discreet step closer to him. "If you're expecting an appreciative audience, you've picked the wrong people. I personally don't endorse this sort of thing."

Noah could respond either way.

He could lash out in anger or lose his focus. All I needed was to distract him long enough to make him turn that weapon away from my friend. Even if it was for a millisecond.

"I told you, this is the right number!" Russ was shouting now.

A loud bang made us all jump. Randy let out a string of obscenities, followed by another thump. He was punching the wall in frustration.

Noah clicked something on his phone and muttered darkly to himself. I peeked at the screen. He had opened a text message. I squinted to make out the words.

4469018

That could be a password, the number of a safe deposit box, or a code for something. I branded it into my brain.

"Guys," Noah called through the open doorway, his voice strained.

Randy and Ross were too busy arguing to hear him.

Noah raised his voice. "Hey!"

The shouting stopped, and Randy's flushed face popped out of the doorway. "*What?*"

Noah held up his phone.

"He sent it again."

He? Who's that?

"He's asking why it's taking so long," said Noah.

Randy stomped out of the vault and stepped over the bag to grab the phone.

"He said—" began Noah.

"Shut up and keep the girls in line," snapped Randy, before spinning around and marching back inside. I flinched as he almost stepped on the end of the bag that looked like the person's head.

The voices inside quietened.

The mechanical whir of a combination lock came to us. The room fell completely still. It seemed like everyone was holding their breath to see if it would work. Even us.

Russ let out a triumphant yell. Then the sound of steel clanking against steel came from inside.

Noah let out his breath, but his hand holding the weapon was shaking ever so slightly.

"Hurry," he said, his voice wavering. "Hurry up, guys."

Randy and Russ were busy, heads down by the box, stealing whatever they came here to take.

I had little time.

Win was leaning against the wall next to me, her eyes closed tightly. Her face was a sickly pallor, like she was using all her energy to stay upright.

I stepped away from her, keeping Noah's profile in my periphery. I needed space for my next move, and I wanted to eliminate collateral damage.

Noah let out another exasperated sigh. "Come on, guys!"

"Shut up!" yelled Randy.

Katy shot me a fearful look. I gave her an imperceptible nod. I couldn't tell her of my plans. After all these years, she should have guessed, if only she had been lucid enough.

I stepped closer to Noah.

Keeping my feet solidly on the ground and taking a deep breath to steady myself, I brought my elbow up and curled my right hand into a fist.

Noah noticed the change in my posture and snapped my way with a frown.

Now!

I slammed my elbow into his chest and ground my right heel into the soft part of his foot.

He doubled over in pain.

I elbowed him again.

He threw his arms across his chest to protect himself, letting his gun fall with a clatter. I barely noticed it slide across the concrete floor toward the body bag.

Katy jerked her head back, as if she had just woken up from a daze and realized what was going on.

Noah looked up, his face red in fury and his mouth opened to roar.

I jammed my open palm under the bridge of his nose, smashing the soft tissue, sending him reeling back against the wall. His head slammed against the concrete with a sickening thud.

He raised a fist and whacked it against the side of my head. I saw stars, but spun around, grabbed his lapel, and kicked my knee into his groin. He let out a yell and crashed down with a loud groan.

Almost there. One last hit and he'd be out like a light.

I raised my foot.

"Stop or I shoot!" came Randy's voice.

I froze.

Chapter Eleven

Randy was standing by the open door.

His gun was aimed at Katy's head.

Noah's weapon had slid across the floor and stopped by the body bag, but Katy hadn't been able to retrieve it.

Stars flickered in front of my eyes, and blood pounded in my ears.

I took my foot off Noah's back and straightened up slowly. He groaned in pain, but stayed down.

Russ was still inside the vault. I could hear him rummaging in the safe deposit box.

How do I distract Randy and grab that gun without getting Katy killed?

He had seen me search for the weapon. It was closer to him than me. He knew what I was thinking.

I stood in place, my hands curled into fists, still panting from my fight.

"What do you want from us?" I spat out.

"Who trained you?" Randy pushed the gun against Katy's head, making her bend her neck to the side. "You have two choices. Follow my instructions or let your friend die." He grinned. "Check mate."

I didn't move.

"Come and join your friend over here. Don't be shy." Another creepy grin. "It's nice and cool inside the vault. You'll like it, I promise."

My eyes darted across the corridor. There had to be another way out. *Think, girl.*

That was when Noah grabbed on to my ankle and pulled me down.

I crashed to the floor with a yell. I raised my arm and punched Noah's face. He yanked my hair. I wrapped my hands around his throat and squeezed. He kicked and flailed.

"Stop or I shoot!" hollered Randy.

But Noah didn't let go.

"What the hell you doing, man?" shouted Randy.

I squeezed Noah's neck tighter. He bucked violently. I moved to the side to avoid his feet, but he kicked and hit something.

Win!

With a shriek, she toppled back, hitting her head on the concrete. With an angry roar, I smashed Noah's head on the ground.

Randy swore.

I was about to slam my fist into Noah's face when a shot rang through the corridor. It was so loud, it shook every cell inside of my body.

I dove.

Noah pulled away from me, like he'd been stung.

For one split second, I was so sure a thunderbolt had crashed around us. But the smell of hot gun powder permeated the stale basement air.

I whirled around.

I could almost see the smoke coming out of Randy's Glock, but Katy was still standing, trembling, and staring at me, her face pale in fright.

I turned toward the other end of the corridor. The steel door across from us had a large dent. The bullet had missed me by a few inches.

My head hurt and my shoulder stung, but there was no time to check my wounds. I needed a better plan.

I was three feet from Randy and Katy, the body bag being the only barrier between that gun and me.

Randy smirked. "You're no accountant. I wasn't sure, but you just confirmed it, and you signed your death certificate."

Katy looked at him, her eyes widening.

"None of you are going to see tomorrow," smiled Randy. He pointed his chin toward the vault. "This way, ladies. It's lovely inside. I promise."

I turned back to Win. She had slithered to the floor and had buried her head in her hands. Next to her, Noah was lying down, holding his head and moaning, but he didn't get up.

"Do you want your friend dead or alive?" said Randy, pushing Katy toward the open vault door.

I took a step forward. *Two more feet and that gun is mine.*

Randy lifted his foot and kicked the weapon inside the chamber. *Shoot.*

He turned to Katy and leered. "What's your name again, honey?"

I gritted my teeth. *You touch her, and I'll shove that gun down your throat and pull the trigger.*

"You're very pretty, you know that? I'm glad she brought you along with her."

He shoved her inside.

"Asha!" cried Katy.

I jumped inside the vault. "Let her go. Now!"

Russ looked up in surprise, stopping midway through zipping up his bag.

Randy had Katy against the steel wall at gunpoint, one hand on her chest, his face inches from hers.

I was about to lunge at him when a whimper came from behind me.

I whirled around to see Noah stepping over the threshold. He was limping, but his hand was around Win's neck. She was stumbling, like she was blind.

"Oh, man, did these girls do that to you?" said Russ, pointing at his face. "You're such a wuss."

Noah had taken a good beating and would sport a black eye soon. He glowered my way. If his eyes had laser beams, I would have turned to cinders.

He pushed Win toward me. I caught her in my arms before she fell. Her right temple was bleeding from where she had hit the floor. She buried her head in my shoulders, shaking.

"We're done here. Done like dinner, people," said Russ, hauling the unicorn bag on his back and squeezing past Noah, like he didn't care to know what was going to happen to us.

He turned around when he got to the threshold and grinned at his partners.

"Tomorrow this time, we'll be in Jamaica drinking rum and Coke on the beach, boys."

"Get that bag inside," snapped Randy, not budging from Katy's side.

Noah lumbered out the door with Russ. The two of them hauled the body bag and dropped it with a sick thud on the vault floor.

Randy turned to me. "You girls will stay right here."

I turned my furious eyes on him, wishing I could beat him to a pulp.

Outside, I could hear the rumble of gears. The thunderous sound got louder and louder until I felt like my eardrums would rip open.

Randy grinned, his hand still on Katy's heaving chest.

"You didn't know this when we picked you up at the airport, but this is where you're going to die. I chose this coffin for you personally. Hope you like it."

Fury spiraled up my spine.

"You'll pay for this!" I yelled. "The airport cameras will have your faces. The bank's cameras as well."

"Seventeen hours," said Randy, grabbing Katy and pulling her toward the door with him.

As long as he had her, I couldn't do anything.

"That's how much air you have in here. By the time this place opens on Monday, you'll be dead on the floor. Enjoy your stay in Seattle."

When he got to the door, he let go of Katy. Without another word, he slipped through the crack, just as the men closed the last few inches.

I sprang toward them.

Randy shoved the barrel of his gun through the slit. "One step closer and I'll put a bullet right between your eyes."

"Heave, boys!" he shouted, his eyes and gun on me.

The steel door moved the last ten inches and slammed shut.

The room descended into an inky darkness. An eerie silence fell around us.

They had trapped us in.

Chapter Twelve

I floundered around in the pitch darkness.

Something rustled by my feet, and I felt around it with my shoe. It was soft and lumpy.

The body bag!

I recoiled in horror.

I stepped away from it and felt my way in the dark until I touched the cold, hard surface of the vault door.

"Open up!" I banged my fists on the steel surface. "Hey! Open the door!"

I screamed, throwing every ounce of energy into my fists. My heart pounded in my chest and sweat rolled down my back. I didn't know how long I hammered, but I kept on until Katy shouted from behind me.

"They can't hear us!"

She was right. This was a futile exercise. The vault was as soundproofed as it was airtight.

I let my hands fall to my sides. My throat was parched, and my legs felt like jelly, ready to give way at any moment.

Swallowing the panic threatening to implode inside of me, I moved my hands over the edge of the doorframe and onto the wall, trying to adjust my eyes to the darkness.

All I could feel was the smooth, cool surface of the steel. There had to be a light switch somewhere.

There.

Something small and circular bulged from the surface, at head level. My fingers sensed its contours. On it was what felt like braille dots. A ribbed surface. It had to be a switch of some sort.

With trembling hands, I pushed on the ribbed piece, hoping against hope that I wouldn't put us in further danger.

Bright florescent light flooded the room.

I blinked.

A cry came from behind me.

I whirled around, disoriented. It took a few seconds for my eyes to adjust.

Katy and Win were huddled together in a corner, a few feet behind the body bag.

"You guys okay?" I stammered.

What a stupid question. Of course, they're not OK.

Katy stared at me, her eyes wide in fear. Win let out an anguished cry. "We're going to die!"

Before Katy or I could do anything, she turned her head toward the wall and threw up, her back bent and her shoulders convulsing.

I watched her helplessly, bitter bile coming to my throat.

"How long do we have?" cried Katy, one hand holding on to Win's shoulder.

I didn't answer. I was barely coming to terms with our situation myself.

Katy was breathing heavily, the beginning of a panic attack. "He said this place was airtight. He said they'll find us dead, didn't he?"

With the three of us in here, I doubted we had enough air till someone opened those doors, but the more we panicked, the less oxygen we had. Then, there was the mysterious stranger in that bag who might or might not be alive.

Win wiped her mouth and whimpered.

I stepped up to my friends, my arms reaching toward them.

"Come over here," I said, nudging them away from the vomit. Things were going from bad to worse. That was going to get rancid fast in this enclosed space.

Katy and Win shuffled backward on their haunches. Then, Katy leaned against the wall of safety deposit boxes, while Win lay down and put her head on her lap, curling into a fetal position.

"We have almost a day's worth of air," I lied.

That was an exaggeration, but the last thing we needed was to lose hope.

"It's Friday," said Katy, her lips quivering. "We'll never get out of here."

I squeezed her shoulder. "Hey, I'll figure it out. I brought you in here, and I'm going to get us out. That's a promise."

She stared at me like she didn't hear me. Her normally beautiful green pupils were small black dots now. I could smell her primal fear.

I softened my voice. "I need you to help me. Will you do that?"

Katy nodded. Win didn't speak.

"Stay absolutely still and breathe normally. Relax as much as you can. That will save up oxygen. Do you understand?"

Another nod from Katy.

"Now close your eyes," I said, lowering my voice to a whisper.

"Katy, pretend you're back home, sitting on your favorite yellow couch with a book in your hands. Breathe. Chantelle's playing in her room next door. Dinner is warming in the oven, and Peace will be home soon. Just breathe. You're in your chair, safe at home. Stay still. Just like that."

Katy swallowed hard but was breathing normally now.

I reached down and pushed Win's hair off her face. Her eyes were closed, and her breathing was raspy, like she was having trouble taking in air.

Whatever drug she had ingested was still affecting her.

"Win, sweetie." I reached for her hand. "I'm going to get us out of here. I need you to stay strong for me, okay?"

She didn't answer, but she gripped my hand.

"Pretend you're going to sleep in your bed back home. Luc is right there with you. Just relax. You're going to be fine. Trust me."

Her right hand moved, and she flexed her fingers.

I had no idea how I would follow through with my promises, but Win closed her eyes and settled into Katy's lap.

I removed my jacket and gently wiped the blood from Win's forehead. She'd had more than her share of pain tonight. I placed my jacket over her like a blanket and stood up.

My body felt numb, but my mind was still working. That was all I needed.

I took stock.

We no longer had our phones. David, Peace, and Luc knew we had a late arrival and wouldn't expect a call from us until the next day.

The bank employees wouldn't open the vault till early Monday morning. Tetyana wouldn't be back in town until late Monday afternoon. Our downtown hotel wouldn't inquire about us. We hadn't even checked in for the night. They'd mark us up as no-shows, and may even charge us for it.

That left Chris Grayson.

My meeting with my client was at noon the next day. We had planned to discuss his case at his home over lunch on Saturday. But that would be ten hours from now.

He would wait for me for a few hours, possibly get frustrated and irritated at my unprofessionalism. There would be no reason for him to call emergency services.

Then again, he might already know we were here. Perhaps he was behind all this, whatever *this* was.

I had to admit the ugly truth. We were alone.

I surveyed the space, looking for an emergency lever, an intercom button, a telephone, anything to let the world outside know where we were.

The shiny safety deposit boxes stared back at me, as if mocking me.

This room wasn't built for humans. This space had been optimized to store money, gold, precious stones, and important papers, which all required a cool, dry, and climate-controlled atmosphere.

I turned around and walked toward the other end of the room. I doubted there would be other exits, given this was a vault, but it was worth the check.

At the very end, and installed in between a row of safety deposit boxes, was a temperature gauge encased in glass.

I peered into it.

It was as cold as a walk-in fridge and the temperatures were dropping. I tapped on the glass, then pulled it, but it was solid. This was just a thermometer. The actual climate control panel was probably a software program in a computer room upstairs.

I shivered. It was only going to get colder, now the door had been shut.

They're going to find us here dead and frozen. All three of us.

No.

Four!

I whirled around and my eyes fell on the body bag.

It was time to find out who was inside.

Chapter Thirteen

I scurried in between the walls of safety deposit boxes toward the front.

Katy and Win quietly held on to each other in their corner, their eyes closed.

The body bag was lying on the ground, the top part leaning against the steel surface, like the person had been propped up by the neck.

I hadn't heard more sounds or seen the bag move after Noah and Russ had unceremoniously hurled it inside. I wondered if the person was still alive.

I bent low to examine the bag. It was made of a heavy-duty vinyl material. A long black zipper ran the length of one side.

I was reaching over to unzip the bag when I spotted it.

My heart leaped to my mouth.

Hidden behind the top part of the bag was a long red handle with the words EMERGENCY written on it.

The emergency lever!

My heart pounding, I threw my hand around the bag, grasped the red handle, and yanked it.

It came off.

I reeled back and clutched at the wall to stop myself from crashing onto the body bag.

Did I just kill our only chance of escape? Or is this how emergency levers work?

I pushed the gear wheel on the door. It didn't budge.

I turned the red handle around in my hand.

Something was wrong.

That was when I saw the serrated edge.

I scrutinized the door where the handle had been attached. Those thugs had sawed through the handle but put it back in place.

A vicious trick.

That was when it dawned on me. This heist had been plotted out well in advance. They had planned to shove us in here all along.

Had they known I was coming? But why target me?

If Chris Grayson hadn't wanted me around, he wouldn't have deposited a ten-thousand-dollar retainer in my account. He would have simply told me he didn't need any help.

Could he have been related to the traffickers who'd attacked us in our youths?

I shook my head. That made little sense. That was ages ago, and they had no advantage in targeting us any more.

Or did they?

Was it *Chris Grayson* who was inside that bag?

A shudder went through me at the thought.

The moan had sounded like it came from a woman. Then again, it had been so peculiar, I may have misheard it.

Taking a deep breath to steel myself, I kneeled by the bag and gingerly pulled at the zipper. It glided down easily. I moved slowly, holding my breath, feeling like I was defusing a ticking bomb.

"Hello there?" I whispered to the stranger inside. "Chris Grayson, is it you?"

No answer.

"Whoever you are, I'll get you out soon."

I wished my hand would hold steady, but I couldn't help but conjure a slimy alien hurtling out and clutching my face in a foul-smelling mouth filled with fangs.

The zipper stopped halfway. A piece of a white cloth was stuck underneath it.

I pulled it free and kept pulling on the zipper, a feeling of dread settling on me. The person hadn't moved or uttered a sound so far.

The bag was half open when I caught sight of a pale thin arm through the narrow opening. An icy shiver went through me to see a part of a human being.

The zipper was all the way down now. The bag was open. All I had to do was flip the top cover.

My imagination conjured up a bloodied zombie as I reached for the flap.

Stop it, I scolded myself. We wouldn't live for long inside here, zombies or not.

With a quick twist, I flipped the cover away.

My heart dropped.

It was a young woman, in her late teens or early twenties, dressed in a white shirt and a short tartan skirt. They had unceremoniously shoved her into this bag. Her limbs were bent awkwardly, but it was her face that left me thunderstruck.

The deep red welts meant a toxic liquid had burned half her face into one big, contorted scar. I had seen acid attack survivors during my travels in India, targeted by misogynistic men whose attentions had been spurned.

But we were in North America.

Who did this to her? Was it an accident? How could such a thing happen?

I inspected the scar. It wasn't new. This unfortunate incident had occurred years ago.

On her right arm was a small black mole in the shape of a heart. A birthmark.

I touched the side of her dainty neck that had been spared of the scar, hoping to feel a heartbeat.

Nothing.

My heart fell. I drew my hand back, a pang of sorrow crossing me.

That moan had been her last sound.

I wondered if she would have survived if I had acted sooner. An impossible task with a gangster holding a weapon to your friend's head, but still.

I stared at the young woman.

Who was she? Why did those men toss her in here like unwanted garbage?

While her face was a mess, the rest of her body was intact.

Her clothes weren't ripped or torn. They looked like they were made of quality material. Her shoes were sensible flat-heeled pumps. A small silver ring hung from her left nostril.

She looked like the typical young woman you'd meet around the corner of a suburban street, waiting at a bus stop on their way to class or work.

Reaching into the body bag, I touched her wrist, wondering if I was wrong. Her body was still warm. I pressed on all sides of her hand, trying to feel a pulse, but her heart had stopped.

That was when I saw it. The image of half an angel tattooed to the back of her right hand, where the thumb met the index finger.

Strange.

Why only half an angel?

Something pulled my eyes toward a bulge in her skirt pocket. I reached in and felt something plastic. I pulled it out and gasped. It was a small see-through bag filled with a white powder.

Drugs?

Just when I thought things had become strange, they took a weirder turn. This young suburban girl may not be as innocent as she looked.

Why had those thugs targeted her? How did she die?

My eyes traveled down her body, seeking clues. I searched for bullet holes, knife slashes, or bloodied bruises, but there was nothing other than her horrifically burned face. But those burns hadn't killed her. It was something else.

A chill went through me as I realized what might have happened.

That champagne.

My stomach sank.

Did they feed her the same drink? Did it kill her?

I turned to my friends. Katy and Win were still sitting quietly in their corner, their faces ashen and haggard like wearied refugees lost at sea. Both had their eyes screwed tight, like they were trying hard not to panic.

It was a relief to hear Win's raspy breaths. But the longer we stayed locked up in here, the shorter her chances of staying alive.

I turned back to the gruesome body in the bag.

The young woman reminded me of us when we were ten years younger. Whatever she had done, she didn't deserve a horrific ending like this.

A fiery thought spiraled up my spine. I clenched my teeth.

I'm going to find out who did this to you and I'll make them pay.

Chapter Fourteen

A rustle made me turn.

Katy had spotted the opened bag by the door.

Her eyes widened at the sight of the deformed corpse, but she didn't speak. She screwed her eyes shut again, as if she didn't want to believe what she had seen.

I leaped to my feet and stepped away from the body.

We need to get out of here. Alive.

All sophisticated security systems had built-in fail-safes. I moved my hands from the bottom to the top of the wall, touching every bit of the surface, looking for a hidden button or switch.

Then I scrutinized the door again, willing it to help me, but we might as well have been stuck in Fort Knox. There wasn't much I could do to help Win if I didn't get this opened soon.

I was running my hands along the upper half of the door when I realized what had been staring at me all along.

The camera!

The round security camera on the ceiling just above the door made half a turn as I looked.

It's working!

I waved.

"Help!" I shouted, though I knew it only conveyed visuals. "We're stuck down here! Help!"

Someone had to see this footage. Someone had to notice something was wrong with this picture.

"Anybody there? Help us!" I yelled, jumping up and down like a shipwrecked survivor.

I stopped as a sudden realization dawned on me.

If anyone was watching the cameras, they would have seen the footage of the men break into the building, then the vault. They would have seen Randy shooting in the basement corridor.

These men were more sophisticated than I thought. To carry out a heist without getting caught meant they had disabled the entire bank's security system. They might have even wounded or killed the security personnel. Either that, or Randy, Noah, and Russ were a part of the team.

If no one came during the initial chaos, what would make anyone come now?

All I was doing was expending more of our precious oxygen.

But the security system had to come back online at some point. The question was when. Would it be the next day? Or Monday morning, after the employees returned to work?

I looked back at my two friends sitting collapsed by the wall. They were staring my way, eyes wide.

They looked so vulnerable. They had fought with me, stood by me through the most difficult times in my life. They were my sisters, my family.

That ball of fury spiraled around my spine again.

I curled my hands into fists and gritted my teeth. I'm going to get them out of here alive, if that's the last thing I do.

I spun around.

Cameras, intercoms, motion detectors, escape levers, trip wires. What else did banks employ to secure their valuables?

My eyes followed the rows of safety deposit boxes from one end of the wall to the other. I stepped away from the door and walked to the back of the room, passing Katy and Win, who were now watching me intently. I squeezed Katy's shoulder to let her know I hadn't gone completely mad.

I stopped halfway down the room in front of the box Russ had opened and rifled through.

I reached over and pulled the handle, but it was sealed. My gut tightened like it was trying to tell me something. Digging into my memory banks, I pulled out the digits I'd memorized from sneaking into Noah's phone.

4469018

I reached toward the combination lock and tried the number, whispering it under my breath.

An idea was slowly forming in my mind. Even if it didn't work, I was keeping my brain and hands occupied. Any action meant I didn't have to think of the inevitable worst-case scenario.

I dialed the numbers, scrolling back and forth.

Click.

Goose bumps sprang up on my arm.

I jiggled the handle. It moved.

I yanked the drawer open and cringed as the steel bars screeched against the metal rollers. The sound echoed in the confined space like fingernails on a chalkboard.

I pulled the box out until six inches of the container was out in the open, but the wall behind the vault was thicker than was visible to the eye. I kept hauling. It kept coming.

The long steel box finally came loose, and I felt its weight.

Balancing it with both hands, I placed it on the floor to examine it. There was a latch on top of the main box. This was only an outer casing.

I pulled the latch open. A smaller steel container was inside the casement. I pried the inside box out and removed its lid. A thick purple velvet cloth greeted my eyes.

Whatever had been stored here had been liable to be scratched or damaged. That signaled expensive jewelry, precious stones, or gold bars.

I tugged at the cloth, but something was weighing it down. I unfurled it slowly.

What were the men after? Why steal from one box when this entire vault was probably filled with valuables?

As I pulled on the velvet cloth, something heavy fell onto the ground with a thud. I whipped the cloth away and stared at my find.

A rectangular piece of gold bullion winked at me from under the harsh light. I reached in and picked it up. Russ must have missed this in his hurry to get out.

The middle of the bar was engraved with small lettering.

FINE GOLD, 999.9, 200g

The bar was smaller than a smartphone and could easily fit into my palm.

How much would a steel box filled with these gold bars amount to?

It had to be worth enough for those men to set up such an elaborate scheme, one that included a dead body in a bag and our potential murders.

If this box had been filled with gold bars like these, those men had got away with a fortune.

I looked around me.

If even half the deposit boxes in this vault had been leased to host treasures, we were surrounded by multi-millions of dollars' worth of wealth. There could conceivably be even billions. Gold bars, precious stones, heritage jewelry, antique pieces, papers that recorded stocks and bond ownership, and who knew what else?

I winced as I realized the irony of our circumstance. I would have gladly given away all of it in a heartbeat for just a few more hours of oxygen, so my friends and I would live.

As I straightened up, I touched something hard with my feet. It was the empty steel box. I let the gold bar fall to the ground. There was a more formidable tool right by me.

I turned to my friends.

Win had closed her eyes again, but Katy was watching me.

Her eyes widened as she caught sight of the gold bar glittering under the fluorescent light.

"Cover Win's ears," I whispered. "This is going to be loud."

Chapter Fifteen

"What are you doing?" Katy's voice was heightened with anxiety.

"I'm going to trip an alarm," I said.

"Didn't those guys disable everything?"

"A bank's security system is more complex than a locked door and a camera. They should have layers of double or triple alarms. I'm betting they didn't turn everything off."

I wished I could be more certain of what I was about to do, but we were running out of options.

"It's worth a try," I said.

Katy turned away and put one hand over Win's ear and another over hers.

This was a guessing game. The bank may not have installed fail-safes, and some of these boxes could be empty with no alarms turned on. But I didn't have the luxury of time to ponder.

I heaved the heavy steel container up. I was no longer holding a safe deposit box. This was my battering ram.

I picked a combination lock randomly.

After placing one leg back and one in front to get into a solid and balanced position, I rammed the edge of the steel box into the lock. The loud slamming reverberated through the small room.

Behind me, Katy gasped loudly. Win said nothing.

I hit the combination lock again and again, ignoring the pain of the recoil in my arms. The sharp edges of the box cut into my skin, but I kept beating until a dent showed on the lock.

I stepped back and glanced at my handiwork.

Did that do the trick?

No alarms went off. No sirens sounded, and no lights flashed.

I selected the safety box next to it and hit the combination lock in a frenzy. I was eating up our limited oxygen supply, but it was better than sitting around and waiting to die.

After beating the second combination lock till I bent it out of shape, I started on a third. This time, I hit the edges of the box, battering it until my arms hurt.

I stopped to catch my breath and wipe the sweat off my face. I was debating whether to continue or come up with a better plan when an ear-splitting siren wailed above us.

My heart leaped to my mouth. I dropped the steel box and whirled around.

A red light was flashing above us.

Did I trigger a hidden alarm? Did someone see us?

A loud rumble came by the door. The gear locks were turning.

The door was opening!

Katy scrambled to her feet. Win stayed on the floor, either asleep or too weak to move.

I gestured for Katy to come and join me. We stood shoulder to shoulder by the door, our backs up. If Randy and his men were returning, we had to be prepared.

The sonorous sound of the gears filled my ears. I could feel the vibrations of the heavy steel door's motions in my bones.

Sweat streamed down my back and my heart pounded like mad, but I kept my focus on the entrance.

The door cracked open an inch. Then another inch.

Shouts and yells came from the other side.

The door opened a few more inches. More hollering. Within seconds, a phalanx of police officers was facing us, their guns trained our way.

"SPD! Hands up!"

Katy let her shoulders drop and stepped up to them.

"Thank goodness you're here," she said, breathing a sigh of relief. "We were going to die—"

"Hands up!" screamed the officer, shoving his handgun in her face.

Katy threw her arms in the air and faltered backward, her face draining of color.

"Don't move!" hollered the cop. "Or I shoot!"

Katy froze in place.

"Stand right there!" yelled a second officer, turning his weapon on me.

I took a deep breath in to steel my anger. I understood their reaction, but we deserved a better reception after all we'd been through.

"What's that smell?" said a third officer, stepping inside, her eyes darting back and forth.

She stopped as she spotted the dead woman in the bag.

I had covered most of her body with the top flap. It was the decent thing to do. Her ghostly and immobile face was all that was visible now, but even that would have been an unnerving sight for the most hardened of beat cops.

"What in good heaven's name?" said the officer, her eyes bulging.

She surveyed the open safe deposit box at my feet, the gold bar lying in the middle of the room, and Win on the floor several feet behind the body bag, her eyes closed.

"What the heck happened in here?" she hollered, turning to me.

I swallowed hard. Where to even begin?

"Please check on my friend," I said, pointing to Win with my chin. "She's been drugged. She needs a doctor ASAP, or she'll die."

"*Drugged?*" said the first officer, who still had his weapon trained on Katy.

"Who the hell are you, and what the hell were you doing here?" snapped the young officer next to him, his aim at me unwavering.

I took a deep breath in and let it out. "Three thugs locked us in here."

My heart was beating fast, but the last thing I needed to convey was fear or nerves.

"We arrived from New York at midnight to meet a client. Two men picked us from the airport saying our client sent them. We didn't know they were bank robbers. We hadn't even seen them before tonight. They brought us in here at gunpoint and locked us up in here with that dead woman."

The officer, with his weapon aimed at me, raised his eyebrows.

I looked him in the eye. He had a blond crew cut and looked like a recent recruit, keen to do his job. His name badge simply said DAVIES.

"We're still coming to terms with what happened too," I said. "They brought that dead woman in the bag with them. We have no idea who she is, why those men picked us, or why they brought us here."

"Lying to law enforcement is a serious obstruction of justice."

"I know how out of the world this sounds, but check the cameras at the airport, the bank, the vault and you'll see. We're the victims here."

The female officer walked over to Win and kneeled next to her to feel her pulse.

"Is she okay?" I called out, hearing my voice crack.

Instead of answering me, she barked into her shoulder radio.

"Eleven-twenty-four. We need paramedics down here, now!"

I wished I knew what that code meant. Was it a person injured or a person down?

I turned back to Davies, the officer who was staring at me like I had two heads.

"They brought us in a limo. I have the license plate number. There were three men. One of them was driving a white cargo van behind us. Did you see them?"

"We'll ask the questions," he snarled.

"Gold!" cried another officer, who'd walked toward the back of the room to investigate. "They were stealing gold. Oh, man, check this out."

In his hand was the gold bullion I'd dropped.

"All right," said Davies, waving his weapon in my face. "Out. March!"

Chapter Sixteen

"But, we're not—" started Katy.

Davies motioned to the doorway. "I said, out! You'll have time to talk at the station."

Just as we were about to step outside, I heard footsteps rushing down the corridor. Two paramedics barged inside the vault, carrying a stretcher. They stopped, startled at the sight of the woman's body in the bag.

"She's already dead," I said, turning to them. "Check our friend in the corner. She's really sick. The bank robbers drugged her with something."

Their eyebrows shot up.

"She threw up, but she still has more of the toxic stuff inside her."

All eyes turned to me. I must have looked an awful sight, disheveled and sweaty, in my crumpled and dirty yoga pants I'd worn for our red-eye to Seattle.

"She needs help fast," I snapped. *"Do* something."

The paramedics turned around and hustled over to Win.

I crossed my fingers. If anything happened to her, I wouldn't know how I would live with it.

After handcuffing us, the young officer, Davies, pushed Katy and me out of the vault, through the corridor, and up the fire escape flight of stairs. With a cop in front of us and another behind, Katy and I plodded along, retracing our steps toward the front entrance.

The bank was teaming with uniformed women and men. Police sirens echoed outside, and the street was flashing in red and blue lights.

The limo had vanished from the curb. As had the cargo van. It was strange to think of a limousine being used as a getaway vehicle, and that might have worked to their advantage.

As Davies pushed us out of the door, a black armored vehicle that looked like it belonged to the anti-riot squad came trundling down the road. Everyone moved aside to let it through.

Where were you when we needed you? I thought silently, as Davies pushed us into the back of a squad car and slammed the door.

The noise dimmed.

Katy leaned back in her seat, her handcuffed hands on her lap, and closed her eyes like it was all too much. I watched the scene unfold around us.

Officers and paramedics dashed back-and-forth, shouting in code to each other. A small group of cops stood huddled by the main door conferring, and once in a while, shot confused glances our way.

I guessed we didn't resemble typical bank robbers.

It felt like forever before the paramedics brought Win out on the stretcher. Her face was covered with an oxygen mask.

With a sinking feeling in my stomach, I watched them put her inside an ambulance.

"Who hired you?"

Officer Davies' flinty eyes bored into mine.

He was even more bullheaded now we were in his territory at the downtown police precinct.

He strutted around the small interrogation room like he owned the place. There was not one crease in his blue uniform, even after the commotion at the bank. He had the physique of a Marine and an attitude of one who'd just rounded up a duo of international terrorists.

Katy and I had waited in the windowless room for an hour for the cross-examination to begin. With only our worries about Win to keep us occupied, we sat close, leaning against each other, exhaustion creeping into every cell in our bodies.

I was thankful for Davies' older partner in the room. Officer Thomas was a big man who looked like he had given up the street beat and the gym a long time ago and spent most of his time behind a desk.

He had brought us water. He had also informed us that Win was at a local hospital, under observation by an emergency medical team. *They say she'll be fine*, he had assured us.

This older cop was quiet, but I was glad for his presence.

He sat across from us, watching us with gentle creased eyes, rolling his coffee cup in his hand, while his partner did the talking.

Davies paced the room, harping at Katy and me to tell the truth, treating us like we had planned to blow up Union Lake Bank, instead of getting locked inside with a dead body and depleting oxygen.

"Let the ladies answer your questions," said Thomas in a soft voice, giving his partner a look as Davies interrupted me for the tenth time. "They're willing to talk, so let them."

"They're lying!" shouted Davies, slamming a fist on the table, making Katy jump. "People break into banks to take things out, not leave things in. This makes no sense."

"If we took the gold, how come we didn't have it on us?" I said, trying to control my voice.

"You handed it over to your accomplices."

"What accomplices?" blurted Katy.

He glowered at her.

"Don't play with me. You were working with a gang. Did they leave you behind? Did you decide to stay back so you could steal more stuff?"

"You think we *purposefully* got stuck in that underground kill box?" I said, suppressing the urge to yell right back in his face. "Bank vaults are airtight, soundproofed, and controlled at freezing temperatures. They're made to store metal and paper, not people. If you came tomorrow morning, you would have found our dead bodies."

"I'm going to ask you one last time," said Davies, leaning in. "Who hired you?"

"Chris Grayson," Katy and I chorused in unison for about the tenth time that morning.

"You don't have a license to operate in this state."

"We came because of a request from a friend," I said. "Mary Hudson is Jane Grayson's only cousin. She begged us to check up on Chris, and I never refuse a call for help."

Davies glared.

"Right now, I'd really like to give Grayson a call," I said. "He'll corroborate our story. I'm supposed to meet him at his home today. I'm sure you've heard about his missing wife. It's been all over the news."

I bit my lip before I said what else was on my mind. *Grayson called me for help because you lot haven't done your job and found her.*

Officer Davies got the hint. His face flushed.

"So he hired some fancy, dancy private eyes from New York, did he?"

"Why don't you do a background check on us instead of coming up with these outlandish claims?" replied Katy, her voice high-pitched.

Davies stopped pacing, put his hands on the back of his chair.

"Do you want to know what I think?" he said, glaring at me, then at Katy and back at me.

That wasn't worth an answer. He had made up his mind about us and anything I said would only rile him further. What we needed now was a lawyer. It was time to phone Peace.

"This PI stuff is all made up," glowered Davies. "It's a front."

"A front for *what*?" I spat out, unable to stop myself.

"You two are part of a drug cartel who were looking for extra cash. That's why you came here. That's why there was a dead body with a packet of drugs inside that vault. You broke in, but things went wrong."

Davies' eyes narrowed.

"You killed one of your partners, and now you're making up this stupid story of phantom men who supposedly abducted you at the airport so you can play the victim."

He paused to take a breath and glared.

"Do you know how many years you'll get for perjury?"

Katy and I remained silent.

"You're looking at ten years!"

Chapter Seventeen

I stared at Davies.

His beady eyes darted from Katy to me and back. His shoulders were tense, like he wanted to pounce on us. Something about us had put his back up, and I had a good inkling of what it was.

Davies wasn't just a keen rookie who wanted to impress his superior. It was the minute I told him Chris Grayson had invited us to help him with his missing wife that he had turned ugly.

That meant only one thing.

The file on Grayson's vanished wife was his—a case he had failed to deliver on.

"You're wasting time," said Katy with an exasperated sigh. "You should be looking for the three thieves, not haranguing us."

I looked Officer Davies dead in the eye. "We couldn't make this story up, even if we wanted to."

Thomas gave a nod, while Davies let out a raspberry.

I turned to the older cop. "If you have any evidence of wrongdoing, charge us formally. If not, let us go. That way, we can check up on our friend and figure out who did this to us."

"You wanna go around playing detective, do you?" sneered Davies.

"Because you're certainly not doing a great job at it," snapped Katy, shooting him a nasty look.

This time, both men glared at her.

I had seen my share of corrupt law enforcement officers, especially in Asia, where they seemed to get away with even murder, but we were in America. Citizens had rights here.

I wasn't about to let Davies intimidate us. He knew that. Otherwise, this interrogation would have happened in a dark alley behind the bank with a few threats thrown in for good measure.

"Why isn't the FBI involved in this?" I said.

Davies' face turned a slight shade of purple. "Are you questioning our—"

Thomas put a hand up to stop him and turned to me.

"This is a local co-op bank, so we're taking care of it for now."

"I want to find out who kidnapped us and what their motive was," I said. "I want to know who that dead woman was. And that white packet? It needs to be tested and its origins traced."

"Our lab is looking into it," said Davies through clenched teeth, his jaw tightening. He leaned across the table, his face inches from mine.

"You think you're one smart cookie, don't you?" he hissed, his spittle falling on my face. "You have some nerve."

I repressed the urge to wipe my cheeks. I didn't want him to think I was weak.

"No one's going to believe your story, not us, not a judge, or even a jury!" He was shouting again. "You're this close to being put in jail. I'll personally escort you in and throw away the key."

Thomas shook his head at his empty coffee cup.

"In all my years of law enforcement, I've never seen anything like this. I've seen banks broken into and valuables taken. I've seen emptied vaults. But never have I seen three live people and a dead body left behind."

I turned to him.

"We know you're doing your job and your job isn't easy. What you walked into was a freakish nightmare. None of us could have imagined it."

Thomas nodded and for once, Davies didn't shout.

"I pledge to you we will share everything we know," I said. "We'll answer all and any of your questions and stay in Seattle as long as you need us to. I'm pleading with you to check on the cameras everywhere, then call Grayson. That should piece together most of what happened."

Officer Thomas raised an eyebrow.

I felt a fire burn in my eyes. "Do you think I want the men who almost killed Win to get away? I'd do anything to find the thugs who did this to us."

Katy looked away, tears welling in her eyes.

Thomas turned to his partner. "Davies, we gotta meet with the DA. I'll call her."

He dragged his chair back, got up with his empty coffee cup in hand, and trundled out of the room.

Davies straightened up, smoothed his shirt, and glowered. "I'm not done with you two yet. I will hold you as long as I'm legally able to and I hope that will be a long time."

If that was an intimidation tactic, it wouldn't work on us.

I kept my gaze steady and my voice firm. "I think it's time to speak to our lawyer."

Davies spun on his heels and stomped out, slamming the door shut. The bolt turned with a loud clang.

For the second time in twenty-four hours, we were locked up.

Chapter Eighteen

"It's urgent," I said, breathing into the phone.

Katy and I were at an empty cubicle at the edge of a bullpen at the police station.

Around us, teams of civilians and uniformed officers were bustling around. No one had looked up when we walked in, but I was sure more than a few pairs of ears were listening in.

I waited for Peace, my attorney, to walk to a spot on the camping grounds with better cell phone reception. In the background, I could hear Chantelle asking her dad who it was. I hated to interrupt their father-daughter weekend, but I had no choice.

Katy sat nervously next to me, itching to talk to her little girl, but we had to figure out how to secure our freedom first.

The door to the interrogation room had banged open a few minutes after Davies had stormed out. Katy, who'd put her head on the table, jerked up, and clutched my arm.

The female officer who'd been part of the rescue operation at the bank had been standing at the threshold, one hand on the doorknob, the other on her hips. Her name badge simply said LEE.

Officer Lee held the door open, an annoyed expression on her face.

"You have ten minutes, ladies."

Katy and I had got up and followed her out. She'd pointed at the landline on a bare desk that contained the telephone, a notepad, and a stubby pencil.

"Make it quick," she had barked before spinning around on her heels and marching out.

I took the chair while Katy rolled over an uncomfortable-looking office seat and huddled close to me. After Katy explained to Peace what had happened, I plucked the handset from her.

"How do we get out of here?" I asked.

"They'd be hard pressed to hold you for over twenty-four hours if they don't have any evidence to arrest you," came Peace's calm and steady voice down the line. "I'll get a legal rep to come and see you ASAP, but you have to be patient."

"How long do we have to stay stuck here?" said Katy, as she leaned in to listen. "And what about Win? She's all alone in some strange hospital."

"We have a satellite office in Seattle. I'll call someone there and ask them to visit her and make sure she's being taken care of." He paused. "How are they treating you?"

"They haven't put us in jail yet," I said. "Kept us in an interrogation room all morning, but they're not letting us out."

"An attorney needs to be present when they talk to you."

"But we didn't do anything," said Katy, her voice plaintive.

"That doesn't matter, hun," replied Peace. "Don't say another word without us there, okay?"

I hung up, grateful to have Peace on retainer and a quick call away. He always responded immediately, especially when Katy was with me.

"They can't pin that awful heist on us, can they?" said Katy, giving me a wide-eyed look. "And how can they think we killed that poor girl?"

Several officers looked up.

I motioned to her to keep it down.

"You said we came to find a missing woman," whispered Katy, leaning closer. "I'm not going on trips with you anymore. I don't care how loud anyone cries for help, even if it's a crazy multi-millionaire—"

"Grayson!" I said, leaping on the phone.

Officer Lee hadn't come to get us yet, and I was going to take advantage of every minute I had. I dialed fast from memory. The phone rang three times before I heard the click.

"Chris Grayson?"

Silence. But I could hear his breathing.

"Are you there?" I tried again.

"This is he," he replied cautiously.

Relief flooded through me to hear his voice.

"We arrived in Seattle last night, but I won't make it to the meeting today because we're at the police station."

A sharp breath came from the other end.

I spoke quickly. "Two men who said they work for you picked us from the airport last night. They kidnapped us and took us with them as they robbed a local bank. Union Lake Bank."

Dead silence.

"Do you know anything about this?"

"What on *earth*?"

My voice hardened.

"They left us locked inside a basement vault. We spent the night in that confined space with depleting oxygen and with the body of a young woman."

"What?"

"You have some explaining to do, Mr. Grayson," I said, trying not to clench my teeth. "We spent the morning in an interrogation room with police detectives trying to figure out what's going on. I'd like to know too."

"My goodness," he breathed.

"I think you know something about this, and you damn well owe us an explanation."

"I, er, I don't... oh, my...," stammered Grayson. "What a nightmare. I swear, I had no idea."

"How did these men know we were coming to town?" I snapped. "How did they—"

Katy nudged me.

A man strode to a cabinet, passing by us with a file in his hands. Several officers had gathered by a water cooler, but they each had a notepad in hand and were deep in discussion.

I leaned closer to the table and lowered my voice, wishing I could reach through the line and shake Grayson by the collar.

"I brought my team to help you, and now my computer security expert is in the emergency ward because those men tried to *poison* her. What is going on?"

"My gosh, oh, my…" He stumbled over his words. "I didn't know… I'll, er, I'll get you out right away. I know some people in the precinct."

"Time's up."

I looked around to see Thomas towering behind my chair.

Had he been listening in?

"You had better," I said to Grayson, before slamming the phone down.

I got up and pulled myself to my full five feet. "Officer, we'll need our lawyer with us for any further questioning."

Thomas raised a brow.

"You're spending precious time with us when the real gangsters are getting away. It's unconscionable."

To my surprise, Thomas said nothing, but turned around and gestured for Officer Lee to approach us.

"All yours," he said.

Without another word, he turned and plodded through the bullpen toward his office.

Chapter Nineteen

"**Y**ou may leave," said Officer Lee.

"We're free to go?" said Katy in surprise.

Lee's face remained stoic. "I believe that's what I just said."

In her hurry to get up, Katy swept the pad and pencil to the floor. She reached down to pick them up.

"Chop, chop, ladies," said Lee, tapping her foot. "Unless you plan on sleeping in the station."

"We can find our way out," I said. "We don't need an escort."

Officer Lee nodded, as if she was glad she didn't have to babysit us. She pointed to the long corridor through which Davies had brought us earlier.

"Straight down and to the left. Just follow the green exit signs."

"Thank you."

"We found your luggage in the limo."

It was my turn to be surprised. "You found the car? Have you arrested the men?"

Lee gave me a dismissive wave. "Your luggage is at the reception desk in front. All items have been inventoried. You'll have to sign a form before you retrieve your bags."

"What about our phones?" said Katy. "I need to call my family."

"No phones. They probably threw them away."

"Where did you find the limo?" I asked, frowning.

"Abandoned on a side street."

"Any sign of the men?"

Officer Lee let out an impatient sigh. "I'm afraid I can't comment on an ongoing investigation."

"Why are you releasing us now?" I said. "Neither my lawyer nor Chris Grayson had time to call you and make arrangements, so what happened?"

She grimaced when I mentioned my client's name. If Thomas had convinced the district attorney to let us go, this place worked faster than any government office on the planet.

I observed the officer carefully. "You found the men who broke into the bank, didn't you?"

"You weren't under arrest," said Officer Lee, impatience laced in her voice. "We just wanted to ask you a few questions."

"You held us here all morning. Davies even threatened to jail us. We cooperated as good citizens—"

"That's why you're on your way out." Lee whirled around to leave. "Y'all have a good day."

"Wait," I said, following her. "What are you going to do now?"

She let out an exasperated sigh. "We have the case in hand, ma'am. We'll be taking the appropriate steps as needed."

"When you catch the thugs, I'll have a few questions for them," I said, holding my ground. "And some choice words."

"You need to leave now."

"They nearly killed us. We have the right to know if you've caught them or not."

"I wouldn't hold my breath. They're probably in Jamaica by now."

I stopped, startled.

That was the second time Jamaica had been named as a getaway. The first time was by Russ just before he took off from the vault with that purple unicorn backpack.

Was it a coincidence? Did the police know who the goons were but were withholding that information from us?

Without another word, Lee snapped around on her heels and disappeared from view.

I felt eyes watching and turned my head.

Davies was standing not too far from our cubicle. He shot me an indignant sneer as he saw me look. His expression told me he would rather see us in jail. Within seconds, he'd slipped into a closed office.

With a resigned sigh, I turned to follow Katy down the corridor toward the main entrance. We walked in silence, digesting what had happened.

The smell of coffee and breakfast wafted from somewhere. My stomach growled. I was running on pure adrenaline. My body and brain were numb with fatigue. We had been in Seattle less than twenty-four hours and had already had a lifetime of experiences—experiences I would rather have done without.

I felt naked without my trusty phone on me. I was dying to call the hospital about Win and to talk to Peace and Grayson. My client knew more about what was going on, I was sure.

We stumbled through the corridor, following the exit signs. A handful of workers hurried by us, but didn't give us a second glance.

We were halfway down the corridor to the main lobby when I saw the sign.

Medical Examinations.

Katy shuddered as we passed by it.

"That's where that poor woman is right now," I said. "They're probably cutting her up as we speak."

"I don't get it. Why put a body in a vault during a heist?" said Katy. "That's worse than leaving fingerprints."

The image of the young woman's scarred face sprang to mind. She had looked so vulnerable. Then, I remembered the drug packet.

Why kill her?

I swiveled my head. We were far from the bullpen and the interrogation rooms. Officers Lee, Davies, and Thomas were nowhere to be seen.

I nudged Katy.

"Detour," I whispered.

"What do you mean?" she whispered back.

"We have a body to check in on," I said as I pushed through the swing doors and into the Medical Examinations wing.

Chapter Twenty

A door opened, and a man in green medical scrubs stepped out.

Katy stiffened.

"Act normal," I whispered, fixing a polite smile on my face.

But the man in scrubs stepped through a set of swing doors at the other end of the corridor. He hadn't even noticed us.

I scanned the signs over each door as we strolled down, doing our best to act like employees, interns, contractors—anything but recently released suspects of a major crime.

The corridor was silent, a contrast to the hustle and bustle elsewhere. The smell of antiseptic and formaldehyde pervaded the air, unlike the odor of old sweat, musty files, and stale sandwiches that emanated from the other side of the building.

I stopped by a hermetically sealed green door, which looked more reinforced than the rest of the entrances along this passageway.

I pressed against the steel bar handle, expecting it to resist, but it clicked open. Using my shoulders, I pushed on the heavy door and peeked inside. There was no one.

No one alive, at least.

Gesturing for Katy to follow me, I slipped in. The door closed gently behind us.

A row of what looked like oversized stainless-steel boxes lined against one wall. It took me a second to realize these were temperature-controlled fridge compartments used to store murder victims.

"It's freezing in here," said Katy, wrapping her arms around her shoulders.

There was no sight of the body bag anywhere. But two cadavers lay covered on the steel examination tables, their outline clearly visible through the sheets.

The faint noise of a far door closing from somewhere along the corridor made me look up.

We didn't have a lot of time.

I swiveled around, looking for the hygiene station. A long stainless-steel counter with two enormous sinks was attached to the far wall. On one end hung a row of rubber aprons. On the other was a cardboard box with the words *disposable gloves* on it.

I scurried over, pulled out two pairs of gloves, and handed one to Katy.

"You check the one by the fridges. I'll check this one."

"You want me to inspect a dead *body*?" said Katy, making a face but taking the gloves with trembling hands.

Without answering, I strode up to the closest gurney and flipped the plastic cover back.

It was the body of a young African-American man who had died well before his time. The gun shot to his forehead was unmistakable.

I spun around.

Katy was still standing on the spot, frozen, a grimace on her face like she'd just swallowed something bitter. The gloves I'd handed to her lay limp in her hands.

I whipped around her and stepped up to the second gurney by the fridges.

I flipped the cover, expecting to see the young woman, but it was another man. This time, a Caucasian male, who also looked too young to be dead, stabbed right in the chest.

I flipped the cover back over his body.

Where is she?

The sound of a door opening made me jump.

Katy grabbed my arm. "We have to get out of here!"

A phone rang outside in the corridor. My heart raced.

"No time," I hissed, stepping up to the hygiene station to grab two face masks and two rubber aprons from the hangers.

I shoved a pair toward Katy. "Put this on!"

It took her a second to realize what I was asking her to do. I put mine on with shaking hands. If they found us here, we'd get a one-way trip to a jail cell for certain.

"Ready?" I said, pulling Katy toward the nearest gurney. I threw open the cover and pretended to scrutinize the corpse.

The door clicked open.

I froze.

"Hey."

I looked up, feeling a river of sweat trickle down my back. A man in civilian clothes was standing by the door, his head in but his body firmly outside, like he didn't dare walk in.

"Doctor Melnyk? Detective Garnier's looking for him."

"Just stepped out," I said, my heart thudding in my chest. I had no idea what I would have said if the medical examiner himself had walked in. "Come back in fifteen."

The man retreated and closed the door.

Katy and I let out a breath of relief.

"Let's get out of here," I said, reaching for my apron when the door clicked open again.

Katy and I jerked our heads around. It was the same man, poking his head through the opening, but this time, he had a frown on his face.

"Hey, not seen you around before. You new?"

I nodded. "Interns from the university hospital."

His face cleared. Then the frown returned.

"Don't want to tell y'all how to do your job or anything, but I thought you were supposed to be at the orientation on the second floor. Meeting's already started."

"Jeez!" I said, hoping I sounded sufficiently panicky, though it wasn't hard to pretend. "We're late! Thanks. Don't tell Dr. Melnyk."

He withdrew with a low chuckle and closed the door.

Katy and I stood in our spots, staring at the entrance, waiting for it to open again.

But he was really gone.

"Let's go!"

I pulled my apron, mask, and gloves off in a hurry. I didn't want us to be hauled in front of Davies so he could sneer at us some more.

Katy and I slipped out the door and back into the passageway. It was empty. We hurried toward the main corridor of the building.

I only started breathing again when we were close to the lobby.

"I still don't get it," whispered Katy as we scurried along. "Why stick a dead woman in a bank vault?"

"Could it have been a message?"

"To whom?"

"The Mafia is known to send dead bodies of rival gang members to their families to show who's boss of the territory—" I paused. "But this wasn't a rival gang. This was an established bank."

"Do they have a Mafia in Seattle?" said Katy.

"Where there will be humans, there will be villains."

I scrunched my forehead. Something was nagging at me in the back of my head. "This might have been a message to the local police. That would explain why they're so tight-lipped."

"What possible message could that be?"

"The most plausible answer is that dead woman was a police informant. Once the gangsters found out, they silenced her, but wanted to make sure the police knew they knew."

"My goodness."

"It's just a guess. If this had been a normal Mafia killing, they would have thrown the body bag into the river. Tied it with a few bricks and no one would have discovered her until the body had fully decomposed."

"Or maybe never," said Katy with a shudder.

We were in the lobby now.

The double glass doors to the station were sliding back and forth as foot traffic streamed in and out. The police were busy that day.

Something tightened in my gut. I was missing a huge clue that was staring in our face.

I turned to my friend. "Katy, I don't think this had anything to do with the bank or the police."

"Then who? Was it us? Someone from our past?"

I shook my head. "It's Grayson. He hasn't told us the complete story. This whole incident revolves around—"

Katy clutched my arm.

"Oh, my goodness. It's them!"

Chapter Twenty-one

Two burly young men in beige uniforms were sitting slumped in the waiting area.

Katy nudged me with her elbow. "What are they doing here?"

The men were in their early twenties, not much more. One had a cut on his forehead, like someone had slashed him with a knife. The other had spots of dried blood on his collar, a black eye, and swollen lips.

The silver name tags pinned to their crumpled shirts said, *Union Lake Bank Security.*

The men were fidgeting and looking around nervously, like they expected an unknown assailant to attack them at any moment. Perhaps someone had jumped on them last night.

I walked over.

The man at the end leaned back as I approached, like he was expecting me to hit him. His companion watched me warily, hiding behind his colleague.

"What are you doing here?" I asked, forgetting to introduce myself.

They stared. One of them blinked a few times, like he couldn't believe his eyes.

I surveyed them from head to toe. Their clothes were wrinkled and dirty, like they had been in a bar fight.

"What are *you* doing here?" whispered the first man, still leaning away from me like I would bite.

"I asked first," I said. "What happened at the bank last night, gentlemen?"

The second man's face had turned pale, and he was staring at me like he knew me.

I bent down, so I was at eye-level with him. "You recognize me, eh? I've been in Seattle only since midnight last night, yet you know me. How is that?"

He rubbed his reddened eyes.

"I saw you," he whispered hoarsely, "inside the vault."

"And you did nothing?" cried Katy, stomping over and standing next to me, her arms crossed. "We could have died. Where were you?"

The men looked away, blinking rapidly.

"A bunch of goons held us at gunpoint and even brought a body bag in." Katy's voice rose by the second. "For goodness' sake, you work at a city bank, not at the corner grocery store."

A few passersby turned to give us curious looks. I motioned to my friend to lower her volume. The security guards merely stared at us, their faces etched in fear.

All along, I had been sure the bank's security team had been involved in the heist, but these two young men looked as scared as we had been inside that vault.

"How did you see us?" I said, softening my voice.

"On the cameras," said the younger of the two. His hands were shaking.

"The security cameras were working all along, then?"

The guards nodded forlornly.

A slow anger burned inside of me as I remembered how Davies treated us like criminals.

"Why didn't you do your job?" demanded Katy.

"Because they tied me and my buddy Tyrone up," said the first man, his voice high-pitched. "They even stuffed gags in our mouths."

I raised an eyebrow. "Who tied you up?"

Tyrone rubbed his face with one hand. There were raw marks around his wrists. These men had been roughed up badly.

"Wish I knew," he mumbled. He turned to his colleague. "They beat Will the hardest."

Will gave a shrug, then winced like that small movement hurt.

"Sounds like you guys had a nasty night too," I said. "Can you tell us what happened?"

The men fell silent, folding and unfolding their hands, looking around, every movement jittery.

I pulled a chair and sat across from them. "I'm Asha Kade and this is Katy McCafferty. We're private investigators from New York."

Tyrone and Will's eyebrows shot up.

"We came to Seattle to help a client find his missing wife. We arrived at the airport at midnight last night when those men abducted us."

The fidgeting stopped. They were listening intently now.

"Two men who called themselves Randy and Noah picked us up from the airport," I continued. "They told us our client sent them to take us to our hotel, but guess where we ended up?"

"The vault," said Will haltingly through his swollen lips.

I nodded.

"That's crazy," said Tyrone. "How...? *Why?*"

"That's what we'd like to know," snapped Katy.

"Have you seen these men before?" I asked.

"No... have you?" said Will, his eyes wide. I stared at him for a second, unsure if he was playing with me, but that was a genuine question.

I sat up straight.

"If I knew who those thugs were, I'd be going after them and making them pay, not sitting here, having a chitchat." I leaned in. "So, tell us what happened last night."

Tyrone pointed at Will, who was rubbing his face like he was in a bad dream and desperately wanted to wake up.

"He was doing the rounds as usual, and I was in the security booth, watching the cameras like I was supposed to."

"Was it just the two of you on watch last night?"

"Jaime does the rounds outside, but he gets off at midnight. After they put in all that fancy computer security stuff last year, they fired the rest of our team, so it's just us two for the night shift."

"How did these men walk into the bank with all the security systems in place?"

"They turned it off."

"How?"

"Beats me." Tyrone stopped as if to think. "They planned this. I swear someone fixed it that morning, you know what I mean?"

I nodded. "Do you have any idea if this was a local gang?"

Both men looked away, blinking rapidly.

"All I know was they wanted us out of the way while they did their job," said Will, hesitating with every word.

I wasn't sure if it was the pain of talking through his swollen lips or if there was something else that made him too frightened to speak up.

"How did you end up tied and gagged? Didn't you see them coming?"

"It was around ten o'clock," said Will. "One second, I was checking the service door at the back, the next second I had a gun to my head. No idea how he got in."

Ten o'clock? We were still on the plane at that time, less than two hours from Seattle.

"Did you catch his face?"

"He said hands up and pushed me with the barrel of his gun on my back. I just kept moving, you know? Man, I wasn't about to turn around and argue. I have a little girl at home...."

Will choked up and covered his face with his hands.

"So, you never recognized the men?"

Tyrone's eyes flickered.

"They didn't bother to conceal their faces," I said. "What does that tell you?"

Tyrone shrugged and looked down at the floor. Will still had his face covered.

We hadn't been the only ones who'd been victimized by those thugs. But something told me Will and Tyrone knew more than they were telling.

Chapter Twenty-two

I turned to Tyrone.

"You must have seen *something* on the cameras. They couldn't have materialized out of nowhere."

"Saw a black limo come around ten," said Tyrone.

Katy gasped. "It had to be the same one that kidnapped us."

"It parked in front of the bank. Thought it was some kids off to a late party and they stopped by to get money from the cash machine. It's just outside the main entrance."

"Did anyone get out of the car?" I asked.

"That was what was really weird. The limo kept revving and reversing, a few feet back and forth like some kid stole it and was having fun. So I kept my eyes on it, wondering if I should call the cops on them. Wasn't watching anything else..."

"A distraction while they grabbed Will," I said, turning to his partner.

Will wiped the sweat off his forehead. "The dude with the gun told me to go to the second floor. That's where the security booth is, where Tyrone was, so they knew what they were doing. They knew our layout."

I nodded.

"A second guy was waiting for us at the top of the stairs," continued Will. "He had short dreads and a Glock."

"Did you recognize either of them in the vault later on?" I asked.

"I think the man with the dreads was there with you, but I didn't get a good look at the white dude."

"Randy," said Katy. "The leader of the ring."

Tyrone and Will raised their eyebrows.

"That's what he called himself, anyway," said Katy.

"They forced me to open the security booth door," said Will. "When Tyrone got up to see who it was—"

"They whacked me," finished Tyrone, showing me the gash on his head. A large cotton swab covered part of it. I could smell the disinfectant.

Will rubbed his face again.

"They roughed us up quite a bit and tied us to our chairs. Hands, feet, everything. Then they left, just like that. They didn't talk or say anything. No idea where they went until they came back with y'all at a half past midnight."

"They left you to take us from the airport," I said in a quiet voice.

"We sat like that for hours," continued Will, as if he didn't hear me. "There was nothing we could do, you know what I mean? Couldn't talk, couldn't reach the emergency button or the phone. We tried everything, but they tied us real good."

Tyrone looked up, his brow creased with lines.

"The cameras were still rolling, so we saw you on the screen. I was so scared for you. All you girls with those psycho men. I nearly pissed my pants when you opened that body bag, I tell you. Man, what a nightmare. Who is she?"

It was my turn to shrug. "I wish I knew."

"Crazy stuff," said Will, shaking his head. "No one's gonna believe me when I tell them what happened. I'm just doing this job for college money. I never expected any of this. I'm so sorry for.... I'm just happy they did nothing to you ladies, you know what I mean?"

I straightened up and glanced around me. The morning crowd in the lobby had dispersed, and it was quieter now. There was no sign of Davies, Lee, or Thomas, but we couldn't hang around here for long.

"The good news is," said Katy thoughtfully, "there's camera footage."

I turned to my friend. "That's why they let us go just now. They saw what happened."

She nodded. "This was obviously an insider job, planned and executed professionally."

"Wasn't us," said Will, shaking his head.

"That's what I told them too," said Tyrone, spreading his hands. "I told the cops we were doing our jobs, but someone was working with them. There was no way we could have stopped them."

"If the cameras captured everything, you have nothing to worry about," said Katy, her voice softening. "That's probably why you're not in jail."

The two men exchanged an alarmed glance, as if they hadn't considered the possibility until she had mentioned it.

"What I don't get is why those thugs didn't cover their faces," I said, leaning back in my chair to think. "Do you think they forgot to turn off the cameras?"

Tyrone shook his head. "They saw them rolling. They even put our chairs in front of the screens, so we'd see what happened."

The more I talked to them, the more I felt they weren't guilty, but they had evaded me every time I asked about the men.

What were they frightened of? A powerful gang? The mafia? The police?

"One reason they didn't turn the cameras off is because they were sure they'd get off scot free," I said, turning to Tyrone and Will. "That means they have connections. You must have an inkling who they could be, no?"

They didn't answer, but they weren't making eye contact anymore, either.

I changed tactic. "What are you doing at the station now?"

"The cops took us to the hospital so we could get checked up last night," said Will. "The ambulance just dropped us here so we could give our statements."

Katy let out a disgusted hiss. "At least they believed you. We just spent three hours in a torture room getting interrogated by a mini Gestapo who wanted to throw us in jail."

Tyrone looked up, a worried expression on his face.

"You think they're going to arrest us too? My mama saved all her money to send me to college. She'll kill me if she—"

"Ms. Kade?"

I spun around to face Thomas, coffee cup still in his hand, only five feet from us. His earlier gentle creased eyes had hardened.

"I believe you were on your way out." His tone was clear. That wasn't a suggestion.

I stood up. "You've been asking questions all along, and now it's our turn."

Thomas leaned in, his giant frame towering over me. "It's time for you to return home."

I didn't budge. "I'd like to know who held us in that death trap. Did you find out who those men are?"

He took a deep breath, like he was trying hard to hold his anger in check.

I had pegged him to be a mild-mannered bureaucrat who would rather be fishing, but there was something hard underneath that teddy bear physique. He was a police officer, after all.

"They tell me they'll discharge your friend from the hospital tomorrow," he said. "If I were you, I'd start planning to fly back to New York."

"I made a commitment to my client."

Thomas let out an exasperated sigh. He spread his arms wide and leaned in, his expression that of a concerned uncle again.

"I've been in this business for a long time, Ms. Kade. I was chasing criminals while you were learning your ABCs in kindergarten. When I say you'd best leave town, I'm saying this for your own good."

"Officer Thomas, I'm an adult woman, not a kid in a playground. I can take care of myself."

He raised a brow. "That's how you got locked up in a bank vault."

"They took us at gunpoint!" cried Katy.

"We have our best officers on the case. I promise to get to the bottom of this, and when I am at liberty to share, I will answer your questions. That's a promise I will make to you. Give us time."

His eyes narrowed.

"What would really help us is if you and your friends leave as soon as you can. I can't promise these men won't come back and I don't have the resources to protect you."

My conversation with Peace sprang to mind. As nice as this cop came across, I wondered if his concern was more about avoiding a potential lawsuit for holding us this morning than our well-being.

Before I could reply, he gestured at the two young guards. They had been listening quietly, fearful expressions on their faces.

"This way, boys," said Thomas.

The men stood up shakily and shuffled toward the police officer.

"Tyrone," I said, as he passed by me. "Do you need a lawyer?"

He shot me a frightened look but didn't reply.

Chapter Twenty-three

"False imprisonment," said Peace.

I was on the public phone at the nurses' station while Katy sat beside Win's hospital bed, waiting for her to wake up.

Behind me, a lone security guard patrolled the ward near Win's room, a bored expression on her face. The police had contracted her with special instructions to ensure no one other than medical personnel entered the room.

I was glad she was there, bored or not. I hated to think of Win lying alone in this room, vulnerable to anything.

The guard saw me look and gave me a nod. I nodded back in acknowledgment.

"Someone goofed somewhere," said Peace, bringing me back to the conversation, "and they'd rather you not ask too many questions."

"We shared everything," I said. "I don't enjoy being yelled at, but the more the police knows, the quicker they'd catch those thugs."

"Given there's no evidence against you, you have the right to lodge a complaint of false imprisonment. They know you have the resources and an attorney on standby. That's what they're afraid of. That means paperwork, court dates, and long hours, enough to make any civil servant quake in their shoes."

"I don't care about Thomas or Davies. What I don't get is the motivation for anyone to pick up three strangers from the airport and take us with them to witness a grand crime."

"They were betting on you panicking, freezing, then dying from lack of air in a few hours. They didn't expect you to live."

"It doesn't take a genius to figure out there might be failsafe trip alarms in a bank."

"You're giving the average Jane too much credit. A normal person shoved in a vault at gunpoint with a dead body would scream and hyperventilate until they die of fear, well before they lose air."

"But why did they do it? What was the point?"

"That's the million-dollar question." He paused. "Let's not forget the dead body. How does she figure into this? Who is she and why was she thrown in there?"

"This wasn't a normal heist. There's a lot more going on behind the scenes and the cops know it. They're being cagey, but we deserve answers."

"They don't think that way. Davies is a hardliner and Thomas sounds more like a bureaucrat than a cop. Right now, their concern is to how to best cover their bums, for their sake and their superiors'."

"We should have answers once they identify the body, except I have a feeling the station will keep that info close to their chests. Thomas is literally chasing us out of town."

"I'm glad to hear the doctors will let Win go in twenty-four hours," said Peace. "Luc bought a ticket over. He almost had a heart attack when I told him the news."

"Please tell him to stay home," I said. The last thing I needed was more folks to worry about.

"I told him you were coming straight over when they discharge Win from the hospital."

"I'll pack her and Katy on the first flight as soon as they release her, but I'm staying."

"Asha."

I knew that tone. Peace was always calm and respectful, but he was shifting into his big brother mode.

"I won't let a cop or a gang of heist men intimidate me," I said.

"You have no skin in this game, girl. You've already gone through the ringer for something you had nothing to do with. Leave it. Come home."

"Mary asked me for help. I promised."

"If she knew what you had gone through, she wouldn't expect you to stay."

"You don't understand. I promised that dead girl I'd find out who did that to her."

"Asha," came the big brother voice again. "Send Grayson back his retainer and wash your hands off this case. Don't get involved."

"That's the thing. This has his name all over it. I want to meet him and find out what hand he played in this." My mind whirred as I thought of my next steps. "Don't worry. Katy and Win will be on their way back, even if I have to handcuff them to their seats."

Peace let out a sigh.

"David thinks you're coming home soon too," he said in a tired voice. "I don't want to be the one to spill the news."

"I'll handle it—" I stopped as I saw someone hovering by Win's open door. I twisted around on my stool to see a nurse enter with a food tray.

"Win's up," I said, turning back to the phone. "Gotta go. Talk soon."

After hanging up, I stepped into the small single room. Win hadn't moved a muscle since we found her curled up under a blanket in her bed, surrounded by beeping machines and screens.

It had been a relief to learn they had transferred her from the emergency wing to a regular ward where they were observing her.

Katy was wiping Win's brow with a towel. Win was still lying in the same position as before, immobile, but breathing heavily.

"I'm going to leave this here," said the nurse, placing the food tray on the bedside table.

The PA system in the corridor crackled to life. "Visiting hours end in ten minutes."

"Can we stay till she wakes up?" said Katy.

"This is not the emergency ward, ladies. You can come again during the regular visiting period."

"Can we wake her up to say goodbye at least? I'd hate for her to wake up to an empty room."

"She needs her rest." The nurse turned a stern face at Katy. "If she's sleeping, that's what her body needs. That's the most important thing for her recovery."

"Is she going to be okay?" I said.

"They flushed the toxicity out. Her body needs to recuperate now."

"Any idea what was inside that champagne bottle?"

The nurse raised an eyebrow, but didn't ask.

"The lab is testing the contents." She paused and let her shoulders drop, and gave us a sympathetic look. "She's in excellent hands. We'll take care of her."

Katy and I stood by Win's bed long after the nurse left, long after the visiting hours ended, ignoring the PA's announcements.

Win's face was pale, and her lips were slightly tinged in blue, but her body was warm and her heartbeat was strong.

I didn't know how long we'd been standing there when a loud voice blasted through the open doorway.

"Visiting hours are over!"

Katy and I jerked back, startled.

It was the security guard. A fierce frown had replaced her cordial expression and her hand was hovering over her gun on her belt.

Her glare deepened. "Leave now, or do I escort you out?"

Chapter Twenty-four

"Keep your voice down," said Katy, glaring at the guard. "She's sleeping."

Katy stomped out of the room in a huff. I followed her with an apologetic smile. We needed the security guard to stay on our side.

"Please keep an eye on her," I said.

The guard's glower remained, but her hand moved away from her holster.

"By the way, do you know where the morgue is?" I asked.

Her response was automatic. "West wing, first floor. By the kitchens."

If there was one thing I knew, it was that hospitals didn't advertise their mortuaries. With a nod of thanks, I hurried away before she realized what I had asked and stopped me.

It took us longer than I expected to find the morgue. I hadn't realized how immense a major city hospital could be.

Katy and I plodded through the labyrinth of never-ending corridors. We passed the main cafeteria, which, according to the guard's brief instructions, should be in the morgue's vicinity.

"I can't wait to hear Chantelle's voice," said Katy, as we stumbled along, her face scrunched with exhaustion. "I hugged her yesterday, but it feels like years."

"We've gone through hell and back," I said, rubbing my tired temples. "We haven't got any sleep since we got here either. It's a wonder we're still standing."

Soon after we'd left the police station, we had hailed down a cab to take us to the nearest car-rental company. Though Officer Thomas and his colleagues were keen for us to leave town, I signed a lease for a week, that dead girl's face flashing across my mind as I did.

I couldn't let this go. I was going to sort this out, no matter what.

After we'd packed our luggage in the back of the car, we'd stopped by a mini mall to rent two burner phones and grab takeaway sandwiches before driving over to the hospital.

Neither Katy nor I had spoken during the drive. We had too much to ruminate on.

The attack on Win was what haunted me the most. I prayed silently to whatever angels were watching over her. If she had sustained permanent damage, I would never forgive myself.

I cursed myself for letting her get into that limo, and then for letting her drink that champagne. I had been suspicious all along, but I hadn't stopped her.

That bizarre limo ride seemed a lifetime away now.

"Where are we going to sleep tonight?" said Katy. "I'm so ready to crash."

"Hotels usually keep reservations for twenty-four hours," I said, pulling my new burner phone out of my pocket. "They might charge us for not showing up last night, but it's worth a try."

We trundled along the corridor while I tried to negotiate with an unfriendly hotel receptionist. After hanging up, I pocketed the phone with a resigned sigh.

"Fully booked."

"They gave up our room?" said Katy.

"Supposedly, there's some major convention in town."

"What do we do now?"

"There must be a motel or a room-share available."

"If there isn't?"

"We sleep in the car—"

I stopped as I spotted the sign with an arrow pointing toward the end of the corridor.

Main Kitchens.

The sound of people hollering, taps running, and plates clinking came to us. I could hear diesel trucks idling in the parking lot just outside the kitchen, their throaty roars mixed with the hum of industrial-strength refrigerators.

"This way," I said, hastening my pace.

"Terrible planning," said Katy, glancing around her. "Why would you put dead bodies next to the hospital kitchen?"

"Convenience. Some trucks bring the food. Others bring in the bodies."

"Gross. I'm never eating from a hospital again. Neither is Win. I'm bringing her a sandwich this afternoon."

I stepped up to the large white door. The sign said *Staff Only.* There was no indication it was the mortuary.

Katy pulled on my arm frantically as a cook strolled by, taking a cigarette out of his pocket. He gave us a curious glance, but a phone call took his focus away.

"They'll never let us in," whispered Katy.

I peeked through the glass panels on the swing door. Inside was yet another barren corridor that seemed to go on forever.

Several heavy, stainless-steel doors lined both sides of the corridor, looking like entrances into surgery rooms.

People rushed past us, clutching clipboards or phones. Some were clearly kitchen and restaurant staff in their black chef caps and striped aprons. Others were uniformed delivery drivers. A couple of medical staff in scrubs walked toward the back entrance, laughing, like they were about to start their breaks.

In our crumpled street clothes, Katy and I stuck out. We couldn't hang around here too long before someone started asking questions.

I pushed the swing door open. "Coming?"

We stepped in, and the doors closed gently behind us. The air was cooler in this wing.

"How do we know she's here?" whispered Katy. "Even if she's here, how do you know they won't kick us out before we see her?"

"Nothing ventured, nothing gained," I muttered as I walked up to the first door to our right. I gently pushed the handle using the side of my body and peeked through the narrow opening.

It was a storage room.

Two young workers were unloading a large cardboard box filled with paper towels. Both had earphones on and were singing to themselves. I let the door close quietly.

The next entrance was a hermetically sealed door with an ominous sign over it. *Limb Freezer*.

"Creepy," whispered Katy, huddling closer to me as we walked over to the next entrance.

I pushed the door ajar and squinted inside.

Floor-to-ceiling stainless-steel fridges lined the walls. A cool burst of air wafted out of the narrow opening.

A lone woman in a yellow plastic coverall was standing by a sink, scrubbing her hands. The water running off her hands was a bright blood red. Next to her was a body on a gurney.

As she turned to get more soap from the dispenser, I noticed the surgical mask on her face. As if she had felt me watching, she turned around to look.

I closed the door quickly and stepped back, almost tripping over my friend.

"Well?" whispered Katy.

"It's all one long hall from here on," I whispered, pointing down the corridor. "All those doors enter the morgue."

"Did you see the dead girl?"

"There was one body on a trolley, but it was a man. There were more, but I couldn't see all the way down the room."

The corridor was quiet, except for the subdued hum of truck engines and restaurant noises coming from outside. But anyone could walk out of these doors at any moment and raise the alarm.

"There's a small crowd of doctors huddled at the end. Maybe that's where she is. Let's try the last door."

I was about to walk over when a door to our left banged open and a man bustled out. He gave us a startled look and frowned, but rushed toward the main entrance.

"Hurry," I said to my friend.

We scurried down the corridor toward the end. I walked up to the last door and gently clicked it open.

This part of the morgue was busy.

Closest to us was a body covered in a plastic sheet. A medical examiner was arranging her tools in one corner. The blinding fluorescent light glinted off an autopsy saw in her hands.

"I couldn't do that job for a million dollars," whispered Katy in my ear. I hushed her quickly, but I had to agree.

The doctor placed her tray of tools at the foot of the body and reached for a tablet.

Another examiner in full overalls, gloves, and mask trudged over and casually flipped the cover away from the gurney. He started calling out snippets of data while his colleague recorded it on her tablet.

Neither of them noticed us peeking in.

I pushed my head in an inch farther. The dead body was male.

"Who are you?" came a sharp voice from my left.

My heart jumped to my mouth.

Two medical officers were standing by a second dissected body behind the door.

Chapter Twenty-five

My eyes flew across the room to the body by the two medical examiners.

It was the corpse of a middle-aged woman.

"Yes?" One doctor frowned at me over her mask. "May we help you?"

"We're l... looking for a f... friend," I said, adding a stammer. Not that hard to do as my heart was racing. "She, er, died last night."

I rearranged my face to appear mournful, hopefully distraught.

"You can't come in here," replied her colleague, pointing at me with her bloodied scalpel. "The family officer will notify you and give you the required information at the right time."

"I just... I just wanted to see her one... one last time."

I paused, swallowed hard, and scrunched my eyes like I was trying not to cry.

"She's twenty-one, in a kilted green skirt, and white shirt. Her face was.... Her boyfriend hit her face so bad.... Did you see her?"

I gave them my best pleading look.

The second woman shook her head. "I'm sorry. There is no such person here."

The first doctor frowned. "This is a restricted area. No one is permitted without protective gear. You shouldn't be here at all."

The second doctor gave us a sympathetic look. "No one was brought in last night or this morning that fit that description."

"But... but I was so sure.... They said the ambulance brought her."

Her partner glared at us. "You must leave now." She made a move toward the red phone hanging on the wall behind her.

"Thank... thank you," I stammered as I closed the door.

"Let's go," I whispered to Katy.

"Strange," said Katy as we scuttled down the hallway, back toward the swinging doors. "If she's not at the police station and she's not here, where is she? Did they take her to another hospital?"

My mind was buzzing, but I had no answers.

"Hey!"

Katy and I stopped in our tracks.

It was the man who had rushed out through the doors just as we'd stepped into the wing.

"Who let you in?" he said, frowning. Without waiting for an answer, he banged the storage room open and hollered.

"Someone call security!"

A scared face popped out of the doorway. It was a young man with headphones. He stared at us mutely.

I grabbed Katy by the arm. "Run!"

We raced through the corridor and burst through the swinging doors.

"Main entrance!" I cried as we dashed through the passageway, weaving in and out of the lunch crowd.

No one seemed surprised to see two adults sprint through a hospital hallway. Everyone gave us space, moving away quickly. We would have made an even faster getaway if we had on scrubs, but this was infinitely better than trying to make an escape at the police station.

I glanced behind me, trying to spot a security uniform. So far, nothing.

"Exit!" shouted Katy, pointing to the sign. We darted through the hospital's main entrance and dashed out to the parking lot.

"Where did we park the car?" cried Katy, frantically whirling around.

"This way!" I yelled, pulling her by the arm toward a low gray concrete wall. "Near the emergency ward. We thought Win was still there, remember?"

"Are they after us?" cried Katy, as she jumped a small concrete barrier.

I spun around, but no one was chasing us.

Not yet.

But it was only a matter of time.

"Faster!" I said.

We were almost there.

A handful of people were lumbering around the parking lot across the road, looking lost and confused, searching for their cars. Unlike us, they were in a lot less of a hurry.

We had just approached the emergency entrance when the sound of rubber squealing on asphalt came from somewhere.

An ambulance was parked by the entrance, but something else was barreling around the corner.

"My goodness," said Katy. "Sounds like someone's dying."

She stepped onto the road to cross it and head into the parking lot.

The tires screeched louder. The vehicle was crashing toward us. But something was missing.

The ambulance siren.

"Get back!" I said to Katy, pushing her onto the walkway.

Suddenly, a white cargo van came careening around the corner, its gears screaming. Katy and I flattened ourselves against the wall. The van came to a screeching halt inches behind the ambulance.

The back doors of the van banged open. While we watched in horror, a body rolled out of the back and hit the pavement with a sickening thud.

Katy gasped.

The van reversed.

For one split second, I was sure the back tires would roll over the person's legs.

"Hey!" I yelled. "Stop!"

I dashed toward the vehicle, shouting. I reached the car just as the driver changed gears, its grinding sound pummeling my eardrums. I banged on the van's back panel with my fist.

The engine revved, and the gears screamed. My eyes flew to the license plate.

Oregon plates.

Wait. I know this van.

I leaped backward, my heart pounding.

The vehicle lurched forward. Then it took off like a rocket, speeding across the driveway, and disappearing around the corner.

I sprinted after it, barely registering the footsteps running behind me.

"Stop! Stop right there!" I hollered. "Stop that van!"

The van gunned out of the hospital grounds, jumped the curb, and turned onto the main road.

I halted in the middle of the road and put my hands on my knees, panting hard. I would never catch it on foot.

The security guard who'd been running with me stopped as well.

His were the footsteps I'd heard. I wanted to tell him to call for backup, but he was hyperventilating so hard, I was worried he would have a stroke.

We exchanged a dismayed glance as we stood bent over, trying to catch our breaths.

"What the hell was that?" he said, finally.

I shook my head, barely able to speak myself. "They dumped a body."

"Jeez."

He didn't make a move to arrest me or ask why Katy and I had been running through the hospital parking lot only moments ago.

He lowered his chin toward the radio on his shoulder, which was crackling loudly.

"Body dump by entrance three-seven-one...."

Leaving him to report the incident, I turned around and walked back to the emergency ward's entrance. I turned the corner, feeling like a hurricane had whirled me through the air. It had happened so quickly, I wondered if I had imagined it all.

No, it had all been only too real.

The body was lying next to the ambulance. Katy kneeled by it, a shocked expression on her face. A handful of onlookers had gathered at a safe distance, gawking.

A yell came from somewhere, and two paramedics with a stretcher rushed out of the main entrance, steamrolling through the crowd. One of them pushed Katy away. Another shouted something into her radio.

The crowd was getting bigger. I elbowed through them and got closer.

It was a young man, and he was still alive. He was curled in a fetal position, his eyes flickering, and his body convulsing.

His hand was crudely bandaged with a dirty white cloth that was seeped in blood. I peered over the paramedic's shoulders. With an icy chill, I realized he no longer had a hand. That bandage was covering a stump.

I moved closer.

He was barely twenty. His short brown hair was stuck to his skull, wet with sweat. Tears rolled down his face.

"I know that van," I said out loud to no one in particular.

"What?" said one of the paramedics, snapping around with a frown.

"I've seen that van before. The one that dumped him here."

"Are you related? Family?"

I shook my head numbly.

He pushed me aside roughly and turned back to attending to the young man.

I stepped back. I was in the way.

"What did you say?"

I turned around. The security guard who had run with me was back. He squatted next to me, his eyes bulging as he noticed the bloodied stump.

"I got the plate," I said. "The license plate of the van."

The guard's eyes widened. Then he scrambled to pull his radio mouthpiece. "Tell me," he said.

I was spelling it out when a strange cry startled us.

"Please!"

We all turned to the young man on the ground. He was looking at me. His eyes locked with mine.

"Please!" he cried, his good arm reaching out toward me. "Help me!"

I stared at him. I had never seen him before in my life. He wasn't part of the gang who had abducted us, but something told me he recognized me.

Had he been in the bank's security booth with the other guards? Wouldn't they have told us if that was the case? Had he been in the van last night? Had he seen the thugs take us into the bank at gunpoint?

He lifted his head as the paramedics moved him onto the stretcher, his eyes pleading.

"Find my baby girl," he cried, his voice cracking but loud enough for me to hear. "Please find her before they—"

"Going in!" shouted a paramedic, interrupting him. "Make way, people!"

"Find her!" screeched the young man, as they lifted him up and carried him toward the door. "Find her!"

I wanted to race after him, ask him what he meant, but the guard had a hand on my arm now, restraining me.

"Give them space," he said quietly.

"Find my baby!"

The young man's desperate screams came from the entrance, but I could no longer see him.

Hidden Cove

Luxury Float Home Community

Chapter Twenty-six

"**I** had nothing to do with it."

Chris Grayson was lying.

I glared at him as he sat slumped in his electric wheelchair.

"You can take back your retainer," I said.

He shook his head sadly.

With his uncombed hair, and in his old-fashioned tweed cardigan, he looked more like a humble schoolteacher who had seen better days. It was a complete reversal from the photos I'd seen of him online, smiling, shaking hands with tech CEOs, and speaking on international conference panels.

Still, I was having a hard time pitying him.

Katy and I were in the living room of his five-million-dollar opulent home that floated in one of the most exclusive neighborhoods in the country.

The expansive view behind him was spectacular. A flotilla of massive float homes was docked alongside the concrete pier that cut through the private lake. Moored beside each home was a sailboat or a speedboat, sometimes both.

Next to the jetty was a larger marina where a handful of small yachts were moored, sparkling and shiny, waiting for their owners to take them out for a ride.

This was a gated community belonging to some of the wealthiest families in this state. A unique summer playground for the privileged few.

And a secure one.

Grayson had shared a code for us to use at the automated gates.

We couldn't believe our eyes when we drove through them. We sat in the car and stared out at the midday sun glinting on this emerald-green water. It was a magical land.

From the research I did before we came, I knew you could only purchase a home here on invitation. Invitees were hand-selected and the wait list was a mile long. Very few people knew of this paradise on water tucked away a half-hour drive from Seattle.

The heaviness of what had happened to Win and the dead girl were the only things that stopped me from getting distracted by the beautiful vistas outside the large bay windows.

Grayson lifted his chin and gave me a sad look. It was strange to see a multi-millionaire who had made a name for himself appear so vulnerable.

I wondered if it was all an act.

"I need your help," he said, his face sufficiently crumpled in sadness.

"I'm not putting my team in danger again," I said, shaking my head.

"I swear on my daughter's grave," said Grayson, his voice cracking. "I would never do anything like this to you or anyone."

Katy leaned in, her eyes balls of fire.

"Do you know why our friend is in the hospital?" she spat out. "Your people poisoned her!"

"They're not my people!" Grayson cried.

His hands were trembling like he had Parkinson's, but Mary hadn't mentioned it. All I knew was he had mysteriously lost the use of his legs after his daughter disappeared. More to do with unbearable grief than a true physical illness, she'd said.

She had been right about one thing, though. Grayson looked like a man at the end of his tether.

He stirred in his chair.

"I made my money, honestly. I did everything the right way, even if it meant I wouldn't make as much as I could. I may have made mistakes, but for the love of everything, I have never, ever hired a gang of goons to rob a bank, kill a girl, or poison your friend."

He let out a sigh. The lines creased on his forehead made him appear a decade older.

"Please believe me," he said.

"But you know who did it, don't you?" I said.

He put his hands to his face and rubbed hard, like he wanted to scratch his skin off. When he looked up, his eyes were bloodshot red.

"If I knew this was happening, I would have called the police station last night. All I'm trying to do is find my wife, not..." He trailed off.

Outside, a pair of seagulls swooped low and squawked before ducking behind a sailboat. Through the window, I could see the masts of the boats gently swaying in the wind. Subdued but happy voices were coming from somewhere along the pier, and the smell of an early afternoon barbecue wafted through the open window.

Grayson turned his head and stared into the distance, like he was trying to think. I leaned back in my chair, my fingers in the steeple, waiting for him to speak, wondering what would make him tell us the truth.

I glanced around me.

The first floor of this house looked like a showroom you'd see in a luxury home deco magazine. There were no personal items, photos, or pictures anywhere.

"Ever since Lily died," Grayson started, his voice hollow and low, so low I had to lean forward to hear, "everything turned upside down. It's like someone has a vendetta against me and they're doing everything to make my life miserable until I... until, I guess, I decide to end it all."

Katy let out a gasp.

I raised an eyebrow.

End it all?

"Lily was your daughter, wasn't she?" I said, feeling my voice soften.

He nodded. His face drooped as he stared at his trembling hands on his lap.

"Everything fell apart after her death. One of my companies went under. Then Jane started... I love her more than anything, but she started drinking. She took off for days, weekends, without telling me."

He looked so gray and shriveled, I couldn't help but feel a pang of empathy for him.

"Mary thinks I've gone mad, but I'm not. Strange things are happening. I may not be like my old self, but I'm not blind or deaf."

He banged his fist weakly on the side of his chair. It hardly made a sound.

"What strange things?" I asked, frowning.

He raised his eyes. "My personal savings account to start."

"What about it?"

"Someone is siphoning my money, little by little. I hardly even noticed."

"How long has this been going on?"

"Ever since Jane disappeared."

Katy leaned in. "Does your wife have access to the account?"

Grayson shook his head.

"It's my personal trust, the one my parents opened when I was a kid. I added to it over the years. Jane and I have other joint accounts. She uses those."

"Is there any money missing from *those* accounts?"

Another shake of his head. "I'm the only one who knows about my account.... about my trust account." He stumbled over his words. "These things shouldn't be happening. Someone's trying to drive me mad."

"How much money has been drained so far?" I asked.

"Around five thousand a day to a total of fifty thousand," he said. "I hadn't checked for a while. It's set up so withdrawals over one hundred thousand would send me an alert email, but these aren't sizeable amounts."

He took a raspy breath in and pulled at his collar.

"I only noticed it last night as I was preparing for our meeting today." He looked up again, his face flushed.

"I swear it's the truth when I say what happened to you is the most outlandish thing I can ever imagine. I can't believe anyone would go to such lengths."

"Do you know who these men are?" I asked, for what felt like the hundredth time that day.

"I only know they tried to kill you as a proxy."

"Proxy for what?"

"Because they failed to kill *me*."

Chapter Twenty-seven

"They knew I called you for help," said Grayson, his grave eyes on us. "And they wanted to stop you."

"Quite a complicated plan when they could have dumped us in a river somewhere," said Katy. "Why would they do that?"

"What I'd like to know is who they are," I said. "If we knew that, I'm sure we'd find where Jane is."

Grayson's head slumped on his chest. "I'm sorry you had to go through all that. I truly am."

We fell silent.

An excited squeal came from outside, followed by a loud splash and gleeful laughter. The early afternoon sun was shining pleasantly over this idyllic neighborhood, but the inside of Grayson's home felt dark and claustrophobic.

I turned to him. "You said strange things have happened. They might give us clues to who is behind this. Can you tell us more?"

"I was sure my phone got hacked at one point. That's the only way they would have found out you were coming. It's like a ghost has infiltrated my home."

"Who would target you?"

"If I knew, I'd tell you. That's why I hired you."

I bit my tongue. "Mr. Grayson, for us to help you, you need to tell us everything."

He furrowed his brow as if he was trying to think.

"Someone was reading my emails last month, because I found strange notes in my draft folder. Only I could have written them, but I hadn't. I was sure someone bugged my house, so I hired a computer security firm to check everything, but they found nothing. Nothing on the computer, on my phone, or in my house."

Grayson rubbed his face again. "I feel like I'm going mad."

"Whoever it is," I said, "nearly ran over Katy and me back in New York. They threw an empty water bottle with a message that said we would regret it if we came to Seattle. Your enemies have a long reach."

It was Grayson's turn to raise his eyebrows.

"The man, if it was a man," said Katy, "wore dark shades, a hat, a scarf, and a brown beard. A disguise, obviously, but does it ring any bells?"

Grayson gave a start, but shook his head quickly. Too quickly.

I leaned in.

"Who are your adversaries? Your competitors?"

"I run several businesses. Over the years, I have fired a handful of bad performers, some from executive jobs, but they usually got hired elsewhere or landed on their feet quickly. I have a trustworthy senior management team. My board of directors is on my side. I've always collaborated well, except...."

"Except?"

"When you're in my position, you tend to attract many fair-weather colleagues. Let's just say after Lily died and Jane disappeared, my social circle shrank to nothing. No one wants to hang around a man with so much bad luck hanging over his head."

"Would any of them want to harm you?"

Grayson gave me a pained look.

"They're cowards and bad friends, but they're not criminals."

"Tell us about the day your wife disappeared."

"Jane went shopping ten days ago. She took her own car, left it at her usual spot in the parking lot at the mall. She does this every week. She had a dress tailored for a charity event, but she never picked it up. No one saw her get out of her car or walk into the mall."

"What about the security cameras?"

"The funny thing is, the footage of the parking lot was all blank. The mall says it was a glitch. The police said they tried everything, but there's nothing to recover."

"Strange coincidence," said Katy.

"Or is it?" I said, frowning.

"Are you saying these mall guards were involved in a kidnapping conspiracy?" said Grayson, raising a brow.

"For someone to break into a bank with a dead body and three hostages in tow means they're sophisticated. This is not a one-man show. There is a team of people working against you. They could have easily paid mall security to erase the footage and pretend it was a glitch."

I looked at Grayson.

"I'd like a list of your business partners. Give me every name, especially those with resources and connections, enough to plan a bank heist without getting caught."

Grayson didn't answer, but with every word, he looked like he was shrinking in his chair, like he was barely holding himself together.

"This could be someone with a petty grievance you've already forgotten about," I said.

Grayson put his head in his hands. "What about Jane?" His voice was barely audible and cracked with emotion. "Where is she?"

"Hey, Chris," said Katy, taking over from me. "May I ask a delicate question?"

Grayson didn't look up.

"Was your wife having an affair?"

Instead of answering, he sunk even lower in his chair and sobbed.

Katy got up and looked for a box of facial tissue. She placed it on the coffee table by him.

"We're only asking so we can find her," she said in a soft voice. "If you know who it is, it will help us pinpoint her whereabouts."

"She didn't run away!" Grayson's voice was warbled. "Something bad has happened to her. I know it in my bones. Find her."

Something bad has happened to her. I know it in my bones. Those were the exact words Mary had said when she asked us to take this case.

Grayson looked up, tears running down his cheeks. "I know she didn't run away because she left a message."

I sat up.

"A voice mail? A letter? Why didn't you tell us?"

"An entry in her diary."

Grayson slumped again.

"I know I shouldn't poke in her personal things, but she's my wife, and she's gone, so I looked in her den."

He pointed a finger vaguely in the direction of a small anteroom next to the kitchen.

"It's her private reading room. I found the diary on her desk."

"What did it say?"

"That she was scared. That she thought someone was after her. It wasn't clear. Her writing was all over the place. The entries were short, and the most recent ones were strange."

Katy and I leaned in.

"Her last entry said someone was watching her, but didn't say who. She also asked for forgiveness."

"Forgiveness for what?" I said.

He let out a heavy sigh. "She didn't say. We had a hard time adjusting after we lost Lily. We became distant. She started drinking heavily and never stopped. I put all my energy into work. We coped the only way we knew how."

His voice trembled. "I should have taken care of her. I should have paid more attention."

"Would it be possible to see this diary?" I said, glancing at the den.

Grayson mumbled something inaudible.

"Do you know where Jane went when she took off for days without telling you?" said Katy.

"I thought it was just vicious gossip," he said, rubbing his temples. "I was traveling, at business meetings all over the country. I only knew because she never picked up the phone and I'd get a text message saying she's taking a break. Or I'd come home to a cold, dark house and there'd be a note on the kitchen counter saying she'll be back in a couple of days."

"Was there a note this time?"

He shook his head. He opened his mouth to speak when a phone rang. Katy and I reached into our pockets at the same time.

"That's mine," said Grayson, staring at his cell ringing on the kitchen counter. There was fear in his eyes.

I got up, walked over, and brought it to him.

"It might be Jane," I said softly.

He reached out with shaking hands, then let his hands fall to his lap again. I clicked on the green accept button and put it on speaker mode.

"Chris Grayson's residence," I said as I laid the phone on the coffee table in front of him.

"Asha Kade?" came a familiar male voice.

"This is she," I said, sitting up.

"What the hell are you doing?"

That was Officer Davies.

"I'm with my client," I replied crisply.

"Get me Grayson!"

Chapter Twenty-eight

"He's in the room with me," I said.

"Mr. Grayson?" said Officer Davies, his voice suddenly subdued.

"I'm here," replied Grayson.

"I'd prefer to speak with you privately, sir."

"You can speak to me now."

"Are you sure, Mr. Grayson?"

"Whatever you have to say, you can say it in front of my team."

Silence.

"Do you have any news?" asked Grayson.

"Yes and no, sir..." Davies paused like he was choosing his words carefully. This was a surprise. I hadn't expected him to have much emotional intelligence or a healthy dose of courtesy.

"There was a heist at Union Lake Bank last night...," Davies started hesitatingly.

Grayson looked up at us. "So I heard."

"Only one safe deposit box was broken into."

"Mine, I presume."

"Yes, sir." Davies stopped again. "They took everything except for one gold bar. We're holding it at the station as evidence, but I thought you should know."

Grayson didn't reply. He stared numbly at the phone like all his words had run out.

"Did you have insurance, sir?" came Davies' voice, concerned.

Grayson nodded, forgetting the officer couldn't see him.

"He does," I said to the phone. I leaned over the coffee table. "What else was inside the safe deposit box?"

It was Grayson who answered.

"Gold bars and a diamond necklace and bracelet set I gave Lily on her sixteenth." He paused. "And an heirloom ring I inherited from my mother."

He took a raspy breath in.

"I rented that box nineteen years ago, the day my daughter was born. I bought one gold bar for every birthday. It was her insurance, her security, in case my businesses tanked. I wanted to leave her with something...."

Davies remained silent on the line.

"How much is it all worth?" said Katy in a hushed whisper.

"Three million, give or take." He looked up, his eyes grayer than before. "But the sentimental value was so much more. It was my only connection to Lily. To me, it was priceless."

"I'm sorry for your loss, sir," said Davies, hesitating over the phone. "We'll be over tomorrow morning to talk to you, if we may."

The junior cop was being overly deferential. Was it the awe of a public servant dealing with a member of society's highest echelon? Or was it guilt because he hadn't found Grayson's wife yet?

"Have you found Jane?" said Grayson, hope rising in his eyes.

"No, sir."

"Then, no need to make a special trip," replied Grayson in a quiet voice, but the disappointment in his face was visible. "Thomas can talk to me anytime. He knows that."

"We need to see you, sir," said Davies, speaking haltingly like he hated to contradict the older man, "in an *official* capacity."

"Fine," replied Grayson, nodding absentmindedly, like his mind was elsewhere.

Davies hung up with a goodbye that sounded like he couldn't wait to end the conversation.

"Do you know Officer Thomas?" I asked, turning to Grayson.

"He's helping Davies with Jane's file," said Grayson, still with that faraway look on his face. "I keep pushing them. I know they're good cops. Davies is new, bright and eager. He's juggling my case with a dozen others, but homicides and assaults get priority."

He turned to Katy and me. "That's why I told Mary I need outside help. There's only so much time in the day those two have to do their jobs."

"A missing woman is a serious matter," said Katy. "The first seventy-two hours are critical. If they don't find a person by then..."

He nodded somberly.

"I know the statistics, but they pegged her as *voluntarily* missing." He shook his head. "The thing is, they all think they know Jane, but they don't."

"What do you mean?" I asked, narrowing my eyes.

"Jane and I regularly attend the biggest fund raisers in the city, so everyone thinks they know us, but everyone was talking nonsense."

"What were they saying?" said Katy.

He sighed and rubbed his face.

"They called her a lush. Then, they said she was a cheater. They said I was going mad. Everyone thought I lost my mind after Lily...." He leaned forward in his chair, his hands clasped in front of him. "It was vicious and nasty. It was like they wanted to see me fail, like they wanted our marriage to die."

"Chris," said Katy, leaning in and putting a hand on his arm. "Are you sure Jane wasn't having an affair?"

Grayson gave a heartbroken look at my friend. His face said everything. "There were some hints...."

"Who is he?" Katy asked softly.

He looked down at his hands again and shook his head.

Something niggled at the back of my brain. There was something I needed to remember, but for the life of me, I couldn't put my finger on it.

"Tell us about your daughter," I said.

Grayson sat quietly for such a long time with his eyes half closed, that I wondered if he'd forgotten we were here.

Next to me, Katy fidgeted. I checked my phone discreetly.

It was late afternoon, and we still hadn't found a place to stay for the night. Win wasn't supposed to be discharged till the next day and I had promised Peace and David that I'd book a flight for Win and Katy as soon as they released her.

"She was eighteen when she disappeared," said Grayson, stirring me from my thoughts. We could barely hear him. It was like he was speaking more to himself than us.

"Jane was upset at Lily because she had started dating a young artist. I don't even know if that boy had a home or a family. Jane was livid. She said he was a homeless bum who vandalized public property with graffiti. Lily called him the *Banksy of Seattle*. Thought the world of him. She was only eighteen, just a misguided little girl in my eyes."

Katy and I didn't breathe a word.

"She brought him over to meet us one day. I was expecting a tattooed, green-haired kid with body piercings, but he looked sensible enough. But Jane was sure he smelled of pot and got even more upset. It was a nasty day."

"What happened?" asked Katy.

"Jane chased him away. Lily and her had the biggest fight. Jane cried all night, saying the boy was going to have a bad influence on our girl. Then, the next weekend, Lily disappeared."

"Did she run away with her new boyfriend?" I asked.

"That's what the police said. She was eighteen, an adult, and everyone on the pier had heard the row between her and Jane. That's the problem with living on a lake. Voices carry far."

He gave a weary sigh.

"I was at the station every single day for months. I was desperate, and I pushed and pushed. I even threatened them. I promised to donate everything I had to their police pension fund. I just wanted my baby girl back."

"What happened to her?" I said.

"They found a tent in the woods, three days after she disappeared."

"Woods?"

Grayson waved a hand vaguely at the open window. "Behind the lake. You can row there by boat."

"Is that how they got there?"

"No one knows for sure, but they found sleeping bags and camping gear in the woods. But they never found Lily or the young man."

Grayson was speaking barely above a whisper now.

"What about the boy's family?" asked Katy.

"He was a homeless orphan. No one inquired about him. It was just me and Jane hounding the police, the DA, victim's rights groups, anyone we could. I didn't know what else to do."

He looked down at his hands.

"I can understand why Jane took to drinking. She was hurting so bad. I was too. I just wanted to end it all."

"Heartbreaking," murmured Katy.

Grayson had turned introspective again, sitting quietly, hands clasped, head down.

I had come here expecting to confront a wealthy businessman who I'd been sure had been playing with our lives. Instead, I had found a broken man.

But that niggling sensation in the back of my head refused to disappear. I was missing an important clue, one that I was sure was staring me in the face.

My gut was telling me to dig deeper, that nothing was what it seemed. I just wished I could see through the fuzziness of my tired brain and the convolutions of this bizarre case.

"I would still have hope if someone hadn't seen her in the woods," said Grayson.

"Who?" chorused Katy and me.

"A toothless hermit with arthritis, he could barely walk."

A toothless hermit?

I stared at Grayson, who looked like he was about to collapse any moment. Perhaps he was losing his mind after all.

"The hermit used to squat in a homemade shelter deep in the woods. It's private land belonging to our community, but we didn't say anything because he was just a harmless man in his seventies. Someone from the Homeless Outreach group did a wellness check once in a while, but he always chased them away."

"What did he see?" I said, leaning in.

"One morning, he saw Lily standing at the edge of the river, like it was too cold to step in." Grayson swallowed hard. "One second, she was standing, staring at the water. The next second, she was gone."

Chapter Twenty-nine

"The police questioned the hermit at the station," said Grayson.

"They arrested him on suspicion of murder until the Homeless Outreach group hired a victims' rights lawyer. The DA confirmed there was no evidence, so they released him. He cried that day in court. Kept saying he was sorry he didn't stop her from getting into the river."

I raised an eyebrow.

Crocodile tears from an unrepentant killer?

Grayson caught my expression and gave a small shrug.

"Even I didn't believe that toothless, homeless man riddled with arthritis and cataracts would be capable of doing anything. He was a frail and elderly man who could barely walk, talk, or see."

He lowered his voice and looked away.

"The next winter, the Outreach team found him by his hut, dead of hypothermia."

"Did he see the boyfriend the day Lily disappeared?" I said.

"He thought he saw a shadow move in the tent and presumed it was the boy. He said he hollered, but he never came out. When the police came to check, the tent was empty. That was the last time anyone saw the kid. He simply vanished."

"Strange."

"The river comes from a glacier up on high and it was early spring when the ice was melting. Everyone said Lily probably went for a morning wash and got caught up in the heavy current and was swept away. The boy probably went to help her but got carried away, too."

Grayson's voice cracked, and he buried his head in his hands.

We waited quietly.

"Jane blamed herself." He mumbled through his fingers. "She kept saying if she hadn't fought with her, she might not have run away."

"Did they find Lily's, er, body in the end?" I asked.

"Police teams swarmed the woods for days nonstop. They searched the lake, the jetty, and even our house. All they found was the empty camp and footsteps by the riverbed, but that was it."

"How long ago was that?"

"Seven hundred and ninety-eight days ago," said Grayson, hunching even further into his chair. "Over two years now."

He looked up, his eyes filled with tears.

"My daughter was a beautiful, talented, smart young woman. She had her whole life in front of her. She was our only child. Her future was so bright and then...."

Katy and I listened silently.

"She dreamed of becoming the next Anne Truitt. She loved to make things from her hands ever since she was a little one. Papier-mâche animals, mud sculptures, even wood carvings."

Grayson pushed his hands on the arms of the wheelchair and struggled to get up.

"Do you need us to take you somewhere?" said Katy, standing up and striding toward him.

He let go and plopped back into his chair with a grimace, and slammed the arms.

"If only I could walk, I could have done more to find her. I'm just an invalid stuck in this damn chair."

He looked at us, a melancholy expression on his face. "Can I show you her room?"

Katy and I nodded.

He pressed a button on his wheelchair and rolled out of the living room and into the corridor next to the open kitchen, with Katy and me right behind him. He stopped in front of a wooden door and pushed a button on the wall.

The door opened with a clatter.

An elevator.

He rolled himself in and turned around. There was just enough space for him and the wheelchair.

"We'll take the stairs," I said with a nod as the doors closed on him.

I swung around and tiptoed over to the den next to the kitchen.

"What are you doing?" whispered Katy, coming up behind me.

"Jane's diary," I whispered back, scanning the small desk in the anteroom that looked out to the lake.

Grayson or someone had tidied up the desk. There was nothing on it other than a lamp and a paperweight.

"Gosh, what a view," said Katy, looking out of the window.

"Where's the book?" I said, opening the single drawer.

Empty.

A loud ping came from above us.

"He's coming out!" said Katy, whirling around.

I pushed the drawer closed and joined my friend as she scrambled up the stairs.

When we got to the second-floor landing, Grayson had disappeared into one of the rooms.

By the staircase were two large bay windows, which gave an even more stunning panoramic view of the watery neighborhood.

We could see the entire lake, the yachts tethered to the dock, and the row of gorgeous luxury float homes moored along the pier.

Further back in the distance was the dark wooded area where Lily and her boyfriend had run off to and had mysteriously disappeared. The lake was so large, I could only make out the outline of the forest from here.

Katy turned around. "What's this?"

I had noticed it too when we had run up. Installed at the level of my waist on the wall across from the windows was a gun case.

I stepped up to it and examined the gleaming handgun through the glass.

"Funny place to store your weapon," whispered Katy.

I read the words engraved on the barrel. "Classic Carry Elite."

The grip was a piece of art, made with polished wood and shining steel. Just what you would expect a tech tycoon to buy.

"Most people store these in their basements," whispered Katy over my shoulder. "Out of view."

"There are no basements in float homes," I whispered back, as I admired the weapon. "Plus, it's the perfect height for Grayson to reach in his wheelchair."

"This is what she loved to do," came Grayson's voice from somewhere on the floor.

Katy and I whirled around.

"She was so talented."

We followed his voice and peeked inside a door at the end of the landing to our right.

We walked into a bedroom painted in bright sea blue colors and decorated just as you'd expect a teen's room to be.

A signed poster of a well-known pop singer decorated one wall. A pink hammock hung in a corner by the window overlooking the lake. Laptops and tablets sat among piles of textbooks. The closet had been flung wide open. Designer clothes and expensive bags hung here and there, but most of it lay on heaps on the floor.

It was a messy room, but it was clearly the mess of a girl with means. What would make her run away with a homeless street kid into the woods?

"This is exactly how she left her room," said Grayson as he saw us look. "Jane always hoped Lily would come back, so we didn't...."

He choked back his words and looked away.

I turned my eyes on the adjacent wall, which was lined with framed photos of the family.

"Is this Jane?" I said, pointing at the woman sandwiched in between Grayson and a teenager, her arms around both of them, her smile wide and engaging.

Grayson nodded somberly.

Thin, fit, tanned, and in a beautiful summer dress and floppy hat, Jane looked like a happy socialite on summer vacation. I knew I shouldn't judge, but I couldn't help wondering why an attractive woman like her would have chosen a frumpy computer nerd for a partner.

As if to rebel against her mother, Lily was in an all-black T-shirt, ripped jeans, and purple tennis shoes with the laces undone, the kind of clothing you'd find in an upscale boutique that presented faux scruffy attire for a hundred times the price of the real deal.

Next to the Grayson family photos were pictures taken with others on the pier and on sailboats out in the lake. Everyone looked like they had just stepped off a luxury yacht for a casual Sunday afternoon gathering. I could smell the money in these images.

But I knew photos never told the whole story. The women in these pictures looked too much alike, the pretty Stepford wives of Hidden Cove.

"This is my favorite piece," said Grayson, picking something up from the bedside table.

Katy and I stepped up to him to see the small wooden sculpture in his hands. It was simple yet striking.

"An angel," whispered Katy.

It was the outline of an angel with a halo around the head and long wings that fell to their feet.

A shiver went through me. I had seen this not so long ago, but in a different format.

"The angel," I whispered to myself.

"What?" said Katy.

"Nothing," I said quickly, shaking my head.

My gut was warning me again. I needed to unscramble my thoughts before I said another word. For that, I needed to rest my weary brain.

I turned to Grayson.

"We've probably run you ragged with our questions. Why don't you get some rest? We'll come back and talk to you tomorrow morning."

"Where are you staying tonight?"

I pulled my phone out of my pocket. "Still looking for a hotel for the night, but you can reach me on—"

"I have a guest house." He gave me a keen look. "You're welcome to stay here."

He pointed out the window.

"It's a small, furnished float house, a few doors down. Jane and I bought it as our guest cottage when we built this home. It's not as big as this, but it has all the amenities."

"That would be lovely," said Katy, her eyes shining, before I could say anything. "We've had the worst day ever, and I just need a bed. A floating one sounds absolutely grand."

Grayson saw my uncertain face.

"This is a gated community," he said. "You and your friend will be safe here."

Chapter Thirty

"**M**ama!"

The kid's screech made us stop. Katy and I had just stepped out of Grayson's home with the guest house keys in hand.

"Shut up, child," snapped a woman's riled voice. "I said, shut up!"

A woman and a toddler were by a large navy-blue float home, two houses down from the Graysons.

The mother stood with one hand on her hip and a finger wagging at the little girl crouching on the ground. The child must have been two or three years old and was sobbing silently, like she knew what would happen if she let out another cry.

I recognized the woman from a photo in Lily Grayson's room.

The kid had on a short dress that was covered in food stains and looked one size too small. She was clutching a brown toy in one hand, like her life depended on it.

"Poor thing," breathed Katy next to me.

Compared to the child's unkempt appearance, the mother looked immaculate in her beige heels and a tailored skirt suit that would have put Jackie Kennedy to shame. Her beautifully tanned legs and perfectly done-up platinum blonde hair told us she was a frequent patron of high-end salons.

But her demeanor and voice said the last thing she wanted was to deal with the child by her feet. The girl stuffed her fist into her mouth like she was trying hard to stop crying, but her tiny chest heaved up and down.

I felt for the little one.

"You never learn," snarled the mother, still unaware of our presence. As we watched, she snatched the toy out of the girl's hands and threw it into the lake.

"One more word out of you and you know what I'll do. It'll be *you* in the water next!"

"My goodness," said Katy, putting a hand on her heart.

The woman stomped up the stairs, leaving the girl on the pier. The child seemed to collect herself, wiped her face, and crawled after her mother, laboriously reaching for each step, one by one.

"What a witch," Katy breathed angrily. "We have to do something."

Before I could reply, the girl lost her footing, stumbled down the stairs, and fell to the pier with a loud cry. With an angry *tsk*, the mother stomped down, grabbed her by one arm and pulled her up. The kid burst into tears.

"Stop this sniveling!" The woman shook the girl so violently, her head snapped back and forth.

My legs moved faster than my brain.

"Hey!" I called out. "Stop that! You'll hurt her."

The woman looked up and scowled as Katy and I rushed over.

"Mind your own business!" she snarled, exposing her perfect white teeth.

Before we could get closer, she stormed up the stairs with the child and slammed the door shut.

We stood in front of their house, listening to the girl crying inside.

"Hasn't she heard of shaken baby syndrome?" Katy's face flushed. "She could have bruised that kid's brain or broken her neck. She could have *killed* her."

I noticed something move on the water near the dock.

The small toy was ebbing up and down, with the gentle waves lapping against the wharf. I kneeled by the edge of the dock, reached into the water, and snatched it out.

It was a handmade doll made from scraps of old cloth, soaking so wet that it had lost its shape. If I hadn't fished it out, it would have sunk to the bottom within minutes.

This had to be that kid's security blanket she probably slept with, ate with, and dragged along wherever she went. This doll had been white once, I was sure.

The little girl's sorrowful face was etched in my mind. My heart ached for her.

"She can afford fancy suits and heels but not a decent toy for her kid?" huffed Katy as she saw what I had hauled out. "People like that shouldn't be allowed to have kids."

A long face popped out of the front window of the navy-blue house.

"There she is," said Katy through clenched teeth. "I should walk up there and give that woman a good piece of my mind."

I lifted the toy up to show it to her. The woman merely glared before turning away and vanishing from sight. Inside the house, the girl had turned silent.

With a sigh, I walked up the stairs to the doorway and placed the toy on the top step, laying it out so it would dry faster. It took me a second to notice what it was. It was an angel with wings and a halo behind its head.

I stepped back, shaken.

I knew about the reticular activating system, the part of the brain that comes to life when you buy a red Toyota and start seeing red Toyotas on the streets all around you. Just like that, I was seeing angels all over the place.

I scampered down the steps to join Katy, who was still glaring at the window like she was deciding whether to bang on the door and give the woman a good talking-to.

"Let's tell Davies and his team when they come to talk to Grayson tomorrow," I said. "They can inquire about the girl and get Child Protection Services involved if needed."

Katy turned to me, her eyes flashing. "If she can afford a house like that, why doesn't she hire a nanny? A stranger would treat that kid better than that."

With an angry huff, Katy whirled around. "All that fancy heels and makeup, and she can't give a decent dress or toy to her own daughter?"

We walked silently after that, making our way toward the guest house along the pier.

My mind was buzzing with questions.

The mother-daughter incident made me realize one thing. Living on the pier didn't grant these residents' much privacy.

Those large bay windows on every side gave million-dollar views, but they also exposed the interiors to outsiders. With only the pier and open water separating each house, there wasn't much you could hide from your neighbors.

Grayson had said everyone had heard Jane's argument with Lily. How much did the inhabitants of this exclusive community know about his wife's affair and her disappearance?

We passed a property with a *for sale* sign. Katy jabbed me in the waist and pointed to it with her chin.

"Two million dollars for a house on the water. These are just glorified houseboats. Do these people even own the land?"

"They own fifty acres of the property surrounding the lake," I said, recalling the research I did after taking Mary's call. "It's communal property, so they have a marina management team who takes care of the pier, the docks, the gates, the garage—"

"Did you see the cars in the garage? There are millions of dollars of vehicles parked just in there."

She was right. After calling Grayson via the intercom at the gate and punching in our security code, I'd driven into the marina building to park our rental. The guest spot was in between a luxury Cadillac sedan and a gleaming Tesla Model-X. This was the playground of the wealthy, after all.

I tried not to gawk at the three-to-four story float homes we passed. Each had been carefully designed and built to spec. None of them were similar. A few even displayed the names of their architect on a discreet sign by the front door.

The smell of the afternoon barbecue still lingered in the air, but lunch was over, and the pier had turned quiet. Everyone had retreated to their homes for a siesta, I presumed.

It would have been a pleasant walk if our reasons for being here had been different. Something told me there was a lot more going on under this bucolic and beautiful surface.

The sound of a lone loon echoed from the middle of the lake.

"Was that a goose—" Katy stopped as I put a hand on her arm.

"Did you see that?"

"What?" said Katy, swiveling her head around.

A glint of the late-afternoon sun bounced off glass from the side of a house down the pier.

I had noticed that glint before. It had kept disappearing and appearing, and moving around as we strolled down the empty quay.

"Someone's watching us," I replied quietly.

Chapter Thirty-one

M y spine tingled.

The glint had disappeared, but I couldn't brush off the uneasy feeling that a stranger was observing us.

We were fifty feet from our guest house, a charming little cottage sandwiched between two mega float homes.

We fell silent and slowed our pace to a leisurely level as if to admire the architecture, but our eyes and ears were on full alert.

We passed by an orange float home, two doors up from the guest cottage. This was where that glint had come from. I gestured to Katy to slow down even more.

"Do you see anyone?" she whispered in my ear.

"Not yet," I whispered back.

The exterior walls of this house were covered by wrought-iron art déco sculptors that looked like they had been cobbled together by a hyper-imaginative child. Heavy curtains hung on all the bay windows, blocking its million-dollar views.

Why would anyone do that?

The wraparound patio was filled with Adirondack chairs, garden gnomes, pink flamingos, and rustic outdoor knickknacks. A row of clay planters hung along the patio, bursting with lilies, honeysuckles, and daisies.

Fallen petals swayed on the waves lapping against the house, just underneath the planters.

It was a colorful and offbeat structure, but something about it made me feel unsettled. It reminded me of my childhood storybooks with pictures of spooky cottages in the woods made of chocolate and candy, designed to lure innocent boys and girls, only to become dinner for a wicked witch.

Katy and I picked up our pace. We had just passed the front door of this house when I spotted our spy.

The woman jerked her head back as if she hadn't expected us to move so quickly. But I had already seen her crouching behind a row of terracotta planters, next to the half-opened side door.

We stared at each other.

She was in her sixties or thereabouts, and was wearing a large, shapeless orange dress that made perfect camouflage against the tangerine walls. In her right hand was a pair of binoculars, and on her face was a guarded expression.

"Hi there," I called out in a friendly voice.

She didn't reply, but her suspicious eyes narrowed.

Her bare arms had old scars and her face was pockmarked, like relics from a bout of childhood chicken pox. She resembled Kathy Bates in Misery more than the lithe and pretty Stepford-like wives of Hidden Cove.

I pasted on a polite smile and put one foot on her floating patio.

"You have a gorgeous home," I said.

Her eyes widened like she was surprised to receive the compliment, but she remained silent.

I pointed at the binoculars. "Bird watching?"

Her face flushed.

"Is it always this beautiful out here?" said Katy, stepping up brightly next to me, her megawatt smile turned on.

The woman shot her a curious look. "You gals here for the house sale?"

Her voice was raspy, like she smoked cigarettes and drank Jack Daniels every day.

"Hi, I'm Asha and this is Katy," I said, not answering her question directly.

I reached out with my hand, but I might as well have offered her a snake. She gave my hand a distasteful glance and stepped back.

Not a handshaker then.

"And you must be...?"

"Geena," the woman mumbled.

"Nice to meet you, Geena," I said.

No answer.

"What's it like to live in a floating house?"

"Okay, I suppose," she said, hesitating. Her eyes flitted nervously from me to Katy and back again.

"I guess you shouldn't live here if you get seasick, eh?" laughed Katy.

Geena smiled a small smile.

"You get used to it. Helps you sleep well at night."

Her body language said she wanted nothing more than to disappear inside, but something was keeping her here. And I knew what it was. Her curiosity was stronger than her need to stay secretive.

Was she the neighborhood snoop? Or was there something more?

"How long have you been living here?" I asked, amiably.

"Ten years or thereabouts."

I gestured to the rest of the wharf. "How many families live here?"

"Dozen or so."

"It must get busy around here."

"Most folks have other houses in the city. Pretty quiet out here till it warms up."

"Are they friendly?" asked Katy in a cheery voice.

Geena's eyes traveled to our crumpled pants and shirts, the ones we'd worn through a red-eye flight across the country, a bank heist, a police interrogation, and a visit to the city morgue. I thought I caught a sympathetic smile. Her face softened and her shoulders dropped.

"So, what are the neighbors like?" repeated Katy. "Snobbish or nice?"

"Different," said Geena. "Not like at the trailer park, that's for sure."
Trailer park?

"There's no fighting too, so that's real good."

Her defensive posture was slowly melting away.

"Nights are quiet. Just the loons and ducks on the lake and the stars in the sky."

"Seems like a tight-knit community," I said. "You must have a lot of lovely parties out on the pier."

"I'm not one of them," she snapped.

Next to me, Katy flinched at the harshness of her tone.

Geena was the last person I would expect to find in this upper-crust community. What was her story?

"I'm not like them, you know," she said, like she had read my mind. "They don't invite me to their fancy barbecues. They stick together, and I stick to me. Just because you live close doesn't mean..."

She trailed off.

I nodded. "We just saw the fancy lady who lives in the navy-blue house with a little girl. Who is she?"

"I wouldn't mess with Nathalie. She's connected."

"Connected to who?"

Geena jerked her head back and stared at us for a few seconds. Her eyes narrowed and her shoulders tightened.

"Wait. Who are you again?"

"Asha and Katy," I said, smiling.

She frowned.

"Johnson only comes down to show the houses on Fridays, but lately, after all the news and all, he hardly has any takers...." She screwed her eyes. "What are you doing here?"

I kept my smile intact. "We're here on business."

That wasn't a lie. I just hadn't answered all her questions, just like she hadn't answered all of ours.

Her eyes widened. "You're the gals Grayson was going to hire."

"News gets around fast here," I said.

She didn't reply, but took a step back as if to leave. Her face had shut down again.

I put a second foot on her patio. "Do you know the Grayson family well?"

"Everyone knows everyone here," she mumbled, looking away. "It's not easy to hide in this place."

I raised an eyebrow. "Hide from the neighbors, you mean?"

Her eyes flittered and her face flushed. She really didn't want to talk but she couldn't help herself.

"Hide secrets."

"What kind of secrets?" I said.

"It's just.... nothing..." she stammered, taking a step back.

"What can you tell us about Jane Grayson?" I said, stepping closer. "Did you see her the day she disappeared?"

A dark shadow crossed her face, but she caught it just in time. She looked away, blinking like she was confused.

"I heard Jane Grayson didn't get along with her daughter," I said, trying another path. "Did you ever hear her argue with Lily?"

Another dark shadow came over her face, and this time, she didn't hide it. She glanced over her shoulder and then from side to side, as if to check if anyone was within hearing distance. But the pier was empty other than us three.

"She argued with everyone," replied Geena, her voice hardening.

"So, Jane didn't get along with anyone?" asked Katy.

"That woman is poison." Geena's voice dripped with venom. "I hate her guts to death."

Chapter Thirty-two

We waited for Geena to elaborate, but she had become tight-lipped.

Time to change tactics again.

"What about Lily?" I said. "What was she like?"

"Poor girl. Always getting in trouble."

"What kind of trouble?" I asked.

"Running around with friends and such. Making everyone sick with worry."

"Running off with her homeless boyfriend, you mean? What was he like? Do you know his name?"

Geena gave me a startled look, like she hadn't expected that question. She turned around and stepped closer to the side door.

"Gotta make supper," she muttered, fumbling with the knob.

The door opened, and I peeked inside. The side entrance led to the kitchen, which was just as cluttered as the patio outside.

Geena was a hoarder.

"We're staying at the guest house for a few days," I said as she lumbered inside. "Would you like to visit us for tea?"

Geena turned to me with wide eyes, like she had never been invited for tea before.

"Do you like cake?" said Katy, taking my cue. "Cake and tea on a floating patio sounds like a dream, but I bet you get to do that every day, don't you?"

"Yeah, I guess," stammered Geena.

I was a foot from the side door, which she was holding open. Her fridge was covered with pamphlets and old photos, and it seemed like the overflow had been pinned to the back of this patio door.

While Katy inquired what kind of cake Geena liked, I discreetly examined the collage of pictures. Most were tattered and yellowed, but one caught my eye instantly.

It was a recent photo of Grayson's daughter, Lily. In it, she had an arm around a young man and a smile on her cute face.

My heart skipped a beat.

I had seen that young man's face before. He was the man in the hospital with a maimed hand.

So, he is the boyfriend!

In the photo, the couple were seated in a rowboat out on the lake. Far in the distance, behind them, was a line of tall fir trees.

The woods, where they had both disappeared.

"I'm busy," mumbled Geena, taking another step inside.

"You're welcome anytime," called out Katy just before she shut the door. The sound of a bolt came from the other side.

"I feel like Alice," Katy whispered as we stepped back onto the pier.

"Alice?"

"In Wonderland. It's like we've walked into the Mad Hatter's neighborhood. Everyone's acting weird and I don't think anyone likes anyone here."

"Did you see the photo?" I said as we walked away from the orange house.

"What photo?"

"She has a pic of Lily and her boyfriend on the back of her door."

"You saw the boyfriend's pic? I wish I paid more attention."

"You've seen him," I said in a quiet voice. "Lying on the road by the hospital emergency entrance."

Katy gasped out loud and spun around to face me. "That's *him*?"

"I'd bet everything it's him."

"My goodness." She frowned. "But what does this mean?"

"Your guess is as good as mine."

"One thing for sure, Geena knows a lot more than she's telling."

"We could be putting more weight on her words than we probably should. She could be just a harmless busybody who loves to gossip."

"A harmless snoop who knows what's really going on here?"

We walked silently over to the guest house, lost in our thoughts.

"Aaw," said Katy as we approached the little float home we were going to spend the night in. "How adorable."

The guest house was a tenth of the size of the giant homes along the promenade. Across from it was another mega float house with a *for sale* sign in front.

I had thought the guest cottage was sandwiched in between two large float homes, but now we were close, I realized the guest house and the empty home were both at the end of the dock, across from each other.

Beyond us was wide open water.

I walked up the narrow dock that led to the guest house, feeling it sway gently under my feet. I slipped the key into the keyhole and unlocked the door.

"Wow," said Katy, looking over my shoulder.

I had expected a rustic cottage. Instead, all the amenities of a luxury hotel room that could fit into five hundred square feet had been added to this space, together with the extra charm of waves lapping against the floats.

We stepped inside and shut the door behind us.

"Italian marble," said Katy, peeking into the bathroom.

I looked up at the chandelier hanging over the bed from the ceiling. "That didn't come from IKEA, I can tell you that."

"What a cute little kitchen." Katy pointed at the stainless-steel compact machine next to the stove. "Check out this all-in-one grinder-brewer coffee cappuccino thingamajigs."

"You don't need Starbucks when you can have that."

"I feel drunk. This entire house is moving," said Katy, standing in the middle of the room, legs and arms splayed out. "How come we didn't feel anything in Grayson's house?"

"His place is much bigger. The floats underneath must be enormous to stabilize it."

Katy dropped her handbag on the floor and threw herself on the bed in the corner. "We lucked out. This is better than any hotel room."

I walked through the open kitchenette and stepped up to the bank of panoramic windows at the back.

The day's events were catching up to me, and I was ready to crash.

My muscles ached, and a headache was coming on. I still needed to grab our bags from the car, desperately wanted to take a shower, and forage for food in the pantry that Grayson said we could help ourselves to.

But my body refused to move.

I leaned forward, pressed my nose against the glass and gazed out onto the lake. I now knew why these homes cost so much. I could just stand here and fall asleep, I thought.

Imagine retiring here with David. That was, if I could ignore the strange neighbors.

The temperature was cooling, and a mist swirled over the surface of the water. Through the smoky haze, I glimpsed something move.

It was a loon. A small, dark-feathered bird ducked its head into the water and lifted its entire body up, spraying water all over itself.

Far in the distance was the dark outline of the mysterious woods. Though the pale gold rays of the afternoon sun glittered on the lake, it felt like night had already fallen over the forest.

The dark green foliage of the trees created an impenetrable wall between the lake and the rest of the forest. It looked like a foreboding curtain that hid untold secrets.

I wondered what had happened to Lily and her boyfriend that day, two years ago. Did her boyfriend fall into the river and get swept away too, but somehow rescued himself?

What had he been up to all these years? Did Randy and his gang find him and kidnap him? Why did they let him go now? Most of all, why maim him so brutally? What had happened to him had not been an accident.

I had so many questions, but no answers.

I stared at the darkening horizon, my gut stirring. Something told me the woods weren't entirely uninhabited.

I couldn't help but feel someone was in that forest, staring back at me, just as I was looking their way.

Chapter Thirty-three

"Hey, you hungry?" I said, turning around.

Katy had already fallen asleep on the bed. Her head was tilted to the side and her mane of hair spread around her like the red halo of an angel.

Let her sleep.

I shuffled toward the fridge, feeling every muscle in my body ache. I needed food or my headache would explode.

A row of copper pans hung above the counter, but I didn't have the energy to cook. I pulled open the small fridge, my stomach rumbling as I spotted the frozen pizza boxes and potato wedges. There was even a box of pre-made pancakes. All frozen, none of them healthy, but I was famished.

I pulled out the pizza and shut the fridge door when I heard the frightened yell. I dropped the box on the floor and whirled around.

Katy!

She was huddled by the headboard, clutching the coverlet to her chest, staring out the window like she had seen a phantom. I dashed over.

"What is it?"

She pointed a shaky finger at the window.

I glanced out, my brow furrowed.

It was quiet on the pier. The wrought-iron lamps along the promenade had come on. A light fog from the lake swirled around the iron posts, giving a ghostly Grim's fairytale feel to this watery neighborhood.

"It was the man with the beard," she whispered hoarsely. "The same one who tried to run us over back home."

"You're dreaming, Katy."

"I'm telling you, he was staring inside. By the window."

If someone had been outside, they would have had to step onto the patio and we would have heard them walk on the wooden planks. They would have had to be really stealthy to not even make the floats move.

I glanced around the perimeter quickly. Though our guest house was small, it was a modern structure like the others, solidly built with good latches and locks. I didn't need to worry about anyone breaking in, but the thought a creep watching us was unnerving.

I frowned. "Are you sure you saw him?"

"Just now. I swear!"

I leaped toward the door and flung it open, but there was no one outside.

I walked around our house, wondering if an intruder was lurking behind. The floats bobbed up and down as I treaded around the patio.

Unlike the larger houses, there were no railings around this little cottage. In an icy winter, this would be a dangerous place to hang out. I peeked over the edges, wondering if anyone had fallen in. Then again, I would have heard the splash.

After another round, I stepped toward our open doorway and looked out at the pier. Lights had been switched on in a few houses now. The lake community was preparing for supper or bed, I imagined. In the distance, the loon called, its eerie sound echoing across the open water.

I felt eyes on me again.

I spun around.

There was a light on the second floor of the neighboring float home. I gazed at the window, wondering who lived next door.

As I watched, the silhouette of a man with a slightly arched back and scraggly gray hair passed the upstairs window. He hobbled behind the half-drawn curtains without seeing me. A large television on the wall by the bay window flickered to life, and soon, the image of a news anchor's talking head flittered across the screen.

It couldn't have been him. Whoever had peeked in had to be nimble and fast. That ruled out Geena as well.

I looked to my right.

There was only one other float home at the end of the jetty. It stood alone, moored further away from the rest of the houses. It was a humongous modular structure, a modern box-like building with a flat roof. It exuded none of the warmth and charm of the traditional float houses on the top of the pier.

The *for sale* sign in front of it swayed to the wind, making a baleful clang each time it swung.

There were no curtains on the windows and no flower boxes on its veranda. There were no boats moored next to its dock, or any hint of human life.

The sound of a window creaking came from the top floor. Through the twilight, I thought I caught a shadow on the second floor.

I blinked.

Was someone inside? What would anyone be doing in a dark, empty home? Did Katy really see the mysterious man with the beard and was he in that lonely house? Or was my imagination running away from me again?

After another glance around the pier to make sure no one was watching, I walked over to the lone house at the end. When I got to the floating patio, I tiptoed over to the nearest window on the main floor, thankful for my petite frame. The enormous floats underneath hardly moved.

Cupping my hands on the window, I peered into an empty room, stripped bare of all furnishings. I moved over to the next window. The previous residents had taken out all the furniture and fixtures. The inside was a hollow shell.

I walked around the patio, moving stealthily, my fists curled and my shoulders tensed, ready for a fight, half expecting to bump into someone. But there was no one.

I shivered.

It was cooler on this end of the wharf, open to the water and the elements. I was the furthest away from land, trees, and other houses, which would have provided some shelter.

"Asha!"

I whirled around.

Katy was at the threshold of our house, waving her arms urgently.

I ran back.

"You okay?" I said, panting, as I got close.

"Come, you have to see this," said Katy, rushing back inside and gesturing to the window by the bed.

"Don't touch it," she said as I reached toward the windowpane.

"Touch what?"

"You don't see it?"

I wiped my tired eyes and scanned the outside again.

"Look closer," came Katy's voice.

I adjusted my eyes. That's when I saw it. They were so faint, I had missed them. Someone had blown on the glass and written on it, using their finger.

Go home.

Chapter Thirty-four

A phone rang, startling us.

Katy jumped toward her handbag to grab her cell.

"That's not yours, unless you changed your ring tone," I said, scanning the room to see where the sound was coming from. "It's not mine either."

There.

A wireless headset was sitting behind the multi-tasking coffeemaker on the kitchenette counter. I pushed the appliance aside to see a tiny green light turn on and off on the headset.

No one knew we were here except for Grayson and the neighbors who had spotted us. Who would call us?

I plucked the headset from its cradle, clicked on the call button, and put the phone on speaker mode.

"Hello?" I said, as I scanned the words scrolling across the top of the small screen.

Unknown number.

"Who's that?" whispered Katy from behind me.

Something crackled on the other end, like someone was crumpling a piece of paper.

"Who is this?" I said, leaning closer to the earpiece, trying to make out the mysterious noises.

The sound of scraping came next, like something was being pushed back. A chair?

"Asha?" said a feeble male voice.

My eyes narrowed. I barely recognized him. "Mr. Grayson?"

"I think you need to come down."

"Everything fine over there?" asked Katy over my shoulder.

"I'd like you to see this." Grayson spoke so low, it was almost inaudible.

A dull thud like something had banged on the phone made me jerk back. What was going on?

"Hey, are you okay?" said Katy.

A fumbling sound came, followed by a crackling noise.

The mysterious bearded man Katy had spotted peeking through our window sprang to mind. I debated whether to call the police, but if Grayson had seen an intruder in his house, he should have called them already.

"Are you in danger?" I said, leaning into the mouthpiece. "Can you speak freely?"

"Sorry," came his shaky voice. "I, er, dropped the phone. I... I don't know what to think. It's so strange—"

"Is anyone with you?"

"What? No... no, I'm alone at home."

I let out a sigh of relief.

It had to be something else.

"Hang tight. I'm coming over," I said. "Stay right where you are. Don't do anything. And please don't open the door to anyone other than me."

Grayson didn't answer, but I could hear his nervous breathing through the speaker.

I hung up, feeling a dangerous undercurrent in this case. With every passing minute since we arrived in Seattle, I had felt a growing dread. We weren't sniffing out a missing wife who'd been having an affair. That was for sure. I just wished I knew what we were about to face next.

"Stay here," I said to Katy.

I whirled around and stepped toward the entrance, but Katy sprang forward as I opened the door.

"I'm not staying alone in here," she said as she brushed past me and slipped out the door.

We started jogging toward Grayson's home.

"I promised Peace I wouldn't put you in any more danger than I already have," I muttered.

"We're sticking together," said Katy, her voice firm.

We were passing Geena's orange house. A quick glance showed that the lights were on, but there was no sign of her.

"Grayson's in bigger trouble than he knows," I said, picking up my pace. "First thing tomorrow morning, I'm going to see where I can rent a sidearm."

"Do you think—"

A door banged open, silencing her.

Yellow light flooded through the open doorway of Grayson's house. The silhouette of a man in a wheelchair was at the top of the ramp that had been custom built for his chair. He was looking our way.

I ran up to Grayson.

"Didn't I tell you to keep your door locked until we got here?"

He gave me a dazed look. The lines on his forehead had deepened like he had aged years in the hour since we left him. Mumbling under his breath, he gestured for us to follow him inside.

Katy and I leaped up the stairs, got in, and locked the door behind us.

I scanned the living room. It looked exactly as we had left it only an hour or so ago.

"Did someone try to break in?" I said.

"What?" said Grayson, rubbing his temple. "No, no. Nothing like that," he mumbled as he rolled across the living room. "I heard a knock a few minutes ago, and I found this."

Katy and I followed him across the living room and into the open kitchen. He pointed at a mid-sized cardboard box sitting on the counter.

"Someone left this on my doorstep."

I got closer to scrutinize the box. There were no markings or shipping labels on the outside. I noticed a pair of scissors lying on the counter next to it.

The box had already been opened.

Grayson reached toward it, but his hands were shaking. He pulled his hands back and wiped his face. He was sweating, profusely.

"What's in there?" said Katy.

"Wait," I said, pulling my friend away from the counter. "It's not a bomb, is it?"

Grayson gave me a shocked look, but didn't answer.

I tried again. "Did you see any wires, anything electric, a detonator?"

"No, no, nothing like that..." But his lips were quivering. He looked like he was at the verge of a collapse. "It's er... er... you really need to see it."

"Step aside," I said, and turned to Katy.

With a nod, she took Grayson's wheelchair by the handles and pushed him to the other end of the kitchen. He wrung his hands, mumbling darkly to himself.

Whatever was in this box had disturbed him greatly.

Using a dishcloth that had been hanging from the oven door, I gently pushed the box toward me. Even through the cloth, I could feel the cold emanating from inside.

Katy watched me, her eyes on the box.

I wondered if Grayson had ordered takeout but had forgotten he did. He had been a nervous man when I first met him, but he didn't seem like he had his faculties intact anymore.

Creating makeshift gloves with the dishcloth, I flipped the top flaps open and peeked inside. All four sides of the box were lined with blue freezer bags, the kind you'd used to create an icebox for a picnic.

I turned the flaps all the way back. Katy came over and leaned in just as I reached into the box.

She sprang back with a cry.

I pulled my hand away and stared at the thing lying snuggled in between the four freezer bags.

It was a severed hand. The dried blood was still visible at the disjointed end.

Chapter Thirty-five

K aty looked away, a hand on her throat, making gagging noises.

Grayson clasped and unclasped his hands obsessively, and continued to mumble to himself like he was repeating a prayer.

"Mr. Grayson," I said. "We need to take this to the police."

He gave a cursory nod, but didn't look up.

"I know who this belongs to," I said.

Grayson looked up and sat up straight, suddenly paying attention.

"There's someone in the hospital right now with a missing hand. The young man who was thrown out of the same van that followed us to the bank heist."

He stared at me mutely. My gut was warning me again. Grayson hadn't told us the complete story.

"Is there anything you haven't shared with us about this case?"

Silence.

He wasn't helping us or himself, I thought. With a resigned sigh, I turned back to the box to close it. That was when I spotted it.

My heart jumped to my mouth.

Using the dishcloth to hold both top flaps, I flipped the box to the side on the granite counter.

"Don't!" cried Katy, stepping back in horror, a hand over her mouth.

The severed limb tumbled out and fell onto the counter.

All the air got sucked out of the room. Grayson stopped muttering and his face turned white. Katy stared at the hand, her mouth open.

I pointed at the grotesque limb. "See this?"

There was a tattoo of half an angel between the thumb and the index finger.

I turned to Grayson. "Can you guess who this is from?"

He shook his head. Then, he looked away.

"Did Lily's boyfriend have any tattoos?"

"No...." He swallowed hard. "I thought... Jane... Jane thought he would be tattooed all over, but he was clean."

"What about Lily?"

His eyes widened.

"What are you...?" He spluttered. "Of course not. Jane would have been very upset if she had got a tattoo. What are you saying?"

"Mr. Grayson, I believe this hand belongs to Lily's boyfriend. He's alive. I'm going to ask you again. Is there anything else we need to know this case? "

Instead of replying, he doubled over. Soon, we heard him retching.

———◆———

We got little sleep that night.

Katy tossed and turned in bed while I tried to make myself comfortable on the couch at the guest house.

Suddenly, a silhouette sprang up on the bed and my friend's frustrated voice cut through the darkness.

"Why do we have to have it in here?"

I turned toward her with a tired sigh.

"Because it's safe here."

"I don't understand why we couldn't have left it at his house. It was sent to him, not us."

"A detached hand in a freezer bag isn't going to bite us."

I could feel her eyes on me like angry laser beams from across the room.

"Yes, but you stuck it in our fridge. That's where we have the pizza, for heaven's sake. Beyond gross."

"We can't leave it outside," I said, now wishing I'd brought my sleeping tablets with me. The low-level headache that had been plaguing me all day was transforming into a full-blown migraine.

"We can't leave it at Grayson's house, either. Didn't you see the way he was? So out of it. He could throw it away or destroy it, and after all that has happened, I don't blame the man."

Grayson had looked relieved when I'd told him I'd take the limb to the guest house for safeguarding till we talked to the police the next morning.

He had agreed to my plan, nodding mutely, and had wheeled himself into the elevator without a word. Katy and I had seen ourselves out, after checking all the windows and entrances, and making sure his door locked from the inside.

"Why would anyone do such a thing?" came Katy's voice from the bed.

I sat up on the couch and pulled my blanket around my shoulders. I wouldn't get any rest until she fell asleep.

"Whoever they are, they're after Grayson," I said. "This has something to do with his missing wife and our stint in the bank vault. It's all connected."

"This is so out of the world. But why?"

I rubbed my temple.

"It's the usual culprits. Money, sex, or greed. We just have to ask the right questions to the right people to get to the bottom of it."

I paused as another thought came to me.

"We need to start with the officers who had Jane Grayson's file."

"Oh, boy. Davies will be super happy to see us, I'm sure," came Katy's plaintive voice. "They're going to tell us to stop interfering and go home, again."

"Grayson hired me for a job, and I plan on finishing it."

"We."

"No, just me. As soon as the hospital releases Win, you and she will get on the first flight back to New York."

"Don't tell me you're doing this because you're having fun. We almost died in the bank."

I silently cursed myself for not leaving Katy and Win behind in New York. "That's exactly why I need you two out of here ASAP."

"And you?" came my friend's high-pitched voice.

"I made a promise. I'm going to stay and finish this job."

"Who's going to tell David?"

"I will," I said in a quiet voice. "I'm not doing this just for the money, you know. I'm also not doing this just because of Grayson."

"Then, why?"

The disfigured face of the young woman in the body bag flittered across my mind. "To figure out who killed that girl."

I turned my head her way. "Please go to sleep. We can chat in the morning."

I listened to her ruffling the sheets as she tried to settle back in bed, my mind fully alert now. Soon, I heard gentle snores from her corner as my friend succumbed to her exhaustion.

There was something else I wanted to speak to the police about, but I needed to be certain before I shared that key piece of information with Grayson or Katy.

I leaned back on my couch and stared out of the large bay windows.

Outside, the moon was almost full. Its pale beams fell on the lake water, reflecting an unearthly green glow.

The loon called again, as if it knew I was awake, listening. That sound should have been comforting, but it felt like a warning.

A warning of things worse to come.

Chapter Thirty-six

"They're not permitted in here, sir," said a familiar male voice.

"I'm not coming in without them," said Grayson through the open doorway.

Katy and I were at the police station after a long, troubled, and sleepless night. But a cold shower and a quick pizza breakfast had been enough for me to wake up and clear my head. I had a job to do.

Katy and I stood behind Grayson's wheelchair while uniformed officers and civilians bustled around us, coffee cups, thick files, and phones in hand. I had the cardboard box in mine, which Katy had refused to carry, let alone touch.

Grayson had sat slumped in my backseat on our way here, his folded wheelchair in the seat next to him. I had checked on him several times through the rearview mirror, but he hadn't spoken or looked up during the entire ride. It had seemed like the only thing that held him upright was the seat belt.

There was something about Chris Grayson I didn't get.

He didn't act like the typical wealthy businessperson I met in my line of work. They were usually extremely confident, strong-minded, results-oriented people who rarely showed weakness, even during the most grueling of circumstances that would break a normal person.

In contrast, Grayson was feeble, frightened, and alone. A part of me wondered if this was an act.

Something also told me he hadn't shared everything about his wife. It would have been because of shame, because he thought it irrelevant, or because he was hiding something from us. I wish I knew which it was.

"Sir, if you'd like to invite your attorney—" Davies began.

Grayson banged a fist on the arm of his wheelchair. "I don't need a lawyer!"

Katy and I reeled back in surprise.

"What a change of attitude," whispered Katy.

"More like it," I whispered back and nodded.

"I just want to find my wife!" Grayson shook his fist in the air. "You lot have done nothing. I don't think you even tried."

Davies' face crumpled for a second, but he recovered quickly. Jane Grayson's file was his kryptonite.

With a resigned sigh, he opened the door wide. Grayson pushed his wheelchair past him without even a glance back. Davies stood in his spot by the doorway, glaring at us.

"Didn't Thomas tell you to leave town?" he hissed as we stepped in to follow Grayson.

"Grayson hired me to do a job, and I mean to finish it," I snapped back.

"Are you aware that I can charge you with interfering with police business?"

I suppressed a sudden and juvenile urge to open the box and throw the severed limb in his face.

"Seems like you're in the mood for wasting public funds. Go right ahead. Good luck finding anything that will stick."

With an incensed snarl, Davies spun on his heels and marched through the corridor to where Thomas was standing with Grayson.

The five of us entered the office silently.

It was disheartening to be back in the same interrogation room where Katy and I had spent hours, only the day before.

This time, the space felt claustrophobic. On top of Grayson, Thomas, Davies, Katy, and me, Officer Lee stood by the door, watching us with a sharp eye.

I wondered why they thought to have an armed guard in here. Did they expect us to get violent?

I placed the cardboard box in the middle of the table.

"A present for you, gentlemen."

Davies and Thomas raised their eyebrows.

"This was left at my doorstep last night," said Grayson.

"What's that smell?" said Thomas, sniffing the air suspiciously.

The severed hand had been sitting in the boot of my car long enough to emanate a slight rotting odor. Either Katy, Grayson, and I had got used to it or it hadn't affected us as much since we knew what it was.

Davies leaned toward it, frowning. "What's in it?"

I pushed the box toward him. "Why don't you see for yourself?"

With an impatient sneer, Davies flipped the top open. He staggered back with a surprised yell, turning his chair over. He careened toward the officer by the door, his face pale with fright.

Thomas stood up and peered into the opened box. He froze as his eyes fell on the gruesome object.

"My good lord," he said finally.

Davies was spinning in place by the door, keeping a safe distance.

"Take that away," he shouted at Lee. "To the morgue!"

Officer Lee's eyebrows shot up.

"Do I call the bomb squad, sir?"

"If it was a bomb, would I ask you to take it to the morgue?"

She didn't move.

"Now!" shouted Davies, covering his nose.

Lee stepped up to the table and, without even looking inside, snapped the flaps shut. Without a word, she whirled around and marched toward the open door, box in hand.

"Put it in the freezer!" Thomas shouted at her disappearing back. "Tell Dr. Melnyk he needs to examine it right away."

I sat in my chair, observing them, waiting quietly for the panicking and hollering to die down.

Thomas and Davies walked back to the table and stood behind their chairs, staring at us, accusing expressions on their faces.

"What the hell were you thinking?" said Davies.

"You could have warned us," said Thomas.

"Someone left that box at Mr. Grayson's doorstep," I said. "That means it was someone inside the gates. If I were you, I'd be questioning all the residents along the pier."

"We're not looking for advice on how to do our jobs," growled Davies.

Thomas frowned at me. "We'll be doing that and much more, Ms. Kade. You need to leave this work for the professionals."

"We saw a man get thrown off the back of a van at the emergency ward entrance," I said, ignoring his snide comment. "His right hand was a stump, covered in blood and patched up with a dirty cloth. I'm sure your people at the hospital already told you about it."

"Your point being?" said Thomas.

"I got the license plate number down and gave it to the hospital security officer. It was the same vehicle that followed us in the limo. That van was their getaway car."

Thomas and Davies didn't say a word, but their eyes darted back-and-forth. Grayson said nothing, his hands limp on his lap.

"There's a connection between what happened to us, the dead woman in the vault, the young man with his hand cut off, and Jane Grayson's disappearance. Figure out what the common thread is and you'll find Chris's wife."

"I love a conspiracy theory just the same as you," said Davies, shaking his head.

"Chris is a well-known businessman in this town," said Thomas with a heavy sigh. "This isn't the first time we've seen such threats sent to wealthy business owners. This hand might have nothing to do with Jane's disappearance."

"Are you saying people cut off each other's hands regularly in this city?" said Katy, giving him an innocent look.

Thomas turned a stern face to her, one a headmaster would give a naughty student.

"We have an entire team of officers on these files. We don't jump to conclusions. We examine facts and make evidenced-based decisions."

"In your haste to get that box away from this room, it seems you may have missed a valuable piece of evidence," I said.

"That box will be examined inch by inch," said Davies. "Don't teach us to suck egg—"

"So, you didn't see the tattoo between the thumb and index finger?"

Thomas jerked his head back slightly. Davies gave me a surprised look.

"Of course I did," snapped Davies, but he wasn't making eye contact anymore.

"I've seen that tattoo before," I said. "I think it's your most important clue."

Chapter Thirty-seven

"Remember the body inside the vault?" I said.

Thomas and Davies exchanged a nervous glance.

"Dr. Melnyk started his procedure this morning and didn't mention any missing limbs," said Davies quietly.

I sat up in my chair.

So they had taken her body to the station's medical examiner's room, after all. She must have been inside the mortuary fridge when Katy and I had walked in.

"Enough!"

We all jumped as Grayson punched the table.

"What about Jayne?" he said, looking from Davies to Thomas, fire in his weary eyes. "Where is she? How do we know she's okay? How do we know if she's still alive?"

Thomas leaned in.

"I told you, Chris, I have my best men on her file. We're looking into it. You know I'm going full throttle."

Grayson's face flushed. "You've been saying this for weeks. What are you doing to find her?"

Thomas put a hand on Grayson's trembling arm, towering over my diminutive client.

These two knew each other from before. Were they friends? Colleagues? Business partners?

"Chris, I have a backlog a mile long," said Thomas in a low and soothing voice, the way one would speak to a close and trustworthy friend. "You know I'm fighting budget battles with my superiors. They cut my team in half. I'm doing everything I can for you."

Grayson looked away, his breaths coming shallow and fast. His face contorted like he was trying his best to contain his anger.

"Why do you raise my hopes like this? Why are you doing this to me? She means everything to me!"

Thomas gripped Grayson's arm tighter.

"Trust me, Chris. We will find Jane."

I pushed my chair back. "I think it's time to search for her ourselves, Mr. Grayson."

"Now, you listen here, Ms. Kade." Thomas whipped around and glared at me, his thick finger inches from my nose. "If you'd stop interrupting and interfering, we would get this business looked after faster."

Grayson pushed his wheelchair back, his body and face crumpled, looking like the defeated man we'd seen yesterday.

"If you have nothing new on Jane, I'm done here."

Thomas let out a sigh and turned to my client.

"Chris, I'd like to speak with you privately."

Grayson rolled toward the door.

"Please, Chris," Thomas called out. "Can we talk?"

Grayson stopped and turned his head. Thomas and Grayson stared at each other for a few seconds, like they were speaking a secret language. These two knew each other well. Why hadn't Grayson mentioned this before?

"Just find Jane," said Grayson in a low voice.

Something nagged at me from the back of my head. A small idea was taking form. My heart beat a tick faster.

"Katy and I can step out," I said, tapping my friend on the shoulder.

I turned to Grayson.

"Might be a good idea to hear Officer Thomas out. Anything he says will only help you find your wife sooner. We'll be outside, waiting for you."

Grayson gave me a confused look. Davies shot us a churlish one and waved at the door, like he couldn't get rid of us fast enough.

Katy and I slipped out, and Davies slammed the door behind us.

"Stay here with Grayson," I whispered to Katy. "If you hear anything, roll him down the corridor until you see me."

She gave me a puzzled look, but the idea had got a hold of me and wasn't letting go.

Before my friend could stop me, I power-walked down the corridor as if I was heading toward the women's toilets. I glanced over my shoulder to see Katy watching me, a frown on her face.

Giving a silent thanks to her, I took a turn to the left and hurried along. Retracing the footsteps Katy and I had made earlier, I slipped into the wing that housed the medical examiner's offices.

I pulled on the heavy green door to the mortuary room when I heard the yell.

"Stop right there!"

That was Officer Lee's voice. I didn't look back. I stepped inside, closed the door, and turned the bolt.

"Excuse me?" said a voice I didn't recognize.

A man in plastic green overalls was standing half bent over a gurney. He had a bloodied scalpel in one hand and what looked like a dentist's stainless-steel tray in the other. He was staring at me over his mask.

I tried not to gag. There was blood everywhere, all over the open body, on the doctor's apron, and on that tray.

Someone banged on the door.

"Open up!"

That was Lee again.

Ignoring her, I peered at the corpse. It was the dead woman from the vault, her mangled face half covered in a sheet.

"What in heaven's name is going on?" said the surgeon, still half bent, staring at me like he couldn't believe his eyes.

I pointed at the woman. "Have you identified her?"

"Open up!" It was Davies now.

"I was with her in the bank vault," I said to whom I presumed to be Dr. Melnyk. "I found her inside that body bag."

The doctor stared at me, his eyes wide.

It seemed like the entire police force was hammering on the door now. Keys jangled loudly. They would soon barge in.

"I believe the next of kin has the right to know she's here," I said.

"I, er..." The doctor straightened up and glared. "Who are you and what the heck are you doing in here contaminating my work?"

"Her father is in this station," I said, speaking fast. I didn't have time. "He needs to see her—"

The door banged open, and Davies rushed inside, his handgun aimed at my head. Before I could do anything, he pounced on me and twisted my wrists behind my back. He pulled out a pair of handcuffs, swearing loudly.

That was when Katy rushed in, wheeling Chris.

Thank you, Katy.

She had known what to do.

"You're not permitted here!" shouted Dr. Melnyk, waving his arms in the air. "All of you! Get out! Now!"

The stainless-steel tray in his hand fell to the ground, dropping various body parts on the floor. Davies jumped to the side with a surprised yell as the blood splattered onto his tunic. He let go of me and the handcuffs fell with a clang.

"I'm working!" yelled the doctor, brandishing his scalpel, his furious eyes bulging over his mask. "You're destroying the evidence. Contaminating this whole space!"

Lee ducked as the scalpel came dangerously close to her head.

"Watch it, man!" she shouted.

I turned to Grayson over the melee.

"The body. You know her."

He gave me a glazed look.

"Check her right arm for the birthmark."

His face turned pale. "Jane?"

"It's a black heart-shaped mole!" I shouted, as Davies grabbed me again and struggled to put those cuffs on me.

Katy pushed Grayson's wheelchair closer.

Thomas rushed into the room.

The doctor turned to him and ripped off his mask. "Thomas! What the hell are these people doing in here? Get them all out now!"

Thomas grabbed Grayson's wheelchair handles from my friend.

"Chris, you can't be in here. Everyone out!"

But Grayson had already seen what he had to see.

He crumpled forward in his chair and fell to the floor, head first. Katy grabbed the back of the wheelchair before it crashed over him.

"Lily! Lily!"

Grayson beat his fists on the ground in anguish, his tormented cries echoing through the morgue.

Chapter Thirty-eight

"I was sure they were going to throw us in jail for good," said Katy, slamming the car door shut.

I slipped into the driver's seat of our rental car and rubbed my wrists. "David held me in that room for a while, handcuffed. I call that an arrest."

If Katy hadn't phoned Peace for help immediately, they would have stuck me in a cell until they decided on a court date. In the end, all they could do was charge me with mischief. They dropped the charges quickly after Peace brought up the question of possible false imprisonment. I simply wasn't worth the paperwork and Thomas and Davies now had bigger fish to fry.

Lily's body in the morgue, years after her supposed death, had reopened that file and posed new questions no one had answers to.

My heart went out to Chris Grayson.

This was not the way I had wanted to break the news to him. But I also knew that mangled face would stump the detectives and DNA tests took time, if they even bothered to do one. Thomas was stressed out about his backlog and his budget, which meant the investigation could have been delayed for weeks, if not months.

That was too long a wait for Chris Grayson to learn his daughter had been alive all along.

He had lain on the floor, sobbing and screaming, until Doctor Melnyk had sedated him and taken him on a stretcher to the station's clinic.

Grayson was still under observation when they let Katy and me go. I had wanted to see him badly, to assure him I would find who did this to his only offspring, but I had lost all my bargaining chips with Thomas and Davies.

After Peace had hung up, Officer Lee had released me from the interrogation room and marched Katy and me out of the station without a word.

I'd followed her through the station's maze of corridors, feeling everyone's eyes on me, like arrows on fire aimed my way.

After pushing us out of the main doors, Lee stomped back inside, wiping her hands like she'd just removed the station of vermin.

"We're making enemies fast," said Katy, putting on her seat belt.

I switched the car engine on. "Where were you when Davies was questioning me?"

"Getting harassed by Thomas in the next room."

"Why didn't you tell Peace? He can't do that—"

"Do you know what he said?" She gave me an indignant look. "He told me we have no business being here. The way he talked was like I should have stayed home and made a sandwich for my husband. That man needs to get with this century."

I rolled the car away from the curb. "And I thought Davies was the mean one."

"Thomas never raised his voice, which was what made me so upset. He knows how to bully without shouting."

I shook my head.

"They're mad because we're figuring things out before they can," I said, doing a shoulder check before changing lanes. "We've progressed far more on their missing persons files in forty-eight hours than they did in years."

Katy let out a sigh. "I just hope Jane's okay wherever she is. Whether she's having an affair or not, Grayson needs to know."

I glanced at my rearview mirror and frowned. For a split second, I thought I'd spotted a white van a few vehicles behind us.

I rubbed my eyes. Every plumbing and roofing company in Seattle probably owed fleets of white cargo vans like that.

This is what happens when you don't get enough sleep. You start hallucinating.

I turned toward the road sign with the large H symbol on it.

"Can't wait to see Win," said Katy. "Poor girl, all alone."

I took the entrance to the freeway toward the hospital.

"She's probably going to be more mad about missing the action than anything else."

"Don't you think it weird no one told us what Lily's boyfriend's name is?" said Katy. "He has no family, no connections. It's like he doesn't exist."

"Except he does. We saw him."

"And his severed hand," said Katy, with a shudder. Her voice turned hard. "If Thomas thinks he can scare us away, he has a surprise coming. We're going to show them, right?"

I got off the freeway and drove toward the entrance of the hospital.

As soon as I turned into the main driveway, a peculiar sense of déjà vu came over me. Every time we came to this place, something horrible happened. I couldn't wait to see Win and make sure she was all right.

"Watch out!" cried Katy.

My eyes flew to the rearview mirror. I yanked the steering wheel hard to the right. My tires squealed on the asphalt, and we leaped over the curb, just as the white van dashed by us.

"Hey!" shouted a man who'd jumped out of our path just in time.

I slammed on the brakes.

The pedestrian lifted an angry fist. "Get off the curb!" he shouted. "Learn how to drive!"

With another shake of his fist, he stomped through the main doors. Two women in scrubs who had been behind him gave us the evil eye.

Didn't anyone notice the white van that almost slammed into us?

With shaking hands, I put the gear in reverse and pulled into the nearest parking lot. Katy sat silently next to me, but I could hear her heavy breathing as she tried to calm down.

It was only after I had parked the car and turned the engine off that I could speak.

"They want to kill us," I said.

"What have we done to them?" said Katy.

"We are principal witnesses to their crimes."

Chapter Thirty-nine

"We just discharged her," said the nurse.

"What do you mean, discharged her?" I said, a sinking feeling coming to my stomach.

Katy stood by me, her hands clutching the counter. The nurse shuffled through a stack of documents on her desk and pulled a paper out.

She squinted at the form. "Forty-five minutes ago."

"Where did she go?" I said, trying to swallow the panic rising inside of me.

We hadn't stopped to report our near accident with hospital security. I didn't even remember if I had locked the car. After realizing the threat, Katy and I had dashed inside and run up to the ward where Win was being treated.

The nurse gave a nonchalant shrug, as if crazy, hyperventilating people like us were an everyday occurrence for her. "We just started a new shift, but I can assure you, the paperwork is all here. She signed out herself."

"Impossible," I said, my mouth dry.

"You shouldn't have let her walk out like that," said Katy, glaring at the nurse.

The nurse pursed her lips. "She's an adult."

I leaned over to read the paper in her hand, but the nurse snatched it away.

"Are you family?" she said, frowning.

"Best friends. Colleagues."

"We don't share patient information with everyone who walks in here. You have to leave."

Something beeped on her desk. She peered at her computer and grabbed a clipboard. "I have to go," she said, turning around.

"Can we talk to the nurse who signed her out?" I called as she moved away from the desk, her attention already on something else.

"Come back tomorrow," she said, hurrying off. "Their shift starts at five AM."

She bustled around the corner without another glance. I looked around for a gate or an entrance to the nurses' station, but a security guard was standing close by, watching us, a stern expression on his face.

I searched the faces of the nurses and custodians bustling around us, but none of them looked familiar. There was no sign of the female guard who had been watching over Win, either.

I should have never left her alone. Please be okay, Win.

I turned to the security guard.

"Did you see a petite woman in her late twenties? Asian. Bob-cut hairstyle."

The man shook his head and turned away.

Katy gave me a numbed look. "What do we do? She doesn't even have a phone."

I glanced at the guard again. He was now observing a lone patient in an open hospital gown, pacing the corridor and shouting incoherently at no one in particular. The guard reached for the radio on his shoulder.

"This way," I said, pulling Katy as I scrambled down the corridor.

We crashed into Win's room. An elderly, frail man lifted his head. His sunken eyes were almost white with cataracts.

"Mary?" he said, pointing a shaking, bony hand our way. "Mary, is that you?"

I stepped back and double-checked the room number on the door.

"It's her room," whispered Katy.

But Win was gone.

We stepped out, walking backward.

"Sorry, so sorry," I said to the patient, feeling bad to have disturbed him.

Katy put a hand to her heart and leaned against the wall outside the room. "Oh, my goodness, I'm never going to forgive myself for this."

I pulled my phone out.

"Whether they like us or not," I said, opening the web app and searching for the precinct's number, "we need Thomas and Davies to help us now."

"Why would she walk out like that?" said Katy. "Why couldn't she call us?"

"Our phones are in a ditch somewhere, remember? And she doesn't have the numbers for our new burners."

Katy started pacing up and down the corridor while I made the call to the station.

"Thomas and Davies are not available," I said, slipping my phone back into my pocket when I was done. "Either that or they're avoiding us."

"What about Win?" said Katy.

"The call center said to come down to the station to file a missing person's report in twenty-four hours."

"Twenty-four hours? By then, who knows what would happen to her?" A red flush flamed through Katy's cheeks. "Bunch of idiot bureaucrats!"

Though I couldn't stand Thomas and Davies either, I still had some faith in the system.

We were in a first-world country with a justice system that worked most of the time. It wasn't perfect, but it wasn't close to the corruption I'd dealt with in our youth in other places.

"She's a smart gal," I said, trying to think. "She couldn't have gone that far."

"It's been almost an hour. Anything could have happened!"

"Before we panic, let's check the rooms just in case she's somewhere here, waiting for us."

The security guard was now occupied with the patient in the corridor, who seemed to be resisting him.

Katy and I tiptoed the length of the corridor, popping our heads into each room and even checking the bathrooms.

It wasn't lunchtime yet, and most of the patients were asleep. Those who weren't didn't give us a second glance, mistaking us for hospital employees, I imagined.

We were coming to the end of the ward, and I was losing hope fast. The white van rushing out of the hospital was a bad sign. If they had kidnapped Win—

Katy grabbed my arm. "Oh, my goodness."

"What?" My heart raced and my hopes rose again. "Win? Where?"

Katy shook her head and pointed silently to the open doorway in the corner, a room I hadn't checked yet. I peeked in.

It was the young man who had been thrown out of the white van.

He was sitting half upright on his bed, surrounded by machines. The hospital staff had bandaged the bloody stub on his arm with proper dressing. His face was sickly, but he was alive.

He was staring right back at us, his good hand gesturing us to come inside.

Chapter Forty

I slipped inside the room before the security guard could spot us.

The young man's eyes flickered and lit up as Katy and I approached his bed.

His face was taut and sickly, but the hope in his eyes was palpable. He kept motioning with his good hand. *Come closer. Come!*

His gestures were insistent.

"Hi there," said Katy.

He drew his lips back as if to speak, but no sound came out.

Is he brain damaged?

All these machines surrounding his bed meant his condition was serious. A human body would react drastically to a severed limb. But something about this setup bothered me.

If anyone needed protection, it was him. Why didn't the police have security watch over his room like they had for Win? On that note, where was that guard, and why did she allow our friend to leave?

The young man tried to speak again, but only a low guttural noise came out, like the sound a cornered animal would make.

He closed his lips and swallowed, his eyes flickering anxiously. His breath came hard and fast, as if the attempt to talk had sapped him of his energy.

We stared at each other while my brain whirred, wondering how to best start a conversation with this stranger.

I had barely registered his face when he was thrown off the van, my preoccupation being with the vehicle. He was in his early or mid-twenties, tall, lanky and wore his brown hair down to his neck. He looked very much like the man in that photo on Geena's door.

That was when I spotted the clipboard above his bed. A nurse had written his first name on top. *Miles.* There was no last name.

"Hi Miles," I said, putting on a friendly smile. "We're here to help you."

He blinked rapidly.

"I'm Asha and this is Katy," I said, softening my voice.

Next to me, Katy shuffled her feet impatiently. "Did you see a petite Asian woman with a bob cut? Have you seen Win?"

Miles turned and stared at her, confusion clouding his eyes.

He opened his mouth.

"Did... you... find... her?"

Katy and I leaned closer to hear. He spoke in a raspy, hoarse whisper. It was barely audible. He reached out to us with his good hand.

"Did you find... my baby girl?"

He wasn't referring to Win. I suspected he didn't even know she existed, unless he had seen us all come out of the limo and into the bank. If I had to guess, though, he was asking about the dead woman in the body bag.

Lily.

"She...." I stopped and bit my lips. "We're still looking for her."

I hated lying to him, someone who had asked us for help, but I couldn't send him into further shock by telling him the truth.

Tears welled in his eyes.

I pointed at his bandaged stump. "Who did this to you?"

He turned and stared at his injured arm like he was seeing it for the first time.

"If you tell us," I said, lowering my voice, "we'll be able to help you. Keep you safe."

He turned to me with a frightened expression.

"Miles, do you know Jane Grayson? Have you seen her recently?"

His eyes widened. He recognized the name.

He cleared his throat as if to speak. He opened his mouth and shut it again and swayed back and forth, his face a picture of misery and frustration. A monitor near his head beeped faster.

"It's okay," said Katy, putting a hand on his arm. "Breathe. Slowly. You'll be fine."

He swallowed hard, like something was stuck in his throat.

"Water," said Katy, spinning around. "He needs water."

She picked up the empty plastic cup on the tray at the edge of his bed and stepped up to the sink.

Miles's eyes followed her, then he struggled to sit up.

"Take it easy," I said. "Don't move too fast."

His good hand clutched my arm and squeezed it tightly.

"You'll be fine. Don't worry. You're being taken care of here."

He let go of my hand and turned his head as if he suddenly remembered something. He pointed at the foot of his bed.

Katy scooted over and picked up the neatly folded hospital towel lying at the end. "Do you need a towel, hun?"

Miles shook his head. More incomprehensible guttural noises came from his throat, but his arm remained pointing her way.

Katy and I scoured that end of the room, trying to figure out what he was trying to say. There were extra bandages, a large empty bowl, and a notepad on the tray, all of which I presumed the nurses had left behind after his last round of medication.

Katy picked up the bowl. He shook his head, but kept his arm up.

I pounced on the notepad and held it up.

He nodded rapidly. The machine was beeping faster. It wasn't long before someone would notice it and come over to check up on him.

I brought it over and fished for a pen in my pocket. Katy brought over the paper cup with water, but he barely acknowledged it.

Miles took the pen in his good hand and reached out to the pad I held in front of him.

Katy and I watched silently as he struggled to scribble on the paper. He was writing numbers. A string of digits.

Is it a telephone number?

When he was done, he dropped his head back on the pillow and his arm to his side, letting the pen roll away. He closed his eyes, breathing hard, like he was exhausted.

He whispered without even opening his eyes. "Find her."

"We will," I said, ripping the paper from the pad and pocketing it.

"Hey, what are you doing here?"

I spun around to see the scowling face of a man in nurse's scrubs by the threshold.

"How did you get in?"

"Sorry to be a bother," said Katy, giving him an apologetic smile. "We were just leaving."

"Who are you?"

"Friends of Miles," I said as I slipped past him.

"Hey, wait," I heard him call out as we hurried along the corridor toward the elevator. "Security! Room twenty-seven. Come immediately."

"This way," I said, pulling Katy toward the stairwell next to the bank of elevators. We dove through the fire exit just as we heard the man yell.

"Stop those two!"

Chapter Forty-one

Katy and I dashed down the fire escape and into the parking lot.

"Why are we always running from this place like criminals?" said Katy, panting.

"Where's our car?" I asked, swiveling my head.

That was when I saw her. Her back was to us, but I would recognize that bob cut and petite frame anywhere.

"Win!" screamed Katy, but it was too late.

She had already disappeared inside the gray Chevrolet sedan. The driver started the engine and took off before we could get to her. We ran after the vehicle, waving and hollering like mad, but it turned the corner and disappeared.

"That's them!"

The male voice came from the other end of the parking lot. It was the same security guard who had chased the white van with me the day Miles got thrown out of it.

Even from the distance, I could see him struggle to put one foot in front of another, but his partner was fitter and faster.

I whirled around.

Where's our rental? Why can't I remember—

"There," said Katy, grabbing my arm with one hand and pointing at a corner of the lot with the other. Being a foot taller than me, she had a much better vantage point. "By the parking meter on the other side."

"Let's go!"

By the time the guards had arrived at the parking lot, we'd scrambled inside our car, and rolled on to the driveway.

The last view I had from my rearview mirror was the first guard leaning against a parking meter, a hand on his heart, breathing hard.

"Where did that car go?" I said, speeding toward the main road. "What make was it?"

Katy groaned. "A four-door gray sedan. There are probably millions of cars like that."

"What was she doing going off with some stranger?" I muttered as I slowed down to scan the road.

Katy peered through the windshield. "I see it! I see it!"

I took my foot off the brake and jumped on the accelerator, rolling our car into the left lane. An angry honk came from behind me, but I didn't look. I pushed forward, my eyes on the gray Chevrolet sedan.

There were no decals or signs on the car's panels to tell us what kind of vehicle it was, but it definitely wasn't a registered taxi.

"Four cars up," said Katy, leaning forward and pointing.

I changed lanes again. More honking. Suddenly, a loud thumping sound came from somewhere, like a car had turned on its radio at full blast. I switched lanes, back and forth, until we were right behind the Chevrolet.

"I see her!" cried Katy, slamming her hand on the dashboard.

My heart raced as I spotted Win's small profile through the back window. She was alone in the backseat, and the only other person in that vehicle was the driver.

"It's got to be a rideshare," said Katy, shaking her head. "She'd never get into a stranger's car, just like that. She's smarter than that. But where's she going?"

I leaned on my horn.

The driver of the Chevrolet shot me a surly look through the side mirror, but Win didn't turn her head. I caught sight of dark shades and a brown beard on the driver, but not much else.

"I know this dude," said Katy, staring at the car in front of us. "It's the same guy who tried to hit us by the bakery. Same guy who peeked into our guest house last night."

"Could be different people," I said, not taking my eyes off the road. "That's a brilliant but simple disguise, and we'd never know who's underneath it."

Katy leaned out of our car and waved, yelling Win's name. But all the windows on the Chevrolet had been rolled up, and Win seemed either asleep or occupied with something. She had kept her head down all this time, even with me blowing my horn to the high heavens.

Was she sedated?

"Music," said Katy in a shocked whisper.

That was when I realized the loud hip-hop thumping noise was coming from the gray sedan. A great way to stop Win from hearing my horn or our hollers.

I gritted my teeth. "We've got to get beside them, so she can see us."

An eighteen-wheeler, which seemed as long as a city block, was casually rolling by us in the fast lane, oblivious to our plight.

"If only this darned truck would move," I said.

"Oi!" shouted Katy through the window as she slammed her palm on the side of her door. "Get out of the way! This is an emergency!"

The truck driver didn't even look.

"They'll never hear us," I said, making a decision.

I revved our car and rushed toward the Chevrolet's bumper.

"What are you doing?" cried Katy, pulling her arms in and covering her face.

I hit the brakes hard, stopping just in time. Katy and I whiplashed forward. The car in front sped up, and the driver shot me a frightened look through his side-view mirror.

If that wouldn't get his attention, I didn't know what would.

But he swerved to the right and took off.

Why isn't Win looking up?

The driver was trying to shed me from his tail, but I stayed close, ignoring the yells and honks around us. I revved again and touched the back bumper of the Chevrolet. He changed lanes again.

"Oh, my goodness, I'm going to have a heart attack," said Katy, holding on to the door handle with both hands now.

"We're not going to lose her," I said, clenching my teeth and clutching the steering wheel.

"Hey! You drunk?" hollered someone from somewhere.

A loud and angry blast made Katy and me jump in our seats. The truck driver had finally noticed us and had blared their mega horn, as if to tell both cars to stop being a nuisance on the road.

"He's getting away!" cried Katy, pointing.

The Chevrolet swerved dangerously to the right and took the nearest exit at the last minute.

"Good," I said, sticking right behind him. "Less traffic."

He sped up as I followed him out. A cacophony of honking and another angry blast from the truck came from the main road, as if all the drivers had decided to give us the collective finger.

Ours were the only two cars on this smaller lane now, and it had only one destination.

A deserted gas station.

I revved up and hit the Chevrolet in the back. It wobbled to the side of the road, like it would fall into the ditch.

"Watch it!" scolded Katy. "Win's in there."

I revved up again, this time pretending to get close, but didn't hit it. The Chevrolet screeched to a stop by the gas station entrance. I jumped on the brakes, hitting the bumper hard. Win's head snapped forward.

"Win!" cried Katy, putting her hands to her head.

I banged open my door and leaped out of the car, just as the driver of the Chevrolet got out.

"What the hell do you think you're doing?" I shouted, then froze on the spot.

He had a gun.

The driver advanced on me.

He had dark shades, a long brown beard, and a gray scarf around his neck, just like the driver who had tried to run us over. Something about him was familiar, but I couldn't pinpoint what it was.

"What stupid game are you playing at?" he snapped.

"That's what I'd like to know," I snapped right back.

He turned the gun on Katy, who had jumped out of the car and was making a beeline to the back of the sedan.

"Hey!" he shouted. "Stop right there."

"Win!" shouted Katy, ignoring him and trying to open the door, but it was locked.

"Who the hell do you think you are?" said the driver, his eyes back to me. "You were trying to kill me, or what?"

"You have our friend," I snarled. "And we'd like her back."

"Your *friend*?" The surprise in his voice was unmistakable.

What's he playing at?

"Open the car," I said, glaring at him. "Let her out. Now!"

Chapter Forty-two

The bearded man kept his weapon aimed my way. But Katy's movements by his car were unnerving him.

He glanced from her back to me, and then on to the highway behind us, like he didn't know what to do next.

I knew why he was hesitating. We had one advantage. We were out in the open, and visible from the main road. Someone should have seen us and called nine-one-one by now.

I didn't care to see Davies and Thomas again, but with Win's life on the line and possibly ours, all I wanted to hear were police sirens blaring.

"Drop your weapon!" I shouted.

"Who are you?" said the man.

"My question to you exactly," I spat out. "Why did you kidnap our friend?"

He jerked his head back as if startled.

"Put your gun down," I growled. "The police are on their way. You can explain everything to them."

That was a lie, but a needed one.

He took a step back.

"I... I thought you were trying to attack me. I was just giving her a ride. You followed me. *You* rammed my car. I should call the police on you!"

If criminals got Oscars, he certainly deserved one.

"Lower your weapon now, unless you want the entire SPD on your back."

"I'll tell them how you hit me. You almost caused an accident."

"Try the driver's side, Katy," I called out, keeping my eyes on the man.

She darted over to the other side, leaned in, and unlocked all the doors.

"What are you doing with my car?" said the driver, turning his weapon on Katy.

I took a step forward. As long as I kept his attention on me, Katy could get Win out and back into the safety of our car.

"I carry concealed," I said. Another much-needed lie.

He swung back to me.

I took another step forward.

"I'm the fastest drawer I know. You pull that trigger and I swear you will die just as instantly."

He didn't move. It was hard to say what he was thinking behind those dark sunglasses.

I could jump on him and twist that weapon out of his hands, but something told me this was a charade, pretending to be an innocent rideshare driver. We were in public. He wouldn't get away easily if he did something rash out here.

Katy opened the back door and pulled Win by her arm. Win stumbled out and gave us a dazed look.

"Asha!" she cried, seeing me.

"Get in the car. Both of you."

"Hey!" shouted the driver. "Who's going to pay my fare?"

"You pulled a gun on us, buddy. If you think we're going to pay your fare, you must be mad."

He glared.

He could be telling the truth, or he could be working for those goons who abducted us on our first night, but there wasn't much I could do.

He had a weapon.

I didn't.

As soon as the car doors slammed shut behind me, I walked backward and slipped into the driver's seat.

I started the engine, my eyes still on the driver.

"Keep your heads down," I said, as I rolled back onto the road.

"You think he'll shoot us?" whispered Katy as she scrambled into the seat well.

My eyes went to the side mirror.

The bearded driver was standing by his car, staring at us, the weapon limp in his hands.

I jumped on the accelerator and headed toward the entrance to the highway, my heart beating fast. I had so many questions for Win, but I kept my focus on the road, searching for any more suspicious vehicles that could be following us.

My adrenaline levels were spiked high. My blood was pounding through my veins like pulsating red hot lava. But a sense of dread was overcoming me slowly, chilling the heat. It was like my body was preparing for something worse. I just didn't know what it was.

We drove in silence, until I realized both Win and Katy were still crouched in their seats, silent in anticipation, just like I was.

"All clear," I said. "But keep your eyes and ears peeled."

Katy slowly unscrunched herself and turned around to face Win in the backseat.

"Where were you going, sweetie? You were supposed to stay in the hospital until we came to get you."

Win gave her a dazed look. "You told me to go to the airport."

"*What?* When?"

"The nurse gave me your message this morning."

Win's words were slurred like she was drunk. She had been drugged again, or she was still under the influence of her medication. I crossed my fingers, hoping it wouldn't be as bad as the last time.

"We never left a message," said Katy.

"You didn't?" said Win.

"And where did you get those clothes, hun?"

"The nurse gave them to me. Another patient left them behind. She said they're clean."

"We have your bag at the guest float house. Your ID and wallet are there too. The police found everything in the limo except for the men."

I looked at Win through the rearview mirror. "How did you end up in that car?"

"The driver came to my room and said you sent him to pick me up. The security guard was there too, but she said nothing, so I thought it was legit."

A shiver ran down my back.

This was a bigger operation than I imagined. That bearded man wasn't an innocent rideshare driver. He had been playing with us. So had the female guard at the hospital. There were more members to this gang than I realized, some who had even convinced the local police precinct to get contract work.

"I tried to call you from the nurses' station," said Win. "I left messages, but then I remembered those men stole our phones."

"Whoever called you wanted you out of Seattle, or they were taking you somewhere," I said.

"Kidnap me? Why?"

I had no answers, but one thing was clear. They didn't want us in town.

"I would have never got in that car if I'd known," Win was saying. "Man, I should have punched his face and run out."

"Why didn't he shoot us?" said Katy.

I raised an eyebrow. "In broad daylight? In public? That gun was just a show."

"That beard was fake too," said Katy, shaking her head. "All of him was fake."

"If I see him again, he's going to regret picking me up," shot Win from the back.

"Guys," I said, turning around to my friends. "We're going to the float house to get your luggage and find the first flight back home."

Katy turned to me. "All three of us?"

I shook my head.

"This case is far more dangerous than I thought. But I have to find out who killed that girl. I owe Grayson and Miles that much."

"Wait, Grayson knows that dead girl in the bag?" said Win, sitting up.

"His long-lost daughter, Lily," said Katy. "The one he thought had run away."

"Oh, man. That's crazy. What else did I miss?"

"Honey, it's Luc who's missing you," I said. "It's time for you to go home."

Win stared at me through the rearview mirror. "But I came to help you."

"Didn't the doctor tell you to take it easy? You've gone through a lot already. And you don't sound too good right now."

"If you think I'm going to let that man get away with trying to kidnap me, you're wrong."

I bit my lip. I would have said the same thing.

"You need me." She reached through the front seats and shook my shoulder. "You need my computer skills."

"You need both of us," said Katy. "I'm not going home to make a sandwich for Peace. Seriously? I'm staying right here so I can find out who locked us up in that vault. That'll show that sexist idiot, Thomas."

I recognized those looks, those determined jaws, those narrowed eyes. It was two against one.

I sighed. "All right, you two. Our first stop is at the rental company."

"Do we need a second car?" said Katy.

"They're watching us. We need to get them off our tail before we make another move."

Chapter Forty-three

We stopped behind a yellow convertible at the main gates of the float home community.

A security guard came out of the guard post, a frown on his face.

"He's new," whispered Katy as the burly man strolled over to our car. "We didn't see him here yesterday."

The gates had been opened, but the car in front of us was sitting idle, with its engine running, on the driveway.

"Management must have brought in extra security," I said. "A smart move after all that has happened here."

I leaned out of my window and gave him a polite smile. "I have the code. We work for Chris Grayson."

"ID please," said the guard as he came up and scrutinized the rental label on my windshield.

I pulled out my driver's license and handed it to him.

He shook his head and passed it back to me.

"You're not residents. I'll have to ask you to turn around and leave, please."

Katy leaned across me, dangling a key ring. "But our luggage and everything is at the guest house. We even have the keys."

"Sorry, ma'am, you'll have to get a resident to get your belongings for you. I'm afraid I must ask you to leave now."

"We're hired private detectives," I said. "We're on urgent business."

He shrugged. "I'm only allowed to let anyone in with a resident's written or verbal permission."

"Oh, no," said Win from the backseat. "What do we do now?"

But the guard had already turned around and was strolling back to his post.

I took stock. We couldn't call Grayson. He was still sedated and lying in a cot at the police station's clinic. But there was always a way if I thought hard enough. *Think, girl.*

"Let them in."

We all looked up.

It was a woman's voice calling to the security guard from inside the closed convertible.

"You have my permission."

I recognized that voice.

"It's Nathalie, the mother with the kid," I whispered.

"Well, well, well," Katy said under her breath. "The last person on earth I'd expect to help us."

Nathalie didn't look at us or wave, but drove through the open gates. The security guard turned to us and nodded.

I followed the cabriolet into the garage in the marina and parked in our designated guest spot.

The front door of the convertible opened and out stepped the woman we saw the day before. She looked immaculate as ever in a smart pink suit, like she had just returned from a ladies-who-lunch session.

"Maybe she's not that nasty after all. Kids can drive you stir crazy some days. I know what that's like," said Katy, as we watched her getting her shopping bags from the back, pointedly ignoring us.

I drummed my fingers on the steering wheel. "What does she want?"

Katy turned to me. "You think she let us in because she wants something from us?"

"People don't change personality overnight," I said, frowning. "She knows something."

Nathalie was texting on her phone now, leaning against her driver's side door.

I turned to Katy and Win. "Watch your backs and stay close."

I got out of the car, feeling like my legs would collapse any moment. So many things had happened so quickly since we arrived, my head was still spinning.

The three of us walked toward the entrance.

"Hello there," I said as we approached Nathalie. "Thanks for letting us in."

She looked up and frowned at Win as if she hadn't realized there were more of us.

"Can we help you with your bags?" I said.

She scowled. "I'm fine."

"May I ask a question?"

She glared.

"Do you know Jane Grayson well?"

Silence.

"When did you see her last?"

Her lips curled back in contempt.

"I don't go around snooping on my neighbors like that fat Geena."

I raised my brows.

She leaned toward me, her beautifully made-up face pinched and tight.

"Aren't you supposed to be the detectives, all the way from New York too? If you're real smart, you would have figured that out by now. Why haven't you?"

I stood in my spot, undeterred. "Part of our investigation is to talk to everyone who lives here. Do you have any inkling where she went off to at all?"

"Let's get one thing straight," she snarled. "I don't know what happened to that crazy, cheating bitch."

I leaned away from her in surprise.

A red flush crept up her neck.

"Everyone is tired of her stupid antics," she spat out.

"What antics?"

But she wasn't listening to me anymore, lost in a world of hatred.

"I can't wait for you to find that stupid woman because then we can all go back to our lives."

So, that's why she wanted us in.

Every gesture and facial expression told me she was being sincere.

"We're doing our best," I replied.

"I don't know where she is, but I'll tell you this. I hope you find her soon and wherever you find her, I hope you'll find her *dead*."

We stared at her in shock.

Nathalie spun around, turned her back to us, and focused on her phone.

The conversation was over.

"Let's go," I said to my friends.

Katy, Win, and I walked past her and out of the garage.

"I take my words back," whispered Katy, as we stepped onto the promenade. "What a mean woman."

Win took a deep breath and spread her arms wide. "Can't say much about the people here, but this place is gorgeous."

"And chilly today," said Katy, pulling her jacket around her.

An icy blast of air was blowing from the lake and funneling through the rows of houses on the pier. I wondered if living on the water, while stunningly beautiful, was all that it was cracked up to be.

Our first stop was to check up on Grayson's house.

It seemed to be in the exact same condition as it had been when we had picked him up to escort him to the station. The curtains were closed on the top floor but pulled back on the first.

A peek through the bay windows in front told us no one was inside, at least on this floor.

"Poor man," said Katy as we withdrew and got back on the dock.

To find your daughter smashed up and cut open on a gurney when you thought she was dead would send any parent into massive shock. Grayson wasn't going to return to his normal self any time soon.

A twinge of guilt sprang up inside me to think of what I'd done to him.

But one troubling question remained. Where had Lily been for the last two years?

"Do we get to stay in one of these cool floating houses?" said Win, as she walked along the pier beside us.

She was getting her color back and was speaking normally again, though she was slightly pale from her ordeal.

"A lot smaller," Katy replied, "but very cute—"

A young child's ear-splitting screech stopped us in mid-stride. We were walking by the navy-blue house that belonged to Nathalie.

Katy turned to it with a frown. "Did that woman leave her child alone while she went shopping?"

"She must have a nanny," I said, more to myself than her. "No one would leave a kid that young by herself."

I turned back to see Nathalie threading along the promenade in her heels, balancing half a dozen designer shopping bags in both hands. Her progress was slow, and her focus was on the wood knots on the pier. It didn't seem like she even heard her child's cries.

"I swear I'm calling social services on her," said Katy.

We stepped away from the house and kept walking silently.

My mind buzzed. At what point do you interfere with a parent who might or might not be mistreating a child? We had already lost the trust of the local police officers for being meddlesome and had barely escaped landing in jail for a few days, if not weeks. But I hated seeing that child suffer like this.

The girl's screeches grew louder.

"My goodness," said Katy, "we have to do something."

I turned around to see Nathalie totter up the steps of her house, balancing her heavy shopping bags precariously. She stepped up to the door and flung it open.

The girl's screams rang out through the doorway, sending shivers down my back.

"For gawd's sake, child." Nathalie threw her shopping bags inside and stomped in. "Shut up, would you? Shut up!"

The door slammed closed, leaving us open-mouthed.

Chapter Forty-four

The feeling of eyes watching us came again.

Silence had fallen on the pier. The floating homes, except Nathalie's, seemed devoid of people.

Grayson had told us most of his neighbors flew south for the winter and didn't come back till summer.

I had been planning on getting an inventory of the residents from him that morning. But that had been before everything had turned upside down. Before the severed limb package, and before we discovered Lily's body at the morgue.

I caught a glint of sun on glass from the orange house. Katy whirled around as she saw me look.

"Geena's spying again," she said. "She could have been at our window last night, in a brown beard disguise."

I raised an eyebrow. "Why would she do that?"

"To scare us off. She has something to do with Jane's disappearance and doesn't want us to find out."

"If it was her at the window last night, she has to move quickly." I shook my head. "It was someone more agile, faster, and who lives closer."

"Who lives next door to us?"

"An older man. There could be others inside, but I saw him on the second floor."

"Every neighborhood has to have a snoop," whispered Win as we neared the orange house.

From the corner of my eyes, I caught Geena's shadow. She was at her window, peering out, but withdrew in a hurry when she saw us.

I turned away. "We need to get her to open up and talk."

"She's totally unreliable," said Katy. "I don't trust her one bit."

"Didn't you invite her for tea? Let's see if there's anything suitable in the guest house pantry. If tea doesn't work, we can offer wine, vodka, whatever she likes."

Katy made a face. "I'm betting what will make her talk is juicy gossip, not drinks or cake."

"This place gives me the heebie-jeebies." Win glanced around her and shuddered. "The lake is beautiful, and these houses are amazing, but something's wrong here. I can feel it in my bones."

"It's the people," said Katy, lowering her voice. "It's like the Twilight Zone over here."

I stopped in front of our guest house. "Katy, didn't you lock our door when we left this morning?"

My friends stopped next to me and stared at the front door.

It was ajar.

"Of course, I locked up," said Katy, pulling out the guest house keys from her pocket.

"Did someone break in?" whispered Win, her eyes widening.

"You two wait here," I said, walking toward the entrance.

I pushed the door an inch and peeked inside.

It wasn't hard to get a snapshot of the small space through the opened gap. Unless someone was hiding in the bathroom, the guest house was empty.

Using the tips of my fingers, I pushed the door open further.

Our luggage had been opened, and our things had been strewn all over the floor.

After scanning the room again, I stepped inside with my hands curled and my shoulders taut. I didn't have my trusty Glock on me, but I was prepared for battle.

I walked over to the kitchenette and plucked a copper pot from a hook on the wall. Holding it in front of my chest like a shield, I tiptoed over to the bathroom door, my heart thumping hard.

It was empty.

Our used towels lay exactly where Katy and I had hung them to dry that morning. Our toothbrushes were in their cups, and the shower curtain was drawn. Nothing was amiss.

I surveyed the space. The windows were still latched tight, and the door hadn't been broken.

"My goodness," said Katy, poking her head through the doorway. "What happened here?"

"Someone was looking for something."

"My laptop," cried Win, pushing Katy aside and rushing inside. She rummaged through her things, talking to herself. "My tablet, laptop, notebook..."

"Did they take anything?" I asked.

Win sat back on her haunches with a puzzled expression on her face. It took us a few more minutes to go over our things and confirm nothing had been taken.

We stared at each other from across the mess.

I frowned. "What were they looking for?"

"It's those men who threw us in the vault, isn't it?" said Win.

I stood up and double-checked the door lock.

"Whoever came in here had the key."

I pulled up my burner phone from my pocket and looked up the local precinct's number online once again.

"Let's hope Thomas and Davies are still at work."

"They're going to tell us to go back to New York again," said Katy.

"They need to know everything that has happened," I said, punching in the numbers. "The more we keep things from them, the less help we'll get, and the more Grayson will suffer."

I was just about to hit send when someone banged on our door.

"When did they start allowing hobos in here?"

I spun around.

We stared at the tall, thin septuagenarian at our threshold, his scraggly gray hair standing on end like that of a mad scientist who had accidentally electrocuted himself. His profile rang a bell in my memory banks.

"You live next door, don't you?" I said.

"Who let you riffraff in?"

"I saw you yesterday," I said, overlooking his rude remark. "You were watching us from the second floor."

"For good reason," he snapped. "I'm sick and tired of this place getting run over by intruders. Who gave you permission to come in here?"

"We work for Mr. Grayson. We're here to find his missing wife. If you have any issues with our presence, I suggest you talk to him."

His eyes widened for a moment, then flashed red.

"I don't care who you work for, but I don't want your kind of people here."

"Your kind of people?" Katy glared at him. "Was it you snooping through our window last night?"

"This is a respectable retirement community," said the man, ignoring her question. "Ever since Grayson started having trouble, this place has gone downhill. What do you think this has done to our property values? We're becoming a slum."

Win gestured at his house through the window. "Mansions floating on a private lake, and you call this a slum?"

"Why do you think two houses have been for sale for months now? No one wants to live here anymore. This community is going to hell in a handbasket right under our noses."

A blood vessel on his neck started to throb.

"People have no values any more. No sense of decorum. Running around the pier in the dead of the night. I know what they're up to. I'm not blind or deaf. Bunch of philistines."

"Who did you see running around?" I said, taking a step closer to him. "When and what were they up to?"

He glared, turning from Win to Katy to me. "I've had enough. I'm lodging a complaint with the community council and I will ask them to fine Grayson for disrupting the peace."

"Go right ahead," I said. There wasn't much I was going to get out of him in this state. "But I have a job to do here, and we will be staying."

He turned his sour eyes on me.

"You'll regret it if you stay another night. I suggest you pack your bags and get out."

"That won't happen."

He wagged a finger in front of my nose.

"Mark my words. Go home."

Chapter Forty-five

I stepped onto the pier to see where the neighbor was heading.

The old man was storming off in such a huff, I could almost see smoke rising from his ears. He stomped up to his house and slammed the door behind him.

I needed to talk to him, but now was not the time.

"Did he just say he saw people running around in the middle of the night?" said Katy, coming up from behind me.

"He spotted something, but has no idea what it was," I said.

I scanned the promenade. A shadow moved by the orange house. Geena.

"Be right back," I called out to my friends, and started marching in the direction of her home.

"Where are you going?" said Katy, running up.

"When you want to know what's really happening in a neighborhood, you talk to the local busybody."

Win rushed over to join us.

"Go back and get some rest," I scolded. "You just came from the hospital."

"I'm feeling fine," said Win, slipping in between Katy and me and linking arms. "It was horrible in the hospital. Bad food, a tiny bed, and the smell of Lysol everywhere. The worst thing was, I didn't have anyone to talk to. I need something to make my brain work again."

I squeezed her hand. Part of me wished Katy and Win weren't with me in this spooky neighborhood, but another part of me was glad to have them.

"Who paints their house orange?" said Win, as we got to the middle of the wharf.

"I'd bet you she's harmless," I said. "Annoying but harmless."

"I don't know," said Katy. "It could be her playing all these games."

"Her motive?"

"She said she used to live in a trailer park before. She could have inherited a ton of money and bought this house, but everyone here resents her. She's the outcast, the hobo, the riffraff that man talked about."

"So, she kidnapped Jane Grayson to get back at the community which rejected her?"

Katy didn't answer.

"What about Lily and Miles?" I said. "Why did they disappear for two years, only to turn up under these bizarre circumstances now?"

My friends remained silent, their brows furrowed.

We approached Geena's front door. I peered through the windows, but the curtains were too thick to see through.

Win gaped at the steel wire art sculptures hanging from the facade. "Cyberpunk on steroids. This house creeps me out. Are you sure she isn't a witch?"

"Shh..." said Katy.

I knocked.

We listened but only heard silence.

I could feel the energy of the woman inside. I imagined her cowering in the back. But there was something more here.

I smelled fear.

I knocked again. Louder.

The curtain on the front window shifted slightly, but the door remained shut.

"Let me try the side door," whispered Katy.

She stepped down from the promenade to the patio and disappeared from view. I soon heard her knock on the side entrance, where we had talked to Geena earlier.

A strange sound came from inside. I leaned in to listen.

What's she doing?

I knocked again.

"Anyone home?" I hollered.

Nothing.

"Come on, open up!" said Win next to me, startling me. She stomped her feet impatiently. "We have some juicy news for you!"

I turned to Win and gave her a stern look.

"To meet a snoop, you need to give them the scoop," whispered Win.

To my surprise, the lock on the front door clicked. I held my breath and hoped Geena didn't carry a gun.

The door opened an inch and a scared brown eye poked out.

"Hello there," I said, putting on my friendliest smile. "I'm so sorry to bother you, but can we talk?"

Silence.

"We have, er, information you might be interested in."

The door opened wider, and Geena poked her head out. She was wearing the same bright orange dress we had seen her in the day before. The smell of stale cigarette smoke wafted from inside.

Geena jumped backward as Katy came over to join us, but relaxed when she saw who it was. What was making her so jittery?

She scanned the wharf over our shoulders.

"All clear," said Win with a smile.

"You girls are going to stir up trouble if you don't watch out," said Geena, her voice gravelly like she had just got up. "Come in before someone sees you."

She held the door open as Katy, Win, and I trooped inside. She closed the door and double-checked the locks before moving the thick curtain aside to peer out the window.

She didn't offer us a seat, so we huddled by the foyer staring at her, staring back at us.

"Geena, did you see anyone near the guest house this morning?" I asked.

"I'm a busy woman," she said, rubbing her bare arms. "I don't have time to watch what's going on outside."

I swallowed the first thoughts that came to my mind. "Someone broke into the guest house and ransacked our bags."

"Never saw a thing," she said with a shrug. "I made a cuppa tea and sat on the back veranda to watch the hummingbirds at my feeder."

Katy gave her a surprised look. "All morning?"

Geena turned a dour face to her. "Saw nothing and heard nothing."

She was lying.

But why? Was it because she was embarrassed to be spying on the neighborhood, or was it something else?

I surveyed the interior of her home.

An old-fashioned yellow lamp on a dusty side table was the only illumination in here. The house was spacious and designed like the Graysons' home, but the insides couldn't be any more different.

Unopened cardboard boxes lay on the furniture like she had just moved in. Piles of knickknacks, old toys, and cracked crockery that looked like they belonged in the seventies had been carelessly thrown all over the living room. Dusty vinyl records lay on the floor next to an LP turntable with a broken arm.

It was like she had started a garage sale years ago but had forgotten to tell anyone.

"You said you had news," she said, giving me a pointed look. "What was it?"

I narrowed my eyes. It was time to put Geena to the test.

"Do you know Lily Grayson was alive until a day ago?"

She blinked. Then her forehead scrunched.

"You mean she's *dead*?"

I nodded somberly. Geena wrapped her arms around her shoulders and swayed back and forth.

Her response troubled me. Lily Grayson was thought to have died two years ago. The Graysons even had a funeral for her. I wondered if Geena had known she had been alive all along.

"Do you know where she is now?" I asked, watching her carefully.

She shook her head, her mouth turned down, still hugging herself and swaying.

"She's lying in the morgue at the police station. We saw her body this morning. Someone had smashed her face. She was in terrible shape."

Geena started to shake.

She staggered over to the dirty couch, pushed a pile of magazines to the floor, and plopped down hard. She covered her face with her hands and was silent for a long time before bursting into tears.

We watched her as she sobbed uncontrollably.

Katy gave me a side-eye. I knew what she was thinking.

Were these crocodile tears?

Had Geena been involved in Lily's disappearance? Did she have a hand in her murder?

Chapter Forty-six

Katy stepped into the living room and poked around the mess before extricating a facial tissue box.

She handed it to the woman.

"I used to babysit the girl ever since she was a toddler," said Geena, through her tears. "She was such a sweet angel."

Angel?

"What did she ever do to deserve it?" Geena's voice was muffled as she held a tissue to her mouth.

"Do you know how she died?" I said.

She shook her head, not looking up. "That poor girl. Chris had so much planned for her. Told me she was going to be famous one day, too."

Her sobs ceased. She blew her nose and hugged herself.

I stepped up to her and kneeled to get to her eye level. "Do you know where Lily was these last two years?"

"What do you mean?"

"She didn't die that day in the river. You know that, don't you?"

Geena blinked rapidly and looked away.

"If you know what happened to Lily, please tell us." I paused. "You can either share with us, or you can talk to the police."

She looked up, her eyes wide. She was paying attention now.

"Tell me what you know," I said.

"It was the hobo," she whispered. "The hobo in the woods that got her."

Did she really think I would believe an elderly man with arthritis could overpower a strong young woman?

I wanted to shake her until all the pertinent information fell out of her. I also knew the only way to get through was by building trust, but I was losing patience fast.

"Please tell us the truth, Geena."

"I am."

"Are you protecting someone?"

She jumped like I'd hit her. "No! How can you say that!"

I reeled back at the outburst.

Geena turned her head away and sobbed loudly again.

Win was giving me the side-eye now.

No human being could cry on demand with such emotional anguish, unless she was an excellent actor—good enough to fool us all.

Katy nudged me aside and moved toward her, an amiable expression on her face. "Hey, hun, can I make you a cup of tea?"

Geena nodded, her crying receding just as quickly as it had begun.

Katy made her way to the open kitchen, treading carefully around the stack of tattered Harlequin novels scattered on the floor.

Silence fell in the living room as Geena kept her face steadfastly away from me and I stayed back, trying to think of the next best question.

Win stooped down, picked up an LP and turned it around in her hands. "What is this?"

Geena turned to her and dabbed her eyes.

"That's how I used to listen to music. A long time ago when I was younger than you are. I used to be skinny and beautiful, you know."

"I'm sure you were," said Win with a polite smile.

"That was my favorite band," said Geena, pointing at the LP in Win's hands. "Put it on. It's easy."

Win fumbled with the LP player, making Geena giggle.

I frowned. This seesawing of emotions wasn't normal. She was having us on, or she wasn't fully there.

"Geena, why do you have a photo of Lily and Miles on your back door?"

She gave me a startled look.

"It was, er, I thought they looked cute together on the lake..." She trailed off like she had forgotten what she was saying.

"Can you tell me about the last time you saw Lily Grayson?"

Her face turned guarded.

"I... I... don't remember. It was so long ago. One day she was swimming and fooling around with Miles and the next day she was gone. Carried away by the river, so the cops said."

"What do you know about Miles?"

"Saw him with her out on the lake, playing on a rowboat a few times. Jane hated him so much and she showed it. That woman was nasty."

"When was the last time you saw Jane Grayson?"

Silence.

I tried again. "It's a small neighborhood. You couldn't have missed her."

Geena rubbed her arms so brusquely that I worried she might chafe her skin.

"T... two weeks ago, I, er, think," she stammered.

"What was she doing?"

"Bringing groceries from her car. Saw her at her doorstep with one of those fancy Whole Foods bags."

"Do you know her well? Did you talk to her often?"

Geena made a face.

"Oh, she never hung out with the likes of me. She was a rich lady who lived up the pier. Never said a kind word to me. When I babysat Lily, it was Chris who hired me and paid me. Jane just wrote long lists of things for me to do. Super bossy, if you ask me, and super mean."

Interesting.

She was talking about Jane in the past tense.

"There are rumors she's having an affair," I said. "Do you know who it's with?"

Geena shook her head, a morose expression on her face. "No one tells me nothing."

"Is it someone who lives on this pier?"

Another shrug.

"Perhaps Jane Grayson is gay?" I said. "Was she dating a woman, perhaps?"

"*Of course not.*"

"So, you do know who it is."

Her eyes flickered, then she looked away.

Time to offer a carrot.

"You're a smart woman, Geena. You probably know everything about everyone here, don't you?" I said, smiling. "I'm sure they all respect you for that."

Geena straightened up, squared her shoulders, and shot me a look with fire in her eyes.

"No one thinks I belong here," she said, the indignant anger in her voice crystal clear. "They all want me to pack my bags and go."

These continual mood swings were giving me whiplash.

"Is that what the older gentleman at the end of the wharf told you?" I said, giving her a knowing nod. "If it makes you feel better, he said the same thing to us today."

"He's not the worst." Geena gripped her arms tightly. "It's the women. They want me out. Ever since I moved in, they complained to their fancy council. Said I brought down the value of their houses."

"That's terrible," I said, shaking my head.

"But I have friends in high places," she said, warming up to the conversation. "Or they would have pushed me out already."

"Who are your friends?"

Her face shut down again, and she looked away.

"Good friends are hard to find," I said. "Nice to have support. Are they your neighbors?"

"The others don't invite me to their barbecues or their picnics on their fancy boats. It's like I'm a leper. You know those people who they used to push out of town because they were ugly and sick? That's me."

Geena was a master at evading questions, whether it was intentional or not.

"What do you know about Chris Grayson?" I said, changing tactic again.

Her face brightened. "I used to babysit him, too. I was only eleven when I started with that family. He was a toddler. It was him and his brother."

I raised an eyebrow. "Chris Grayson has a brother?"

"We all grew up together. I was like a big sister to them. That's what I liked to think, anyway."

"Did you enjoy babysitting, Geena?"

"The boys were a handful, that's for sure. I did my best. Their parents paid me good, and the boys liked me too, so when Lily came along, Chris hired me on the spot. Jane didn't like that. She was always trying to get me fired."

"Here you go," said Katy, coming over with a cup of tea.

Geena took it with shaking hands.

"You were close to Lily, weren't you?" I said. "Did you miss her when she was gone?"

She nodded, but she seemed far away, in another world.

"Did they find her in the river?" said Geena.

"After two years?" I said. "The body would have been decomposed badly by now and all that would be left would be bones."

She didn't blink, but her eyes narrowed.

I leaned in closer. "They actually found her inside a locked bank vault."

This time, she blinked.

"Geena, did you know Lily was murdered?"

She dropped her teacup with a loud gasp. Katy sprang back before the hot liquid splashed on her. Geena sat immobile in her chair, the tea running from her skirt to her legs, seemingly not feeling the burns.

"They *killed* her?" whispered Geena, turning to me, her eyes wide in horror.

Chapter Forty-seven

"Who killed Lily?" I asked, boring into her eyes.

Geena struggled to sit up.

"Poor Chris," she said, shaking her head. "Oh, that poor, poor man." She looked up suddenly. "Does he know?"

Katy nodded. "He's at the police station right now."

"How? How did they...?" Geena faltered.

"They poisoned her," I said.

My voice was harsh. I wasn't sure if she had any involvement in Lily's death, but her caginess was getting to me.

Geena let out a cry and put a hand over her mouth.

"They're still examining her body, so there's no official verdict yet, but I would bet everything that's what they did." I paused. "They beat her before they killed her. Did you know that?"

She let out another cry.

"I think you know who did this, don't you?"

She turned to me, tears streaming down her face.

"How could you say that?" Her voice was high-pitched and rising fast. "You come to my home to tell me the little angel I used to babysit was killed, and you're accusing *me*?"

I stared at her.

Do I believe her?

The connection between Jane Grayson's disappearance, her daughter's murder, the severed hand, the unusual bank heist, and our own abductions was fuzzy, but these weren't random crimes.

The answer lay in this exclusive lake community. Everyone here was hiding deep secrets. Geena too.

Katy took a seat on the arm of the couch. "How long did you babysit for the Graysons?"

"I took care of Lily till she was twelve," whispered Geena, turning her face down at the tea stain on the carpet. "I worked for her grandparents, too. I brought up her father and uncle, I tell you."

She took a breath in.

"But I couldn't help them with their homework. They were so much smarter than me. I dropped out of school. No one at the trailer park stayed past grade five, you see?"

"You grew up in a trailer park?" said Win. "Was that around here?"

Geena wiped her face. "Down by the river. A good half an hour away, but I walked here every day because they paid me good."

"How did you get to live on the pier?"

A twitch came on her face. That normally signaled nerves, but it could also be a sign of a lie to come.

"A present."

"An entire house?" said Win, her eyes widening. "You're one lucky lady. Who gifted this to you?"

Katy leaned in. "I guess it was someone special, someone who really appreciated your work, wasn't it?"

Silence.

"Was it Chris Grayson?" I said.

Geena pulled back at those words. "Jane would have killed him."

"Was it his brother?" I asked.

The twitch in her face became more pronounced.

"Can you tell us about him?"

"He's a good man." She turned her face away again. "They treated him bad, but he's a real good man."

"Who mistreated him?"

"The parents."

"What did they do?"

"Chris always did well, you see. But John... it was like he didn't belong to the family. Chris was the smart one. He even played the piano. Got straight As. Then he became a gazillionaire. He's even richer than his parents now. That's what they tell me, anyway."

Geena turned to Katy and leaned forward as if to tell her a secret. She was doing what she was born to do. Tell stories about other people.

She lowered her voice. "No one knew, but Chris was the adopted one."

I raised an eyebrow.

"Chris was born three houses down from me at the trailer park. They took him when he was a wee boy."

"Whoa," said Win, sitting up. "What a twist."

Geena gave her an appreciative look. Even during a crisis, she couldn't help but tell a story. I just hoped this was a truthful tale.

"He had a very different life back then, I can tell you that. His pa hit his ma every night. A nasty lout of a man. His ma screamed so loud, everyone could hear. Then, she got pregnant with this baby boy her man didn't want."

"So, they gave him up for adoption?" Katy shook her head sadly. "That's harsh."

"She was a crackhead. Worked on the streets, you know?" said Geena, giving Katy, then me, an earnest look.

We nodded.

"Chris's adopted mother was totally barren, you see. At least that's what everyone thought. But you won't guess what happened one year after they adopted him."

"She got pregnant?" said Katy. "Happens all the time."

"You're telling me. Along came John, a year later. No one expected it. Life works in weird ways, don't it?"

We nodded. The less we said, the more she talked.

Win had found herself a box to sit on and had her chin in her hands, all her focus on Geena. That seemed to encourage the woman.

Geena sat back in her chair and settled her dress around her.

"Everyone said Chris was going to turn out bad, the worst mistake they ever made. Trailer park trash, right? But he shocked everyone."

"Wow," said Win.

Geena gave her a satisfying nod.

"Chris was a quiet kid, never gave me any trouble. I watched the soaps all day long, and he sat next to me drawing and reading and such. Such a good boy. If you ask me, he wasn't supposed to be born to his family."

"That's crazy," said Win.

"It gets crazier," replied Geena.

Was she sending us down a rabbit hole? But, unlike the rest of the residents on the pier, at least she was talking.

"John wasn't smart like Chris. He was the dark one."

"Dark?" said Katy.

"Had a hard time. Spent more time in detention and juvie jail than in school. It was like the two boys got mixed up at birth."

"What do you mean mixed up?" I said.

"Poor kid from the trailer park was doing really good, and the kid born to the richest family in town was in trouble most of the time. I tell you, sometimes life likes to poke at you for a good laugh."

She gave me a pointed look.

"Do you know what I mean?"

Chapter Forty-eight

Geena straightened up and glanced around her, as if looking for something.

"I need a cig, girls."

Win moved a broken dish from behind the LP player and held up a pack of cigarettes. Geena took them, but started searching again feverishly.

"Lighter," I said, scanning the room.

Win whirled around and dug a box of matches from under a magazine and set it next to the older woman.

"You're good girls," said Geena as she lit her cigarette. "I knew when I saw you, I could trust you."

She let out a puff of smoke.

"I took a liking to John. Whatever bad things they did to him, he was always a good man."

Smoking gave me a headache, but I had to swallow my discomfort. We couldn't have her stop now.

"Me and him got close. I was eleven years older, but it was like we grew up together. His mother ignored him, forgot his birthday because she was too busy giving her attention to her golden boy, Chris. So, I took care of him."

She jutted her chin out and glared at us as if to challenge her loyalty to this mysterious John.

I hoped this was going to circle back to Lily and Jane Grayson soon, or at least give us a hint to what happened to them.

"Where did John end up?" said Win.

"Quit school, got fired from a job, and two divorces later, he was struggling. I was with him all the way. Don't anybody say I abandon my friends. I was his older sister, his mother...."

She trailed off and took another puff, her eyes flitting over to the window. She gazed at the dark curtains, as if reminiscing.

I couldn't help but wonder. Was Geena this man's lover too?

Katy shot me a surreptitious glance. She was wondering the same thing, I gathered.

"So, where's John now?" asked Win.

Geena sighed.

"When your own family throws you away and treats your adopted brother like he's god's gift to earth, things don't go right, you know?"

"How did things go wrong?" I asked.

"It was Chris who got him the job. It's a good job, but people treat him bad, like they know he's a black sheep. It's not fair. It's not John's fault. He has such a good heart. He just wants to fit in."

"That's understandable," said Katy.

Geena looked up at her, a sudden fire in her eyes. "I think Chris told them to treat him bad."

"Why would Chris find his brother a job, and then tell his employer to mistreat him?" I said.

Geena jutted her chin out again and flicked her cigarette. Katy pushed the half-drunk teacup over to catch the ash. I wondered how Geena had gone this long without starting a fire in her home already.

"He told me the other day they are going to push him out."

"Fire him, you mean?" said Win.

Geena wagged her cigarette at her.

"When the brass don't want you no more, they do everything to make you wanna quit. That's what they do. Don't give any promotions, no pay raises, just treat you like a piece of garbage and soon you quit. But John's holding on."

"Is this in one of Chris's tech companies?" I asked.

Geena gave me a look that said, *Are you stupid?*

Katy and I exchanged a glance. From her face, I could see she was thinking the same thing as me. How much truth was there to this wild and convoluted tale of the two brothers? Did John even exist?

"They're promoting other people over my poor John's head," continued Geena. "He's had it. Just about had it."

"Poor John," murmured Katy.

"This isn't the first time he got pushed around like this, you know?"

She stopped to take a puff. I noticed her hands were trembling. She enjoyed telling her stories, but this one hit close to home.

"It was the day their parents died." She was staring at the curtains again. "That was the day John found out how much his own flesh and blood hated him."

Muffled noises were coming from the pier, but the heavy curtains blocked everything. I glanced at the window, wondering what was happening outside.

My mind whirred, trying to think of the best way to extricate ourselves from here. Was Geena sending us on a goose chase? Were we wasting precious time?

"Do you know who they left the family home to?" said Geena, whipping around and giving us a hard look. "The house, their rental properties, the father's company, everything?"

"The two sons?" ventured Katy.

Geena shook her head violently. "Chris got it all. The lawyer said that's what it said in the will. Can you believe it?"

"Did John get anything?" said Win.

"The will said Chris can decide what to give his brother."

"Wow, that must have stung."

Geena leaned back with her cigarette. "Who does that to their own son, I tell you?"

"Did Chris give his brother anything?" asked Win.

She nodded. "He gave him some of the cash from their parents' bank account. It was a lot of money, a million dollars. I will give you that, but it was still a slap in John's face."

I frowned. A million dollars would have barely covered the purchase of one of these float homes. Why would the brother have spent all his inheritance on this woman? There was more to this story than she was telling. Either that, or she didn't know the whole truth and was making things up as she went.

She turned to us, a serious expression on her face now.

"That's how I got this house, you see? Could never get it on my own. But my John bought it for me. Said it's for taking care of him when his own family threw him out like a rat."

"When did the parents pass away?" asked Katy.

"It was a horrible day. Crushed like baby chickens at a meat factory. I'll never forget the sight."

Geena shivered and hugged herself.

"How did they die?" I said, frowning, paying attention to her story once more. My gut was telling me we had finally arrived at the crux of the story.

"They were coming down the road from some charity gala in town one night. Just as they turned the corner to the lake, this other car banged on them. It was a hit and run. Just like that, they were gone."

"That's terrible," said Win.

"I saw it too, with my own eyes. Their car was wrapped around a tree. Mom and Dad with their heads bashed in, like you wouldn't know who they were, if you didn't know the car."

Geena leaned in.

"You know the funny thing? They never found the car that hit 'em. It was like a ghost. Gone. No one ever saw it."

I straightened up as something niggled in the back of my brain.

"Where were Chris and John that night?"

"At home. John was twenty-one. Chris was twenty-two. It was a horrible way to lose your parents, even at that age. I ran all the way to their house to tell them. It was Chris who opened the door. He cried and screamed like a baby, I tell you. John locked himself in his room and never came out. Too shocked—"

A thunderous banging made us all jump.

I leaped toward the window.

"Hey!" shouted a voice from just outside the door. "Open up!"

It was a man's voice, one I was sure I'd heard before. I turned to the door, fiddling with the myriad of locks, swearing under my breath.

"Help!" cried the voice again.

I finally opened it.

It was our elderly neighbor. His white hair were raised like a collection of live wires, and his arms were flailing in the air. His eyes bulged as he saw me.

"What are you standing there for?" he shouted, his voice high pitched and panicked. *"Do* something!"

Chapter Forty-nine

The old man staggered as a gust of wind blew along the promenade.

I put a hand out to hold him up. "Hey, what's going on?"

He waved his bony arms in the air. "Intruder! Thief! Stop him!"

I straightened up. "The guest house again?"

"Someone broke in!"

I raced past him toward our floating house and slammed the door open. My heart was thumping, my adrenaline soaring, and my anger swelling inside of me as I prepared to confront our prowler.

But our little guest house was empty.

My eyes swept the space from one end to the other. There was no sign of further disturbances.

"What are you doing here?"

I snapped around to see the old man standing by the door, panting hard, and gesturing urgently.

"Someone's in that house!" he cried.

"Which one? Yours?"

He shot me an exasperated look and jerked his arms up. "I told you. The house at the end."

Pushing past him once again, I jumped onto the pier and turned toward the lone float home docked at the bottom of the promenade. The

For Sale sign was swinging back and forth in a frenzy, but there was no indication of anyone nearby.

"Did they break in again?" said Win, rushing up to me with Katy.

I shook my head, staring at the darkened home at the end. "It wasn't ours."

There was only one reason for someone to enter an empty house, and that would be if they were looking for a place to hide.

"Thieves, pests," muttered the older man. "One day, we'll wake up and find everything gone and our throats slit."

I suppressed the urge to remind him that a few moments ago he had called us riffraff. Was he playing us? Or was he just a harmless senior citizen, scared of outsiders and suspicious of everything?

I wondered if there were any sane people in this community.

"What exactly did you see?" I asked, turning to him.

"A shadow on the second floor," he replied in a fluster. "No one's supposed to be in there. I called the police, but they said an intruder in an empty home isn't a priority. Bunch of lazy idiots."

"Sounds like just the thing Davies would say," said Katy, blowing a raspberry.

"How did you see anything on the upper floor?" I said, my eyes narrowing. "Where were you?"

"In my living room upstairs. I have a direct line of sight to that house. I just finished watching CNN and was about to head out for a walk. I wanted to check if it was raining, so I opened the window. That's when I saw him."

"Who?"

"It was too far to see."

Seeing my expression, he spread his arms wide. "I may be a half-blind old man, but I saw someone up there. Believe me."

"Was it the real estate agent?" said Katy. "He could have come to check on the house."

He shook his head.

"He only comes on Fridays. Besides, with all this hullabaloo, no one has come to see the houses in months."

It could have been a bird flying by, or even his own curtains fluttering in the wind. Then again, someone had ransacked our temporary home, and that person could be hiding in there.

"I'll check." I turned around and walked over to the end house, with the others trooping behind me.

I stepped onto the floating patio, my eyes and ears alert, and walked over to the bay windows on the first floor.

I squinted through the glass. The house was eerily quiet and, as I suspected, empty.

I walked around the structure, trying the back door and the windows, but everything had been locked down. My friends and the neighbor followed me a few feet behind, double-checking the latches and locks.

It was when I got to the side facing the lake that I noticed what I had missed before. The window on the second floor was ajar and swinging to the wind.

A powerful gust of wind must have pried it open. The real estate agent must have missed this window when he was locking up. But it was too high up for me to see anything.

"Wait," whispered the old man, poking my shoulder with a sharp finger. "You need a ladder."

"What I need is a key to the front door."

But he was already lumbering back to the pier and heading toward his house. As we watched, he stepped onto his patio and picked up a steel ladder lying on the wooden floorboards. His fingers slipped. The ladder rattled and fell with a loud crash onto the platform.

If an intruder was hanging around, they would know we were coming now.

Katy stepped away from me. "He's going to fall into the water if he's not careful. Come, Win, let's give him a hand."

While my friends went to help the neighbor, I did another round before stopping at the open window. An alarming creaky noise came from the second floor.

Did a bird fly in and get stuck inside? A squirrel?

"He's in there, I tell you. Let's nab him and hand him over to the police. That'll show them."

I turned to see the old man had returned. Behind him came Katy and Win carrying the ladder. They leaned it against the wall.

"Hold this in place," I said to my friends. "The patio wood is slippery."

"What's going on?"

Geena was strolling over, a lit cigarette in her hand, her keen nose smelling another story.

The old neighbor turned around to her to tell her what he saw. The two stepped onto the pier and started an animated conversation about who would dare break into this empty house.

I didn't trust Geena and her wild tales. I couldn't help but feel she had been distracting us while whoever broke into the guest home got away.

"Hold tight," I said to Katy and Win as I stepped up the ladder. A blast of wind whipped my hair across my eyes, almost blinding me.

"Be careful," came Katy's voice from below.

I climbed slowly, watching my footing, and clutching on to the sides of the ladder so the wind wouldn't bowl me over. I would be in for an icy cold bath if I fell, I thought with a shudder.

A storm was coming, making the green lake seem darker and more sinister. A mysterious energy seemed to be growing around the promenade and the forest beyond. I could feel it in my bones.

My head was now level with the second-floor window, which was rocking back and forth. I pushed the pane against the wall, so it wouldn't bang against my head.

"We got you," Win called out.

That was when I noticed the stench.

An animal must have crawled in through the open window and died.

I climbed to the next rung to see better.

Another burst of wind came from the lake, threatening to pull me off the ladder and into the cold water below. I flattened myself against the wall and glanced inside.

The upper floor was as empty as the one below. There was nothing to see.

That was when I noticed something move.

A small wall jutted out on the other side of the room, behind which I presumed lay an alcove or nook. Something was moving behind it.

The old neighbor had been right. There was something or someone in here.

Then something creaked.

My heart missed a beat.

A dark shadow swung out of the wall and swung back again.

My mouth went dry.

I wanted to call out to my friends, but no words came out. I had only glimpsed a part of it. I wished I could rub my eyes, but I didn't dare take my hands off the ladder.

"You see anything?" Katy's voice came from below.

I didn't answer, my eyes glued to the far side of the room, my heart beating fast.

Another gust of strong wind burst over my head and into the empty room.

The shadow moved again. I stared at it, unable to turn my eyes away. I knew where the smell of the rotting flesh was coming from.

It wasn't an animal who'd died in here. It was a human.

Chapter Fifty

I looked down at my friends looking up at me, concerned expressions etched on their faces.

Huddled a few feet behind them were the old neighbor and Geena, also watching me with keen eyes.

They had all turned quiet.

I stepped down a few rungs, so I didn't have to shout.

"There's a dead body up here," I said. "Hanging from the rafters."

"Did you see who it was?" whispered Katy.

The three of us were sitting on the side of the jetty by our guest home. The float house at the end of the pier was swarming with police officers, several with reflective vests with the word *Forensics* on the back.

Officer Lee was placing yellow crime tape around the structure, pointedly ignoring us. One of her colleagues had just finished talking to Geena and was now interviewing our neighbor.

The old man had been relieved to see the authorities finally arrive. He had almost fainted when I had told them of my discovery, but he had recovered enough to tell them what he saw. Geena was standing a few steps away from them, smoking another cigarette.

"All I know is it's a woman," I said to my friends, giving them a glum look.

"How long was she in that empty house?" said Katy. "Hours? Days? Weeks?"

I tried not to throw up as the image of the swinging woman from that rafter on the second floor flashed across my mind. "I smelled rotting flesh from the open window."

Next to me, Katy shuddered.

"My gosh," said Win.

"I really hope it isn't her," said Katy, shaking her head sadly.

"Jane Grayson's the only person missing from this neighborhood," I said. "I can't imagine it being anyone else."

We sat in gloomy silence as law enforcement bustled around the pier, carrying forensics equipment, cameras, a stretcher, and yellow tape.

We had already given our statements. We had also told them about the intrusion into our guest house, but the discovery of the dead body was taking all their attention.

"Here come the boys," said Katy, turning toward the front of the wharf where the garage was located.

Thomas and Davies were walking briskly along the promenade and were passing Grayson's home.

I had called my client several times already, but he hadn't picked up his phone. I worried how he would react to this devastating news, if that body was who I thought it was.

Nathalie opened her door and stepped onto the threshold. She swiveled her head around the pier, like she had just heard the commotion outside. Then she hurried down the steps as she spotted Thomas and Davies, teetering on her heels.

With a polite nod to her, Davies kept walking our way, but Thomas stopped to talk.

As we watched in surprise, Thomas leaned over to kiss Nathalie. It wasn't a platonic hello, not even one you'd give your very best friend.

These two were a couple.

"Whoa," said Win, leaning back in shock.

"Well, well, well," said Katy, staring. "We're in Alice's Wonderland, for sure. Everything's upside down and nothing makes sense."

"What's wrong with a cop dating an Ivana Trump lookalike who drives a yellow convertible and lives in a multi-million-dollar house?" said Win, sarcasm dripping from her voice.

"Nothing at all," I said. "But it is different. And we're not the only ones interested."

We all turned to watch Geena. If looks could kill, Thomas and his sweetheart would have turned into ash.

With an angry curse, Geena threw her cigarette butt down, ground it under her shoe, and stomped over to her house. Her footsteps thumped on the platform so hard I could feel the reverberations from underneath my feet.

Geena got inside her house and slammed the door, but no one else seemed to notice. Except for us.

"They're bringing her out," said Win, nudging me.

Two officers in plastic coveralls were carrying a stretcher out of the front door of the house at the end. We stood up to show respect for the deceased.

It was hard to say who was under that plastic cover. All I had glimpsed was a woman's right side. She had been wearing a pink shirt, black pants, and a kitten heel shoe that was about to drop off her foot. Having seen her profile, albeit briefly, I could say for certain it had been a fit, middle-aged female who had been well-dressed.

I stepped closer to the junior officer who had interrogated us earlier. "Can you tell us who it is?"

He snapped his notebook shut. "This is an ongoing investigation. Step aside, ladies. No gawking."

"You're still here," said Davies with a sneer as he marched toward us. "You turn up like a bad stink everywhere I go."

"And it seems you have a grudge against us," said Katy.

He dismissed her with a wave. "If I were you, I would have taken our advice and skedaddled home yesterday. But since you're here in the vicinity of another dead body, we'll have to take you back to the station for questioning."

"Good." I nodded and pointed at Win. "We can then make an official report about the attempted abduction of our friend from the hospital today."

Davies' eyes widened. He looked from me to Win and back.

"Your front desk said to come back in twenty-four hours, but I'm sure you'd agree things are clearly getting out of hand," I added.

He frowned. "When did this happen?"

"When we went to pick her up at the hospital, but when we got to her room, she was gone."

Davies turned to Win, his brow furrowed.

"What happened?"

"The nurses' station got a call saying Asha and Katy were at the airport and to join them," said Win. "Then a man came to pick me up. He said the flight was in an hour and I had to hurry."

"We had a security guard there. She shouldn't have—"

"She didn't say anything."

Davies' eyebrows shot up. Then he frowned again.

"Why didn't you call your friends to confirm?"

"Because the bank robbers took our phones, and I didn't have their new numbers." She didn't say, but her tone clearly added, *you idiot*.

Davies gave Win a stern look.

"You know better than to get into a car with a stranger."

"I know Krav Maga and jujitsu."

He gave her a doubtful look. "Did you get a good look at the guy?"

"Caucasian male in his mid-thirties, short brown hair, medium build."

"He was also wearing dark shades, a hat, and a long, brown beard," said Katy. "If you ask me, that was a disguise."

"Did you take any pictures?"

I shook my head. "We were too busy focused on rescuing our friend from a moving car."

"How on earth—"

"He said he was a rideshare, but he was carrying a gun. He pulled it out, saying he was protecting himself from us chasing him down. All to say, it wasn't the best time to take pictures."

Davies put his hands on his hips and stared over our shoulders at the lake, silent for a change.

"I don't like it," he said finally, to my surprise. "I really don't like this."

"Neither do we," I said. "I'd like to know why they're targeting us."

"Davies!"

We all turned as Thomas marched over.

He frowned as he spotted us. "Didn't I tell you ladies to take the earliest flight home?"

"I don't abandon my clients, especially under such distressing circumstances," I said, giving him an annoyed look. "How is Grayson faring?"

Thomas stopped and let out a weary sigh. He looked like all the world's problems had landed on his shoulders.

"Still under sedation at the station clinic."

He shook his head and looked down.

"I don't know how I'm going to break this news to him."

"So, it was Jane Grayson then? What was she doing in that empty house?"

Thomas scratched his head as if he was deciding whether to reply.

"What happened to her?" said Katy.

He dropped his chin on his chest and let out a heavy sigh. Then, he turned to us, his eyes bloodshot and heavily lined like he hadn't had much sleep either.

"Suicide."

Chapter Fifty-one

"*S*uicide?" said Win.

"Hogwash," said Katy.

"Why on earth would the police lie about something so significant?" I shook my head. "More importantly, why would Jane Grayson kill herself? Something is seriously wrong with this picture."

We were inside our guest house. I was thankful to get away from the officers' constant glares.

The precinct had slipped up big time. Davies had not only failed to find Jane Grayson, he had failed to stop her death. There was guilt behind those incensed eyes, and they were taking it out on us.

Win shot me a glum look as she sat cross-legged on the bed with her laptop.

"Why are they treating us like criminals? *We're* not the bad guys."

In their defense, Thomas had sent Officer Lee to take our statements on Win's abduction and the guest house break-in.

But our door hadn't been pried open, the windows had remained latched, and nothing had been stolen. Lee's raised eyebrows and pursed lips as she surveyed the mess strewn across the living room told us she didn't believe a word we told her.

Her stern admonishment to call what happened to Win an *alleged* kidnapping told me one thing. My barging into the mortuary had solidified our reputation. Attention-seeking troublemakers.

Our reports would soon get dumped to the bottom of a drawer at the station, only to be forgotten, I was sure.

We had come to a dead end.

All my calls to Grayson's number had gone to voice mail. I had no client to consult and no missing person to search for.

It was hard to justify our stay in Seattle with David, Peace, and Luc waiting for us back home. Katy was already packing her bags, ready to claim defeat.

I leaned over the open window facing the lake to take in the fresh air and to clear my churning mind.

I had made a promise while inside the vault to find out who murdered Lily. Discovering her mother's dead body only solidified my resolve to identify their killer.

It had to be the same person. It just had to be.

I hated leaving open threads. I would never sleep if I left this case unsolved. I shifted in place, wishing I knew what to do next.

That was when something crinkled in my jacket. I stuck my fingers in my right pocket and dug out a small piece of paper. I stared at the scribbles on the page, a jolt of energy going through me.

I whirled around and waved the paper in the air.

"We're not done here yet, girls."

Win gave me a quizzical look.

"The phone number," I said, "from Miles in the hospital."

Katy straightened up from her packing. "Poor guy. He wanted us to find his baby girl. I feel so bad for him. Someone has to tell him she's dead."

I frowned at the squiggly numbers.

"Wait, he made a mistake."

"What do you mean?" said Win, perking up.

"There are only seven digits. Telephone numbers have ten."

"He wasn't in any form to speak or think," said Katy. "Besides, that nurse interrupted him, remember?"

"He handed it to me before the nurse chased us away," I said. "He may not have had his wits about him, but he was deliberate and focused when he wrote this down."

Win jumped off the bed. "Can I see it?"

She grabbed the paper from my hand and scrutinized the note.

"Could be part of a street address."

She walked back to her laptop, clutching the paper.

Katy and I sorted the jumble on the floor, leaving her to do her thing. Figuring out numbers was what Win did best. She tapped away on her keyboard, her face taut in concentration and her fingers moving like they were on fire.

I had just turned the coffeepot on, and Katy had brought down three mugs from the shelf when a squeal startled us.

Win was jumping on the bed, her eyes shining.

"It's a boat."

"A boat?" I said, unsure I heard her correctly. "You mean a marina?"

"A big boat, almost a ship."

"Since when do ships have addresses?" said Katy.

"It's an IMO number. Every large vessel has to have an identification number from the International Maritime Organization. See?"

We walked over to the bed and huddled around her laptop. On her screen was a rusty black and red boat, almost two hundred feet in length, moored at one of Seattle's commercial dockyards.

"Check this out. This boat has the exact same number painted on the front."

"There's nothing like that on the lake," said Katy. "Yachts and sailboats, but nothing so ugly and big. The council would never allow that eyesore here."

"Who's the owner?" I asked.

Win clicked on a plus sign that opened up the ship's specifications.

"A numbered corporation," I murmured as I scanned the details. "Bought three years ago and decommissioned soon after." I turned to Win. "Is this boat still at the docks? Or did they send it to a scrapyard?"

"The last imagery on the dockyard was taken a month ago, and it doesn't show this boat, which meant it was moved for sure."

The shine in Win's eyes grew even brighter. "And I think I know where it is."

"What did you find?" said Katy.

"I don't know if it's a coincidence, and I could be barking up the wrong tree...."

I tapped her arm. "Let's see it, Win."

She clicked on a second tab and pointed at the grainy imagery that filled her screen. Katy and I leaned in closer. It was a satellite map of the area around the lake.

Win ran her finger along a thin green line that went from the lake to the ocean, a few miles away.

"This deep waterway goes from the other end of the lake, through the woods, all the way to the sea. See this blob here? That's a mid-sized ship."

I squinted at the screen. "A ship? Are you sure?"

Win nodded. "It's docked where the lake ends and where the river starts."

"Looks like a rectangular building to me," said Katy, peering over her shoulder. "A large warehouse?"

"It's *on* the water."

"Could also be a very large float home," I said. "Who knew houses could be built on a lake until we came here?"

"Look closer at the profile. That's a ship's shape."

I reached over and clicked on the icon to enlarge the dark spot. The more I zoomed in, the more it took on the shape of a large water vessel.

"You're right, it's a ship. Can we find this IMO number on it?" I said, a hint of excitement in my voice.

Win shook her head.

"I tried. The resolution isn't good enough."

"Wait, aren't we stretching things a bit?" said Katy. "That poor guy was barely recovering from being slashed and thrown out of a van. He was pumped with drugs. We should go back and ask him what he actually meant by these numbers."

Win looked at her.

"Don't you two get chased out of the hospital every time you go there? You're only going to give them a good reason to stick us on a plane out of here. Or in a jail."

Katy sighed. "We were trying to do the right thing."

"Thomas and Davies will have a field day if any of us return to the hospital."

While my friends chatted, I stared at the faint outline of the ship at the mouth of the river, a tingling feeling growing around my spine.

"If we can charter a boat," I said, "we could get there in less than half an hour, and no one can stop us."

Win turned back to her screen and started typing furiously.

"There's a powerboat behind Nathalie's house," said Katy, turning to me. "She let us in to the compound last time, didn't she? And she wants us to find Jane Grayson."

"We found her," I said, giving her a wistful look. "She may not want to help us anymore."

"Wait, didn't Nathalie say she wanted us to find Jane Grayson *dead*?" said Win. "Could she be the killer?"

"I would have suspected her too before I learned about her relationship with Thomas. It makes her an unlikely culprit, but we can't assume anything. But that also means she'd never lend us her speedboat."

"What about the old man next door?" said Katy. "He has a sailboat behind his float home. Could we ask to borrow it for a few hours?"

"The neighbor? I get the feeling he'll rat us out to the police in a heartbeat."

"What about Geena?" said Katy.

"She doesn't have a boat. Neither does Grayson," I said, trying to think.

Katy shook her head. "And there's no place to rent a boat on this—"

"Hey, guys?"
Katy and I turned to Win.
"I think I found a way."

Chapter Fifty-two

"We can drive there," said Win with a triumphant look.

"How?" said Katy, peering at the laptop. "There's no road anywhere nearby."

"There's an unpaved path that goes around the lake," said Win. "It cuts through the woods on the other side. Seems like private property."

"This land belongs to the float home community. Probably taken care of by their council." I traced the route on the screen with my finger. It was a thin brown line, a rough road that looked like nothing more than a hiking trail. I wondered if even an all-wheel-drive could navigate that path.

"What do we do?" said Katy.

I jumped off the bed and walked over to the window that faced the jetty.

The commotion had died down outside. The officers had sealed off the end house and finished their door-to-door questioning. The pier was almost empty, with only a few stragglers by the squad cars next to the garage.

The promenade would soon return to its usual tranquil state that belied the gruesome happenings of this place.

My gut was sending me powerful signals. Win had found something important to this case, and I had to know what it was.

Win was watching me with excitement in her eyes. "There's something on that ship that would explain this whole puzzle, isn't there?"

I nodded.

"Let's go check it out."

***

"Hey, what are you doing?" hissed Katy, pulling me back.

We had locked up our guest house and were walking along the pier, heading toward the garage. If anyone had stopped us, we had agreed we'd say we were going out for an early supper to a nearby pizza joint.

Davies and Thomas had already left.

A handful of police officers were chatting with the security guard by the garage. They turned and gave us a cursory glance, but didn't stop us. By the time we reached Grayson's house, the officers had got into their vehicles and were preparing to leave.

Katy, Win, and I had changed into warm outdoor gear and hiking boots. With flashlights, water bottles, and fully charged mobile phones in our backpacks, we were ready to hike the trail and check out the mysterious boat moored at the far side of the lake.

But something told me we needed to be better prepared than that.

"Detour," I whispered, as I slipped to the side of Grayson's float home. "Look for a spare key."

Katy and Win followed me onto the floating patio with bewildered expressions on their faces.

I flipped the door mat over.

Nothing.

"Check by the flowers," I said. "Sometimes people hide extra keys in the pots."

While my friends searched the planters, I worked my way around the house, feeling each windowpane.

No key.

Anyone could have easily spotted us if they had been watching. Floating homes docked along piers didn't provide good nooks or shelters from prying eyes.

This was one reason I was surprised to hear the police had found no witnesses to Jane's death.

Geena watched everything going on in this tiny community. The neighbor next to us didn't have the greatest eyesight, but his instincts had been honed well enough to spot things amiss on the wharf. But no one had seen Jane step out of her home, walk toward the empty house in the end, and go inside before killing herself.

Something didn't add up.

"No keys anywhere," said Win, coming over to me.

Katy shot me an exasperated look. "What are you doing? I thought we were going to find a big boat."

I was standing by Grayson's back kitchen door that faced the open lake. The wind was getting stronger, whipping our hair around. Whitecaps were rolling through the lake and slamming against the pylons of the pier.

I tried the door handle, but the lock held. I looked up. There were no open windows, but I could see Lily's hammock hanging from the ceiling of her bedroom above the kitchen.

I surveyed the area.

So far, so good.

This was the most shielded part of the house, and no one was peeping our way. Not even Geena, from what I could see.

I reached over and tried the kitchen window. It was closed, but not fully latched.

Bingo.

I pushed on the side of the window frame and jiggled it. It took a minute to loosen it. I pulled the window away and reached in to touch the black mesh screen.

"This is breaking and entering," whispered Katy.

Digging into my pants pocket, I pulled out the Swiss army knife I carried with me all the time, a habit from my earlier days when we had to run in the middle of the night without a moment's notice.

Katy shook her head. "If Thomas and Davies could see us now, we'd be toast."

I cut the mesh where it was attached to the window frame, glad I had my gloves on. When I had loosened enough of the material, I pulled the rest away, cringing at the ripping sound.

"Keep an eye out," I breathed to my friends as I eased myself onto the ledge, using my hands as leverage.

Behind me, Katy and Win had fallen silent. I pulled myself through the opening and onto the kitchen counter.

After jumping down, I turned to face my friends, who were watching me, jaws open.

I put a finger to my lips. "Stay right here."

"What if someone comes?" whispered Katy.

"Tell them we heard a strange sound and came over to investigate."

She let out an exasperated sigh. Win rolled her eyes. Without waiting for more questions or protests, I tiptoed through the open kitchen toward the stairway.

I was at the foot of the stairs when the house groaned loudly. I stopped in mid-stride.

What was that?

The floats.

The waves were slapping hard against the bottom of the house. I felt slightly dizzy as the entire structure moved under my feet, but I had to move fast.

I crept upstairs, keeping my head below the windows in case a neighbor from across the promenade was watching. I didn't realize I had been holding my breath until I reached the second-floor landing and stood in front of what I'd come to see.

The gun case.

A quick peek in the bedrooms confirmed the house was empty.

"Forgive me, Grayson," I said as I reached over to the weapon case with my Swiss army knife. I mentally crossed my fingers, hoping the latch wasn't connected to an alarm system.

Grayson hadn't installed a sophisticated lock on it, most likely for ease of access. A few flicks of my multi-utility knife were all that was needed.

I flipped open the glass cover and stared at the Classic Carry Elite. A ray of late-afternoon light hit the polished steel handle. It winked at me as if it was inviting me to get it out.

I reached in gingerly and plucked the weapon out. It was unloaded. *Ammunition.*

I poked around the case until I felt a small knob on the back wall. Pulling it open, I found a compartment with two boxes of cartridges. I took one and stuffed it inside my pocket.

Beneath me, the house groaned again, making the hair on my neck stand up. It sounded like a monster was prowling on the first floor.

I closed the glass case, hurried downstairs and jumped on the kitchen counter by the open window in the back. It was a relief to see Katy and Win waiting for me with no officers or neighbors interrogating them.

"We're armed and ready," I said, patting my jacket pocket where I had stashed the weapon.

"You stole his *gun?*" said Win, her eyes widening.

"Borrowed it," I said, giving her a grim look. "I have a feeling we'll need it."

Chapter Fifty-three

"**S**low down, will you?" said Katy, grabbing the dashboard.

"We should have got an all-wheel-drive," I said, as our little rental bobbed along the muddy, potholed track.

We were crossing through the woods at the other end of the lake. Tall fir trees lined the narrow trail, looking like angry sentinels, guarding forbidden secrets.

A large sign with angry lettering scowled at us as we took a curve. *Private Property. Trespassers will be shot on sight.*

This road didn't show up on our phones' GPS, so Win was making the calculations in her head. All she had to go by was the dense area on her map that identified the forest next to the lake.

It had taken us half an hour to ferret out this hidden path. We had pinpointed the entrance to the woods only after cross checking several online maps, consulting a compass, and making a few wild guesstimates.

We were flying blind.

Compared to the wide-open atmosphere of the float-home promenade on the other side, this part of the surroundings felt sinister and dark. The trees huddled closely, shutting out most of the light, though there was still daylight out. A chilling silence fell as we crossed into the woods, like even the animals and birds didn't dare traverse here.

"Why would anyone camp in this place?" said Win from the backseat. "It's scary."

"Lily and Miles weren't going on a camping trip," said Katy. "They were running away from home."

"Poor Jane and Lily," said Win. "They had so much. What a way to end their lives."

I swerved to avoid another pothole. "They were murdered."

Win leaned across and stuck her face in between the front seats. "So, who do you think did it?"

Katy turned around. "All surveys show that whenever a woman is killed, it's usually the intimate partner. I bet on Grayson."

"The guy who hired us?" said Win. "I thought you said he was a small, scared man. Plus, he's in a wheelchair."

"He could be pretending," said Katy, "and looks can be deceiving."

I frowned as I tried to focus on the conversation while I navigated the rough terrain. "Hiring us could have been a ruse to divert attention away from his hand in the killings."

"Exactly," said Katy.

"But what would be his motive?" asked Win.

"Jane was having an affair," replied Katy. "He got mad as heck and took revenge."

"What about Lily?" I said.

"He told us his wife didn't like Lily's new boyfriend. But what if it was *he* who didn't like the boy, and what was happening to his only successor? So, he got rid of them. Well, he failed to kill Miles, but he nearly did."

"Remember all those gold bars in Lily's safe?" said Win, poking me on the shoulder. "She would have inherited everything, but she threw it all in his face to be with a wannabe Banksy from the streets. Can you imagine how angry he'd be?"

"If Chantelle ever did that, I'd be hopping mad," said Katy. "Not mad enough to commit murder, mind you..."

"But where were Lily and Miles all this time?" I said. "They were gone for two years."

"They hid somewhere," said Katy. "Then, Jane figured out what happened. Maybe Lily contacted her. That would explain Jane's erratic behavior and disappearances just before she vanished for good. She might even have threatened to tell the police or to go public. That's when Grayson struck her."

I slowed down. The road was getting muddier and my rental vehicle's cheap tires were having a hard time sloughing through it.

"So, who are the bank robbers?" I said.

"Grayson's goons," said Katy. "His companies have thousands of employees around the world. He can afford to hire a few thugs to do his dirty work."

"If you're both right, Grayson's got more imagination than I give him credit for," I said. "But why bring us into the middle of the heist? He tried to murder us too, remember?"

Katy and Win fell silent.

Though the ideas thrown out so far sounded plausible, something told me we still didn't have all the puzzle pieces.

"I wish Thomas and Davies would be more cooperative," I said, shaking my head. "We've been in the thick of things from the start and found the bodies. They don't have the resources and here we are with the skills and knowledge, asking to help."

"And they chase us away like dogs," sniffed Win.

"I don't like Thomas, but Davies is the worst," said Katy. "The way he struts around like an arrogant jerk."

"ETA in approximately ten minutes," called out Win from the backseat.

I looked at my rearview mirror to see her zooming in on her screen. "Can we trek there?"

"Hard to say," she replied, her nose glued to her phone. "Let me check."

Katy clutched my arm. "You want to *hike* there? I thought we were going to drive by the boat or whatever it is at the end of this trail."

"Come on, we're private eyes. Besides, a closer check shouldn't hurt," I said, scanning our surroundings to find a place to park.

"To the right," said Win, pointing out of the window. "There's a small clearing up ahead."

I slowed to a crawl and turned right in between two giant oak trees. I eased in between the trunks, tires crunching on the leaves on the ground.

No one spoke as I nudged the car into the woods, inch by inch, until I parked at the base of a fir tree and switched off the engine.

We sat quietly, letting the gravity of our mission sink in.

"You think the killer is on this ship?" said Katy in a small voice.

"If the killer is here, it can't be Grayson," I said. "It has to be someone he hired or someone else we've overlooked."

"Or someone we haven't met yet," said Win.

I pulled Grayson's weapon and the box of cartridges out of my pocket. After checking the barrel, I loaded the gun while my friends kept watch. Once done, I got out of the car and scanned our surroundings.

Our rental car was an unassuming gray which blended well with road asphalt, but stood out among the dark green foliage. I wondered how much of it was visible from the trail.

Katy and Win got out of the vehicle and stepped up to me. That was when the sound of an engine came from the trail.

"Someone's coming," gasped Katy, a hand flying to her heart.

"Get back!" I whispered, pulling them away.

We scrambled behind the car and crouched low. I peeked out from one end, my eyes on the trail.

The sound grew louder. It was a diesel engine.

A truck.

I cocked my weapon, unsure what to expect, uncertain if they would spot us among the trees.

Within seconds, a white cargo van rumbled along the muddy road, wobbling dangerously as it hit a pothole. It disappeared around the corner within seconds, but none of us moved for almost a minute.

"It's that white van," breathed Katy.

"We're in the lion's den," whispered Win.

Chapter Fifty-four

Katy whipped out her phone and opened the message app.

"Shut that thing down," I said, looking around us. "The screen glows. It'll give us away."

"I know Thomas and Davies hate our guts, but they need to know we found the van."

Katy punched a finger on the screen, muttering to herself about not wishing to get killed.

The van's rumbles had diminished, and a hush had settled in the woods again.

Suddenly, my back tingled.

I spun around, expecting to catch someone watching us. My eyes swept the forest, then the trail, searching for any signs of movement, but there was nothing.

The woods were keeping their secrets. The giant fir trees were looking down on us, sneering, as if they knew the danger we were in.

Stop it, I ordered myself. Now was not the time to let my imagination run wild.

"Turn off your notifications," I said to my friends. "No pings or rings until we get back."

Katy slipped her phone in her pocket.

"This way," I said, stepping away from the car. "Let's see if we can get to the ship without having to get on the open trail."

We got in line, with Win in the lead, Katy in the middle, and me taking the rear.

It was time to track down our killer.

It took us twenty minutes to slip through the woods, taking the circuitous route toward what looked like the oblong blob on Win's phone screen.

The lake was hidden behind the tree line, so all we could see as we hiked was thick green foliage surrounding us. The phone's compass was our only guide.

I did a double take when the trees thinned and the green waters of the lake came into view again.

I hadn't realized how expansive the lake was until now. A hazy mist enveloped the float homes and promenade on the far end of the lake. It was far enough that even on a good day, it would have been hard to make the houses out.

Win had been right.

A rusty barge was moored to wooden stakes at the mouth of the river, just where the lake ended, and the river began.

A low, steady hum came from its vicinity, like an electric generator was working. But the vessel itself looked like it had been out of commission for years.

The river was rushing downstream toward the Pacific Ocean, which wasn't visible from here. The dark river water slammed against the boat's outer shell, making the huge vessel sway gently.

Someone had cleared the trees by the boat, creating a makeshift parking lot. The potholes where the river overflowed or where rain had dug into the ground were visible from our hiding spot behind the tree line.

I wondered how long the barge had been docked here.

A shiver went through me as I realized Lily and Miles had come to the woods on this very same month two years ago.

A black pickup truck was parked next to the barge, its nose pointing at the river. A few feet away from it was the white van that had driven by us, the one that had eluded the police all this time.

I squinted as I read the license plate.

It was the same Oregon number I'd seen on the van at the bank and at the hospital. By some curious stroke of luck, this rogue vehicle had never been tracked down.

Katy was right. The police had far to go to ramp up their game.

"It's the limo guys," whispered Win, pointing with a shaky finger.

Two men were by the pickup truck's tailgate, having an animated argument. They were too far away for us to hear, but I could make out their profiles as they moved back and forth, gesticulating. Whatever their debate, it was taking all their attention, and that was a good thing.

"Randy," whispered Katy as she peered through the foliage, "and Noah."

We watched them for a minute, my gut sounding alarm bells. As usual in this case, something about this picture didn't fit. The men had bragged about running off to Jamaica after the heist, but they had been here all along.

In Grayson's own backyard.

The men's raised voices, littered with curses and threats, rolled our way.

What are they fighting about? Sharing the loot from the bank robbery?

Randy turned around and yelled something. He raised a fist like he was about to punch Noah. Noah pushed off the truck and stomped to the van, giving his partner the finger.

"Back," I whispered, pulling my friends toward a tree.

We huddled behind the biggest trunk we could find, listening to the sounds of their car doors slamming, engines starting, and the vehicles being driven out of the parking lot.

I tilted my head a few inches as the white van drove by us with Noah in the driver's seat. Randy followed closely in his truck, a dark expression on his face.

Where were they going? Didn't they realize a city's entire police force was on to them? Their faces had been uncovered during the heist and had even been captured on camera.

We waited until the sound of the engines subsided. It was time to see what was so special about this lone boat moored in the middle of nowhere.

I scanned the area and stepped forward.

"Coming?"

The three of us kept to the tree line as we treaded around the parking lot and toward the bow of the vessel. We stopped as we got close to the ship.

"This thing is huge," said Katy as we stared up at it. "Must be two stories high."

"It's a mid-size barge," said Win. "Probably transported goods from the port to inland warehouses at some point."

"What's inside?" I said. "That's what I want to know."

The sun was now westward, and its rays were cooling. Pretty soon, it would get dark. While we had packed flashlights and had our phones with us, the longer we hung out by this bizarre boat, the more unsettled I felt.

I surveyed the vessel, looking for an entrance.

There were no security cameras, spotlights, or any sign of guards patrolling. Whatever those men were doing here, they didn't seem to expect strangers to discover their hideout.

"A ladder," said Win, nudging me. "To our right."

I checked my weapon again and gestured to my friends.

"Stay close."

After scanning the area one more time to make sure no one else was in the vicinity, we stepped away from the trees and threaded quietly across the barren parking lot to the barge.

We scooted to the side of the boat where the ladder was.

Pushing aside the gruesome thoughts of what I had discovered the last time I climbed a ladder, I jumped onto the first rung. Balancing my weapon in one hand and holding on to the rungs with the other, I ascended the side of the ship to the main deck.

I prayed I wouldn't find more dead bodies in this boat.

But the top deck was deserted.

I stood still for a few seconds, taking stock. Several yards ahead of me was the bridge, enveloped in darkness. A crane and the mainmast jutted from the top, looking like the antennae of a giant insect.

Someone had boarded the windows of the bridge. I tiptoed toward the door and tried it, but it was locked. If someone was inside, they had shown no signs of seeing us.

I peered over the railing and motioned to my friends to join me. While I kept watch, crouching by the gunwale for protection, Win and Katy climbed up slowly.

Once they were on the deck, I walked over to the only entrance to the innards of this ship.

I pulled on the handle. "Locked."

It was a heavy steel door. There was no way I could shoot through that thickness of steel. Win elbowed me aside.

"It's got a keypad," she whispered. "Let me try."

Katy and I patrolled the deck while Win bent over the electronic lock, working her magic.

My gut told me the boat was empty, but my brain didn't believe it. I was prepared for an ambush at any moment.

A whir and a click came from behind me.

"Done," said Win, her voice high-pitched with excitement. "See? You guys needed me."

"Good job, but stay back," I said as I pulled on the handle again. This time, it moved. The screech of metal against metal made me cringe.

The entire world knows we're here now, I thought as I pulled at the door, my weapon aimed at the opening, ready for someone from inside to jump on us.

When the door was opened a quarter of the way, I released my hold on the handle. There wasn't a sound inside the ship.

I stepped in, my gun at the ready.

Katy and Win followed me in and the three of us stood by the doorway, listening.

"This whole thing is moving," whispered Katy from behind me.

"We're on a *boat*," whispered back Win.

My eyes scanned the white metallic interior. The inside of the vessel looked in better shape than the outside.

A long corridor ran along the length of the ship. The lights along the corridor were on, and the hum of the generator was louder, coming from the belly of the boat down below.

This meant those men weren't going to be away for too long.

"Ten closed doors," whispered Katy, pointing to the right and left of the corridor. "What do you think is in there?"

"Or *who*?" whispered Win.

Chapter Fifty-five

"There's only one way to find out," I said.

I stepped up to the first door and reached for the handle.

The door opened to a windowless cabin, the size of a jail cell.

In the corner was a bunk bed and a bedside table. A stack of cardboard boxes was piled on the lower bunk by an unused roll of packing tape. Opening the boxes, I realized all they contained were packing peanuts and nothing else.

I ran a finger along the side of the bed. "No dust."

Katy raised an eyebrow. "They're using this room regularly."

"It's a packing station," said Win.

I nodded. "These boxes contained something they don't want anyone to find out about."

After stepping out of the first room, we walked the length of the corridor, checking each cabin.

They were all the same. Bare, unoccupied, and claustrophobic cabins with empty cardboard boxes stacked on the bunk beds. Other than a few commercial grade packing tapes left carelessly on the floor, there wasn't much else.

A narrow steel staircase greeted us at the end of the corridor. One by one, we climbed silently to the deck below, with me in the lead.

It was darker on the second deck with only yellow security lights for illumination. The hum of the electric generator grew louder as we got closer to the engine room.

Win fumbled around the wall near the staircase and suddenly, the deck lit up in a bleak fluorescent light. I blinked and surveyed the scene.

A half a dozen cabin doors lined the corridor near the staircase, but the second half of the deck contained an open galley, complete with cafeteria-style chairs and tables, and a hot buffet, now empty. A sign dangled from the ceiling in the far corner, indicating common bathrooms.

"What's that?" asked Katy, pointing at something lying on the floor near the end of the corridor by the ship's kitchen.

"A napkin," said Win, walking over. "Or a towel."

"Careful," I whispered. "There could be someone here."

We tiptoed the length of the corridor until we reached the galley. I treaded around the space, peeking behind the counters, but it was empty, and the cabinets and drawers were bare. It looked like no one had cooked a meal in here in ages.

"Oh, my goodness."

The gasp made me whirl around.

Katy had picked up the piece of cloth from the ground and was holding it up.

"This would fit a one-year-old," she said.

"Baby clothes?" I said, my eyes narrowing as she turned the little white onesie around in her hands. "What on earth is that doing here?"

"They could be holding people at the bottom of the barge," whispered Katy, clutching the onesie to her chest.

"Refugees?" said Win, her eyes widening at the thought. "Trafficking victims?"

I stepped up to the door where Katy had picked up the onesie and thrust down on the handle. It was locked. I rattled it, but to no avail. I tried the next door and the next, but they didn't budge.

"Hey, something's stuck here," said Win, tugging at a small sheet of paper from under a closed steel door.

I crouched by her, while Katy tried the other rooms.

"It's a hundred-dollar bill," I said. "Blood money, most probably."

I looked around us. "They locked these cabins because they have something valuable inside."

"Piles of dirty money," said Win, twisting the bill, willing it to come free. "A dragon's hoard of dirty money."

"You'll rip it," I said. "Leave it."

Win fell back with the bill in her hand. She turned to me with a triumphant grin. "Lookee what I got."

"We need to hand that over to the police."

"Too bad none of these doors have electronic locks. Who knows what else is in there?"

"This one's not locked," came Katy's voice from down the corridor.

We looked up to see her opening the farthest door on the left. She pushed it in all the way.

We jumped up, walked over, and peered over her shoulder as she stood by the threshold.

The windowless cabin was a size and a half larger than the rooms upstairs, but had the same bunk bed and bedside table. In the corner was a baby cot and a narrow wooden door which looked like it opened to a closet or a toilet.

The air smelled musty and stale, like we'd walked into an abandoned building where homeless people took shelter.

Instead of cardboard boxes, piles of soiled clothes lay crumpled on the floor in this room.

On top of the piles was the kid's backpack with the purple unicorn motif, the zipper open and empty, like someone had taken everything out and carelessly thrown it down.

Katy stepped inside and pulled the purple backpack fully open.

"Empty," she said.

She plucked a tiny hat from one pile of clothes.

"More baby stuff," she said, and turned to the heap of clothes on the bed. She picked up a shirt and checked its label.

"Woman's shirt size six. The mother of the baby?" She held up a worn lumberjack shirt. "A small-sized adult male. The father?"

"Wait, what's this?" said Katy, feeling the shirt in her hand. She felt the pocket with her fingers, reached inside and pulled a small white packet out.

Win and I stared.

"Cocaine?" said Win. "Heroin?"

"That looks a lot like the package I found in Lily's pocket in the bank," I said.

Katy gave me a wide-eyed look. "So this is where Lily and Miles were for the past two years?"

"Held against their will, I'd say."

"And they were taking drugs?" said Win, shaking her head.

"Their captors probably fed it to them, to keep them submissive," I said, a pang of sorrow crossing my heart.

I couldn't imagine anyone living in these dank quarters. The drugs must have helped them tune their reality out. The poor baby. I wondered where he or she was now.

I walked over to the wooden sliding door and pulled on the handle. Inside was a compact toilet with a shower and a sink. Black mold had grown around the sink and was encroaching on all the ceramic surfaces.

"Hey," came Win's voice.

I turned around to see her bent over, examining the lock on the door.

"All the other cabins had manual bolts, but this has an electronic one." She looked up with a frown. "And this one is only operable from the outside."

"They were locked in," I said, rubbing my forehead, trying to comprehend what we had discovered.

"Randy and Noah are running a human trafficking racket," said Katy, her face pale. "That's their jam."

"But what were they doing with Lily?" I said. "A local heiress?"

"Kidnapped and trafficked too—" Win stopped and shook her head. "Nah. Why would they do that, when they could have asked Grayson for a hefty ransom and made fast cash?"

"Exactly."

I looked around the room. These baby clothes were disturbing. My memory whirred, trying to dig up something important someone said, but for the life of me it was eluding me.

I turned to my friends. "What's the link between Chris Grayson and these men?"

"He seemed as shocked as we were about the heist and finding his daughter dead," said Katy. "Seemed genuine unless he's a real good actor."

"How did we find this place?"

"By tracing the boat's IMO number," replied Win. "Plus, some deductions and guesswork using Sat maps and a compass."

"Miles gave us the IMO number," said Katy. "The guy we think is Lily's boyfriend."

"The same dude who was thrown off the white van that was also at the bank heist," said Win. "The van that was parked here only a half hour ago."

I nodded. "Katy, what did Miles ask us both times he saw us?"

"He said, *find her. Find my baby girl*," she said, frowning. "I thought he meant Lily."

"Me too," I said. "But what if he was referring to his child?"

Win picked up a tiny torn shirt from the heap of clothes. "So, Randy and his gang kept Lily and Miles captive here for two years, and this is their baby's clothes?"

We didn't speak for a few seconds, staring at each other. None of this made sense, but I knew it had to. We just had to find the right key to unlock the puzzle.

"Horrible," said Win, shaking her head. "I feel so bad for them."

Katy pulled her jacket around her shoulders and spoke in a sad voice.

"Seeing what they did to Lily and Miles, I'd say that poor little baby is in a shallow grave or underwater right now."

Chapter Fifty-six

I still had more questions than answers.

"Why would these thugs go to these ridiculous lengths? Confining anyone is time and energy intensive, let alone a baby."

I turned to Katy. "Did Davies get back?"

She pulled her phone out of her pocket.

"Probably gone home or at a bar having a drink with Thomas," said Win, making a face. "Too busy to tackle the horror happening right under their noses."

"No replies," said Katy, shaking her cell in the air. "There's no reception down here. My bars are all red."

Win and I checked our phones.

"Mine are red too," said Win.

I willed my brain to think fast. It was going to get dark soon and those men could return at any moment.

"If there are any captives on this ship, we need to get them out ASAP." I stepped out of the room. "Let's check the deck below. Ten minutes and we're out of here."

"Got it," said Win, following me out.

It was time to descend to the belly of the ship.

We took the final set of stairs to the engine room, hearing the generator's hum get louder. I was in the lead, my gun out, my flashlight on, bracing myself to find people shackled to the bottom of the boat.

But other than the generator and the smell of diesel, no other sound or noise came from below. A shiver ran down my back, wondering if everyone had died.

I shook my head. *Where's the stench, then?*

Jane's body had only been in that empty house for a few days and already stunk. We would have detected the odor of rotting flesh if people had died down here.

Swallowing hard, I took the last few steps down to the hull and gazed at the wide-open space.

"They gutted it," I said.

The electric generator sat in the far corner, humming away. It was the only machinery down here. The ship's engine had been stripped out and taken, but it was what had replaced it that was extraordinary.

"What a weird place to put a workshop," said Katy, surveying the room.

An electric lathe lay on its side next to a large rough-hewn log. By the log was a set of dented chisels and two pairs of safety glasses. The steel floor was covered in wood chips and sawdust.

"What's this?" said Win, walking over to a table in a corner.

On the table sat a lump of gray clay. Next to the table was a backless stool covered by a canvas cloth speckled with mud and dirt. Two aprons splattered in paint had been thrown carelessly on a steel pipe that ran along the hull.

"A pottery wheel?" said Katy. "This is crazy."

"I don't believe Randy and Noah are artists," said Win, whirling around.

"I told you," said Katy. "This case takes us down one Alice in Wonderland rabbit hole after another."

A rustle came from a corner. I spun around, aiming my weapon.

"Don't shoot!" cried Win.

A large brown rat with a broken tail scurried along a steel pipe. It stopped on the dirty aprons for a second to inspect us, its whiskers quivering, its beady eyes shining.

We stared back, frozen in our spots. Then, as if it was satisfied with what it saw, it disappeared behind the pipe with a squeak.

"Yuck," said Katy with a shudder.

"Poor thing," said Win.

"I'd take Ratatouille over Randy any day," I said. "Time to go back up. I don't like being down here without a cell signal."

We climbed up the stairs.

"Lily and Miles disappeared two years ago," I said, as we trooped along the corridor of the top floor deck toward the entrance. "They were last spotted in the woods not too far from here, never to be seen again."

"Until now," said Win.

Katy nodded. "Randy and Noah kidnapped them, brought them here, and kept them in that cabin in the second deck."

"I know why Lily ran away now," said Win. "Imagine Chris and Jane finding out their daughter was shacking up with a street kid *and* was having his baby?"

I frowned. "Wouldn't those thugs let them go as soon as they found out she was pregnant? It's too much trouble."

"Ransom," said Win. "The Graysons are the victims here. Chris had nothing to do with any of this."

"Randy and Noah are gangsters who were looking for extra money," said Katy. "Then, Jane Grayson found out about it and Randy or one of his men killed her before she could tell Chris or the police."

"Two years is a long time to hold anyone for ransom." I shook my head. "It doesn't add up."

"Maybe Grayson couldn't pay up. Appearances can be deceiving. In reality, he could be near bankruptcy."

"Wouldn't he have mortgaged that mansion then?" I said. "Sold it or re-financed it to buy his daughter's freedom?"

No one had an answer.

We were out on the top deck now.

The wind had died down, but gray clouds streaked the darkening sky. Twilight had descended around us, that strange time between day and night when you couldn't help but imagine shadows hiding in every corner.

We turned our flashlights on to make our way. Our phones still hadn't caught a cellular signal.

I scanned the top deck. The bridge sat hunkered in the middle of the ship, looking as unwelcoming as before. Something about those boarded-up windows bothered me.

"Quick check on the captain's quarters," I whispered, walking toward the bridge.

Like the other door, the entrance to the bridge had an electronic keypad. Katy and I kept an eye out for danger while Win did her magic.

My entire body was tense, and my eyes alert, constantly darting back and forth, watching for danger signs.

We were vulnerable, being out in the open like this. If the men drove up to the boat now, they'd see us the minute they turned into the parking lot.

It took Win longer this time, and the whir and the click were a welcome relief. I pushed the door open and stumbled inside with my friends at my heels.

"Eek!" cried Win in fright.

Katy jumped back, stepping on my feet.

Just when we thought things couldn't get stranger, they just had.

Three faceless ghosts greeted us by the door.

I turned my flashlight on them.

They looked almost human. They stood silently in a row, heads bowed toward the floor.

Katy took a step back, her hand on her heart, gasping. "Oh, my goodness. What in heaven's name is this?"

"What the heck are they?" whispered Win.

I walked up to the closest figure, reached out, and touched the cloth draped over them. It was thick canvas, the same material we saw by the pottery wheel down below.

What's underneath these ghoulish sheets?
I yanked the cloth away and let it crumple to the floor.

Chapter Fifty-seven

A life-sized wood carving stood before us.

It was shaped like a human, but with grotesque features and uneven limbs.

"Whoa," said Win.

I yanked the sheet off the second form, then the third.

We stared at the crudely carved figures. Two were men and one was a woman, all with sorrowful expressions.

"What are they supposed to be?" said Win, circling them. "Totem poles? We're on the West Coast after all."

"Can't be," said Katy. "Totems are beautiful. They have eagles, bears, and symbols representing this land. These are just... *sick*."

"Randy and Noah don't seem like they have indigenous backgrounds. Then again, you never know," I said, staring at the melancholy faces carved into the wood. "If these are a modern version of totem poles, the elders would be rolling in their graves."

Katy reached over and touched a scrawny wooden arm, a disapproving look on her face. "These are so amateur."

"Now we know what they're up to in that workshop below deck," I said.

I shone my flashlight around, but it was hard to make out much more than the silhouettes of smaller sculptures and boxes lying everywhere. Some were covered with white sheets, while others lay in piles, like someone had thrown them haphazardly, turning a ship's bridge into a warehouse for discarded artwork no one wanted.

"This is junk," said Katy. "Why would anyone make these?"

"One man's trash is another man's treasure," said Win.

"Anyone see the light panel?" I asked, turning my flashlight on the walls. I pulled on a switch and a white light flickered above us.

I picked up a clay sculpture with a human face, its lips and eyes contorted into macabre shapes, like it was being tortured by an unseen hand.

What demented mind conjured up these things?

I put it back down with a shudder.

"The devil himself," said Katy, holding up a ceramic skull with horns, its mouth twisted into a deranged laugh.

Randy and Noah weren't the sentimental kind, which meant these items had to be worth something. Worth enough to be stashed on a remote boat in a place where few dared to tread.

I surveyed the room. They had boarded up all the windows, except for one that looked out into the woods below. I made my way around the jumble and peered outside.

It was getting harder to see. I was glad we had our flashlights on us. We could find our way back to the car at least.

"They're not back, are they?" said Katy in an anxious voice from behind me.

"No, but I don't like this window," I said, bending down to pick up the sheet I'd pulled off the sculptures. I draped it over the steel bar that ran along the top of the window to create a makeshift curtain.

"Let's take a few pictures and get out," I said. "We've spent far too long on this boat."

Win was halfway through the bridge, picking up pieces and putting them back down. She straightened up and looked my way.

"Whatever happened to all the bridge equipment? Navigation gear, steering wheel, compass, radio?"

"They stripped it all down," I said.

"For this crap?" She whipped her arms out and hit a clay sculpture which fell to the ground with a crash.

"Oh, no," she said, putting a hand over her mouth.

"I'm sure they can whip another one of those in a minute," said Katy, making a face.

Win bent down to pick something up and held it to the light.

"I know nothing about art, but I can tell you what a USB stick looks like."

I made my way toward her through the mess of items and squinted at the shiny piece of black plastic in her palm.

"Fell right out of that thing," said Win.

I picked up the largest piece of the broken sculpture by her feet and turned it upside down. There was a hollow space underneath.

Katy came over and did a double take.

"An angel?" she said. "This is a sign."

"Sign from a mere mortal," I said. "Poor girl."

"You think Lily made this?"

"Remember the small angel sculpture Grayson showed us in her bedroom?"

Katy took the broken piece from me to examine it. "Miles is an artist too, come to think of it."

I nodded. "If this is an art counterfeiting operation, Lily could have been killed because she refused to do a job. Could be the reason they lopped off Miles's hand, too."

Katy gave a shudder. "Brutal."

"These don't look like masterpieces to me, though," said Win, gazing around her. "Even I'd know these are badly done. Fakes."

"They could have dumbed down their work deliberately," I said. "The angel sculpture Lily had in her room was beautiful, even for one made by a kid. This could have been her way of protesting their captivity. The thugs tired of her and killed her as punishment."

Katy and Win didn't answer.

I felt like we were staring at the final puzzle pieces, but they were still scattered, leaving me with more questions than answers.

Whatever had happened on this ship, it was more horrific than any of us could have imagined when we boarded that flight to Seattle.

I pointed at the USB stick in Win's hand. "Can we see what's in there?"

"I need my laptop. Mine's in my backpack in the car."

"Hey," came Katy's voice, guarded and low. "There's something in here."

She passed the broken angel back to me. "Look inside."

Using my flashlight, I peered inside the curved hollow space. I took a sharp breath in as I noticed the words carved on the clay.

"They'll kill us," I read out aloud, feeling the hair stand on the back of my nape. "Three, seven, four, zero, eight, one—"

"Wait, I know those digits," said Win. "This boat's IMO number."

I looked at the pile of sculptures around us. "Maybe there are messages in all of them."

Win picked up the nearest clay sculpture that was shaped like a football and smashed it against the side of a wooden box. We picked up the pieces to examine them, but there were no words inside. Or USB sticks either.

Katy took a ceramic monkey and slammed it against the hull. We scrambled to find the pieces and put them together.

Nothing.

"We'll be here all night," said Katy, hands on her hips.

Win picked up a clay dog.

"Wait." I glanced around.

There.

I stepped around a pile of boxes toward a corner where three angels stood side-by-side. They were only a foot tall.

"Something tells me these are extra special."

I picked the first angel up and smashed its shoulders on a steel pipe, sending hardened clay everywhere, making clanking sounds as the broken pieces hit the hull of the bridge.

I turned the broken piece in my hand upside down. Like the first one, the inside was hollow. I shone my flashlight and peered inside as Katy and Win huddled around me.

Win read the words out aloud. "Call Chris Grayson. I am alive."

"A call for help," breathed Katy. "That poor girl. Why on earth would they hold them here, forcing them to make this grotesque art?"

I took the second angel sculpture and hit the shoulders against the side of the steel bridge. It broke perfectly into two pieces.

"John Thomas will kill us. Tell Father."

Thomas?

A chill went through me. Katy and Win stared at me.

"Did we get duped?" I said.

"Thomas is a common name—" Katy started.

"Hey!" Win pounced on something on the ground.

"What is it?" I said, peering over the boxes.

"Another USB stick?" said Katy.

Win opened her hand to show us a roll of green paper.

"Money," she said, as she pulled out the rubber band and unrolled it. "All hundred-dollar bills."

We stared at it.

The bills were crisp and clean, like they had been newly minted. Strange. I turned to Win.

"Do you still have that bill you yanked from under the cabin door?"

She pulled the crumpled paper from her pocket. I reached for it and held it up to the light.

"Is it my eyes or are these colors off?" I murmured as I scanned it.

Win leaned in and traced her finger along the right side of the bill. "There's no watermark."

We looked at each other.

"Counterfeit!" cried Katy.

She pointed at the roll of bills in Win's hand. "What about those? Are they fake too?"

I pulled one bill from the wad and held it up.

"This one looks genuine enough, but there's only one reason for us to find a fake one under that door." I paused as I thought this through. "I would bet anything Randy and his men are running a counterfeit operation and delivering them to their clients via these art pieces."

"So, that's what's going on here," said Win.

"Where did you find that roll?" said Katy, scanning the floor.

Win pointed at the broken angel in my hand. "It came from inside there. It was stuck in the hollow space."

"Those cabins on the second deck are locked for a reason," I said. "That's where they're print—"

A loud crash came from behind us, like the bridge had exploded.

"Watch out!" screamed Katy.

"Oh no!" yelled Win, ducking.

I spun around.

The sheet I'd hung along the window had burst into flames.

I grabbed my friends and pulled them to the floor, behind a large box. I shielded my face and peeked over.

The burning sheet had dropped down, exposing the broken window. Shattered glass lay on the ground among the sculptures.

A busted bottle rolled toward the wooden carvings by the door.

Someone had just thrown a Molotov cocktail inside the bridge.

Chapter Fifty-eight

The men were back.

I whirled around, looking for a fire extinguisher. A normal ship's bridge would have had several, but they had stripped the room of everything useful.

There was only one thing to do.

I sprang up from behind the box and ran toward the fire.

"Asha!" screamed Katy.

"Watch out!" shouted Win.

The flames were spreading across the room. We would have an inferno soon. I grabbed the remaining canvas sheets and threw them on the fire to stop it from sucking up any more oxygen.

A thundering crash made me spin around. The bridge door had slammed shut.

"Hey!" I leaped over the boxes toward the door and pulled on the handle. It didn't budge.

We were trapped.

I banged madly. "Open up! Hey! Open up!"

Win got up from her corner and instantly doubled over from the smoke. "We're going to die!"

If we didn't burn to death, we would croak from smoke inhalation first.

"Stay down!" I hollered and put a sleeve over my mouth before I inhaled that toxic air.

I glanced around desperately, my heart hammering like mad. A monstrous wooden statue was standing next to me, its facial expression looking even more hideous to my frenzied mind.

I stepped behind it and tilted it, but it was heavy.

Katy rushed over and took position next to me. Together, we toppled the piece over until it came down on the fire with a crash. We moved to the next carving, and the next, bringing them down on the flames. Anything to smother the oxygen from stoking the deadly flames.

This was a temporary solution. The wood would catch fire and it would grow even bigger.

I turned to Katy and Win, sweat streaming down my face.

"Sheets!" I hollered. "Grab as many sheets as you can!"

Katy and Win scurried around, pulling the sheets off the sculptures.

"Tie them together!" I yelled as I made my way toward the broken window, holding my left sleeve across my nose and mouth.

The sound of an engine revving came from the parking lot below. I kicked myself for not having heard it come in. I had been so absorbed in our discoveries, I hadn't done my most important job.

I glanced out from the corner of the window to see the red taillights of a vehicle disappearing down the trail through the woods.

They were leaving us behind to die.

With the door to the bridge locked, there was only one way out of this hell. Hoping against hope there were no snipers behind the trees, I picked up the largest woodcarving I could hold in my hand.

In a corner, as far away from the fire as they could get, Katy and Win were tying the sheets together, stooping to cover their noses with their sleeves every few seconds.

I turned back to the window and raised the wooden piece. Shielding my eyes with the other hand, I smashed the jagged shards jutting around the windowpane.

The Molotov cocktail had done a good first job. The glass was old and had shattered easily. All it needed was a half a dozen hits, and I had an opening for us to get out without getting cut.

The bridge was as hot as an oven now and my face sizzled like it was melting off.

"Done!" cried Win, rushing over, holding one end of the sheets.

Above my head was the steel pipe I had thrown the makeshift curtain around. It ran up toward the ceiling and out to the masthead. It was as solid as I could find. We didn't have many choices.

With my heart pounding, I threw one end of the sheet over and around the pipe. After tying a knot to hold it in place, I flung the rest of the cloth out the window.

A siren sounded faintly in the distance.

Katy came over, wheezing. She clutched my shoulder.

"Police?" she said.

"Could be Davies. Probably got your message."

I pointed at Win and shouted over the crackle of fire.

"You first."

"Wait!" cried Katy, giving me a terrified look. "What if they're down there?"

"They're gone." I pulled out my handgun and positioned myself by the window. "I'll watch your back. Go, Win!"

Behind us, the largest wood carving was catching fire, red-hot flames flickering around it.

Katy bent over, coughing a rough hacking cough.

We didn't have time.

Win stepped onto the ledge and straddled the sheet.

"Careful," called out Katy in between her coughing.

Win swung from the sheets.

My eyes swept the surroundings, looking for any movement. If I saw a shadow, I was prepared to shoot to kill.

Win slid down quickly.

"Next!" I shouted at Katy.

She put a hand over her mouth, still clinging to me. "I don't know if I can do it. You go."

"Get out, sweetie," I said. "Now!"

I could feel the scorching heat on my back and wondered if my jacket had caught fire.

Katy stepped onto the ledge, her legs wobbly. She grabbed the sheet.

"Slide," I shouted. "It's not that far down. Slide!"

The heat was getting stronger, and sweat dripped down my back like a river. I felt like my hair would catch on fire any moment. I wanted to jump on that sheet after Katy, but I didn't want to scare her or slow her down.

"Just a bit more!" Win hollered from below. "You can do it!"

It seemed like it took forever for Katy to get to the bottom. I doubled over through the window, gasping for fresh air, almost gagging as I did.

"Clear," came Win's voice from below.

I jumped on the sheet and swung wildly, hitting the hull of the barge. Something sharp jabbed on my arm and cut into my skin. I didn't have time to dwell on the pain. I slithered down, trying not to let the sheet slip from my sweaty hands.

When I got to six feet, I jumped down, landing hard on my side. I winced as a searing pain traveled through me like a lightning strike, but I sprang to my knees.

Win and Katy pulled me over.

The sirens were getting louder.

"Let's get out of here!" I said.

Holding on to each other, we hobbled toward the woods. We stopped at the tree line and turned to glance at the horror we had escaped.

The flames were devouring the ship's bridge. The sound of cackling and spitting was growing in intensity.

The hungry fire flared and licked at everything in its path, shooting sparks high in the air. Red-hot embers were dropping on the deck and had already started little fires everywhere.

An ominous white smoke was swirling over the barge and disappearing into the darkened sky.

We could feel the heat from where we were. We didn't need our flashlights anymore.

Soon, this entire vessel would be ablaze.

With it, all the evidence we had discovered would be destroyed.

Chapter Fifty-nine

The three of us huddled by the tree line, catching our breaths. All we could do was listen to the sirens as they got louder and closer. The first squad car came screeching to a halt in front of us.

"What the hell?" shouted Davies as he leaped out. He stopped in mid-stride as he saw our state, our torn clothes, and the scratch marks on our faces.

"Y'all okay?" he sputtered. "What the hell happened?"

I had been prepared for battle.

My heart had been racing, my shoulders up, and my hand gripping the gun behind my back, away from view. The last thing I needed was to have a phalanx of law enforcement pounce on me again, thinking I was the threat.

Behind Davies, four more squad cars screamed to a stop and lined up along the muddy trail. Flashes of blue and red illuminated the fir trees in ghastly shades.

Uniformed officers jumped out and crouched behind their open doors, shielding their faces from the blaze. Their weapons were drawn, and their nervous eyes scanned the area.

"Where were you?" demanded Katy. "I texted you hours ago."

"I came as soon as I got it," cried Davies.

"Did you know about this place?" I said.

A loud explosion came from the barge. We dove into the woods, covering our heads. Davies landed with a thump beside me.

"Anyone else in there?" He raised his voice over the pandemonium.

"Negative," I hollered back. "But someone had been locked up in there for a while."

"Locked up?"

"If you can get the DNA evidence, you might find Lily and her boyfriend had been held captive in here."

"On this ship?"

Win turned to him. "There's a workshop at the bottom deck and a ton of sculptures on the bridge. There was, anyway. It's burning up as we speak."

Davies narrowed his eyes.

"Sculptures?"

I reached into my pocket and pulled out the roll of hundred-dollar bills. "Would you like to guess what was going on here?"

His eyes bulged. He opened his mouth to speak, then closed it again.

Behind him, an officer was barking into his radio, calling for backup. The others were running around with mini fire extinguishers and shovels in hand, removing debris from the ship, trying to contain the fire from spreading to the woods.

What they needed was a fleet of fire trucks.

"It'll all become ash soon," I said, shaking my head. "I'd bet anything this was a money counterfeiting operation gone bad."

Davies plucked the wad of cash from my hand. "My goodness."

"Lily and Miles had somehow got entangled in it and were forced to work for them," said Katy, her voice hardening. "Jane Grayson found out, and that's why she was killed."

"Murdered?" he said, flustered. "What were you...? how did you even find this place?"

Katy shot him an annoyed look. "Whatever was going on here was happening under your watch, mister."

"We're doing everything we can under a tight budget..."

He rubbed his temple and stepped back, like he didn't want to have this conversation anymore.

I gave him a steely look. "Why haven't you captured the men from the bank heist? Randy and Noah were here an hour ago."

"We just found out about this place." His cocky confidence was gone and in its place was an unsettled expression.

"*Right*," snorted Katy. "We nearly got killed because you didn't figure it out before we did."

"Where's your partner?" I called out as he slowly backed away from us and toward his car.

He gave me a startled look, like he was surprised at my question.

"Home with his family. End of shift."

"You might want to ask him about this barge."

He gave me a wild look.

An officer bellowed to him. He spun around. More squad cars were coming over, lights flashing and their sirens overtaking the sound of the cackling fire.

With another strange glance our way, Davies ran over to join his team.

I turned to Win. "Do you still have the USB stick?"

She nodded.

"We need to get to our car," I said, gesturing for them to follow me.

With the officers' attention on the blaze, they hardly noticed us. Katy, Win, and I slipped deeper into the woods.

We trundled in between the trees, using our flashlights to find our way. Dusk had fallen over the forest and the air had cooled. Moving away from the fire made us feel the chilly night air even more. We huddled close together, with Win in the middle.

No one spoke.

My adrenaline was sky high, my heart was hammering, and my right arm stung badly, like I had been stabbed.

We had nearly died.

Soon our adrenaline would subside and the pain in our bodies would take over, but before that happened, we had urgent matters to handle.

It took us a few false stops and starts before we found our rental tucked in between the giant oak trees. We scrambled inside, seeking the warmth and safety of our car.

I locked the doors, switched on the engine, and turned up the heat.

Win pulled out her laptop from her backpack, while Katy and I checked our phones. The red bars were slowly turning green, but it would take a minute before we could make a proper call.

"Tetyana," said Katy. "She's waiting for us at the hotel tonight."

"We'll call her as soon as we can," I said.

"She's going to be mad she wasn't in the thick of things with us, if I know her," said Win from the backseat. "That's if we survive to tell her the story."

"I just want to go home and give a big hug to Chantelle and Peace and tell them how much I love them. Chris Grayson never got the chance to say goodbye to his girl, and she was here all along, not far from his home."

She wiped a tear.

"All the money in the world, and he lost the most important things he had."

I sat quietly, rubbing my hands for warmth. I was bone tired, but my eyes and ears were alert as I watched the road, only half listening to my friends.

If Randy and Noah came back, we'd be sitting ducks. The police vehicles were further down the trail, and the officers were fully occupied. By the time they heard us, those thugs could do anything.

My weapon was on my lap, and I was prepared for an ambush.

"Oh, my gosh."

Katy and I whirled around to the backseat. Win turned her laptop toward us. The USB key had been inserted into the side port.

"You guys won't believe this," she said.

We stared.

"Thomas?" said Katy. "*Officer* Thomas?"

The officer's face was at the center of the screen, but he wasn't looking at the camera. It was a still from video footage, grainy and pixelated like someone had captured it from afar.

Behind him was the unmistakable view of the lower deck of the barge, the workshop, the electric generator, and all.

"John Thomas," I said, staring at his face. "I should have known."

"Can you sharpen the picture?" asked Katy.

"So, he was the uncle all along?" said Win, squinting at the screen as she fiddled with the video settings. "How come he has a different last name from Chris?"

"Remember Grayson was adopted," I said. "He might have kept his birth parents' name for whatever reason."

"Like I did." Katy nodded. "I didn't take any of my foster parents' names. It's just a way to feel less lost when you're an orphan."

I reached over and squeezed her arm. She blinked away a tear.

We had gone through a lot in our childhoods, and had made a promise to never let anyone who needed help down. The only drawback was there was always something in our cases that reminded us of our own pasts. That was never easy to deal with.

"Are you ready to see the video?" said Win, balancing the laptop on her knees.

I nodded. "Roll it."

Chapter Sixty

Win pressed play.

The camera panned out to show us more of the lower hull. Behind Thomas was one of the ugly life-sized sculptures we'd seen inside the bridge.

Katy and I leaned over the front seats to hear better.

Thomas was speaking. "When's the next shipment?"

"Two days from now," replied Randy.

Noah was sitting casually on a stool next to him, and behind them stood a third man.

Katy leaned in closer. "Stop the video."

Win clicked on the pause button.

"I know that profile now," said Katy, pointing at the man in the back. "He was the one with the beard and the hat. He's the one who tried to kidnap you from the hospital."

"His size and shape are close to the rideshare nutcase," said Win, examining the image.

I scrutinized the man's face. "I'd bet that's the thug who drove the van during the heist, too. We never saw his face, did we?"

Katy slammed a fist on the back of her seat. "He's the same bearded twit who peeked through our guest house window and the same idiot who tried to run over us back home!"

I raised an eyebrow. "He must have come over to Seattle on the same flight as us, or around the same time. This was an expensive operation."

Katy shot me a wry look. "What's a few hundred thousand dollars in expenses when you're stealing millions of real money and printing millions of fakes?"

She was right. I turned to Win. "Keep rolling."

The video continued.

"I want you to make it fast and quiet," said Thomas, as the others nodded. It was clear who was the leader of this corrupt crew.

The image shook and became fuzzy, like the person behind the camera was trying to get a better angle. Then everything went black.

Katy turned to me. "Do you think Lily or Miles took this video? Grayson said Lily left everything behind, including her phone. I saw it on her bed."

"She could have had a second cell phone," I replied.

"It could be Miles's device," said Win.

"You'd think the goons would confiscate their phones as soon as they kidnapped them, like they did with us," said Katy.

I sat back to think.

"There is the possibility they got a hold of Thomas's or Randy's phone somehow. We don't know what was behind the locked cabins in the second deck. They could have stolen a phone, taken the video, downloaded it to this stick, and hid it in a piece they were making."

"Brave kids," said Katy, shaking her head. "They were desperate."

Win nodded. "One thing I'm sure of is they were hiding behind the pipes in the engine room when they took this. They were near where we saw the rat."

"It's working again," said Katy, pointing at the screen.

The video had come on again, more clearly this time. It zoomed on the men, but the sound was now muted. Thomas was talking, but it was impossible to make out the words anymore.

"Shoot," said Win. "Shoot, shoot."

"It's good enough," I said. "IT forensics should be able to recover most of it."

"I could too, if I had access to a lab." She moved the cursor to shut the video off.

"Hey," I said. "Let's check if there's anything else on this stick. If Lily and Miles stole this USB from the goons—"

But Win was already ahead of me. She had shut off the video and clicked on another icon.

I squinted at the spreadsheet that had just opened up on the laptop screen.

"I found this," she said, a note of triumph in her voice. "I was going to show it to you next."

"An inventory of their production," said Katy.

"They were churning out cash like they were the Federal Reserve," said Win as she scrolled through the worksheet.

"We need to hand this over to the authorities ASAP," I said. "Can you get a copy to the FBI? You've done it before and we now have a phone connection, so it's possible. Am I correct?"

"Right away." Win turned the laptop around and hunched over it.

I sat back in my seat and scanned the trail. The sky over the woods was aglow from the blaze. Panicked shouts and loud hollering were coming from the direction of the burning ship.

I caressed the gun on my lap, trying to figure out our next best move.

Katy turned to me. "I still don't get why Thomas would kidnap his own niece and then kill Jane Gray—"

An ear-splitting siren stopped her.

"My goodness, that's an air raid!" she cried.

"Fire trucks," I said.

Within seconds, three fire engines sailed by us, sirens blaring, their high roofs pushing away the tree branches. The firefighters inside didn't even notice us, their complete focus on the blaze up ahead.

As soon as the last truck disappeared around the corner, I put our car in gear and my hands on the steering wheel.

"Sent," said Win, closing her laptop with a click. "They have the info now."

"Great job," I said, rolling the car forward.

"Where are we going?" said Katy.

"To have a chat with Thomas."

"Shouldn't we tell Davies?" said Katy. "Get backup?"

"I don't trust him," I said, as I reversed onto the trail. "If he's in on this, he'll try to stop us, and I don't think he's going to be nice about it."

———⋈———

The cries of a screaming child greeted us as we approached Nathalie's navy-blue float home.

Grayson had buzzed us inside the compound.

He had got a ride back home with Officer Lee to recuperate an hour ago, but he had sounded confused, his words slurring, like he was under the influence of strong medication.

I had badly wanted to share our discoveries with him, but he was too vulnerable. I needed hard evidence before I gave him any more distressing news.

I couldn't imagine what it must be like to see the scarred corpse of your daughter and get news of your wife's purported suicide within days of each other. Guilt was still roiling inside of me for shocking him with Lily's maligned body.

There was a time to bring him into this, but it wasn't now.

After parking the car, I stomped up the pier, my weapon in hand, flanked by my friends.

Win and Katy had turned on the audio record apps on their phones. We were going to capture everything we heard from now on.

A slow anger was broiling inside of me. There was one more question I still didn't have an answer for. Why did Thomas and his goons drag us into the vault with intent to murder?

That man had a lot to answer for.

I stomped up the front steps of the navy-blue floating home and banged on the door.

The child shrieked louder.

I turned to Katy. "How old do you think that kid is?"

"Two years, give or take—"

The door flung open.

On the threshold stood Nathalie, still in her Chanel suit and pink heels. But her makeup was smeared, and her hair was undone, like a hurricane had blown through it.

"Go away!" She snapped her hand in front of my face, like she was shooing away a fly.

She pushed the door to close it, but I thrust my boot in to keep it from shutting.

"What do you want?" she barked.

I stepped forward and gave her a hard look. "I'd like a word with Thomas."

Her eyes widened as she spotted the gun in my hand. I wasn't aiming it at her, but she got the message. She staggered backward, turned around, and scooted in, almost bumping into the entryway table.

I kicked the door open and marched inside, with Katy and Win at my heels.

Thomas was sitting on the living-room couch in his pajamas, a beer in his hands, and a game on TV.

He sat up as he saw us.

"What the hell!" he shouted.

Chapter Sixty-one

"Get out of my home!" roared Thomas.

Then he saw my weapon. His face turned pale.

"Good evening, Officer Thomas," I said, stepping around the leather sectional and taking position in front of him.

"What in goodness' sake do you think you're doing?" he shouted, though his voice had lost its initial confidence. "You can't barge in like this."

Win walked up to the coffee table, picked up the remote, and switched the TV off.

"I'm a police officer," Thomas spluttered. "You'll go to prison once and for all, and you'll never see the light of day."

"I believe that's *your* future you're referring to," I said, my eyes boring into his.

He blinked rapidly, like he couldn't believe what he had just heard.

The little girl behind us hadn't stopped crying. I wondered where Nathalie had run off to. Was she calling the police station?

I hoped so.

I would have loved for them to get a front-row seat to this conversation.

"The only way a mid-level civil servant could afford not one, but two, multi-million-dollar float homes in this exclusive community is through a lottery win," I said, watching him carefully. "Or through outright theft."

Thomas blinked again. "It was inheritance money." His voice was faltering.

"We know you bought Geena her house, too."

He looked away, a nervous twitch coming on his face. He spread his arms as if to reply, then he pulled them back again.

The clicking of angry heels on the marble tiles came from the kitchen. Nathalie strutted into the living room, her eyes on her husband.

"What's this?" she said, placing her hands on her hips.

Thomas ignored her.

"You told me Chris bought Geena the house," she said.

Thomas gave her a dismissive wave, but the fire in her eyes was unmistakable.

The toddler tottered from the back of the kitchen toward Nathalie, clutching her toy in one hand, her tiny chest heaving with quiet sobs.

She reached for the woman's leg, but Nathalie shoved her away with her foot, like she was nothing more than an annoying pet. The child fell back on her bum and started crying again, but no one paid attention.

I turned my focus back to Thomas.

"You're Grayson's brother, aren't you?"

"What if I am?" he snapped, slamming his beer on the coffee table. "That's none of your damn business!"

"I make it mine," I growled, a red-hot flash going through me, "when you try to kill my friends and me in an airtight vault."

Nathalie took a sharp breath in.

Thomas got up from the couch and pulled himself to his full height. Even in his pajamas, he cut an imposing figure. I could now see how this man could have influenced others to take part in illicit activities.

He glowered at me. There was a quiet rage in his eyes, but it was mixed with a flicker of fear.

I knew why. He didn't know how much we knew, and that was unsettling him.

A phone rang from somewhere in the room.

"You might want to pick that up," I said, waving the gun in the direction of the ringing. "It's probably Davies calling to report what he and your entire team are up to tonight."

He glared.

"Your rusty barge is on fire, Officer Thomas," said Win, relish in her voice. "It's burning to the ground."

Thomas jerked his head back.

"Your counterfeiting operation has been exposed," said Katy. "You kept it hidden well, using your position to steer everyone away from your criminal activities, didn't you?"

Nathalie gasped.

I wondered if that was because she had just found out this news. Or if it was because she now knew that we knew.

The phone rang again, more urgently this time, it seemed.

Thomas floundered on the couch, searching for his cell. When he finally found it, he put it to his ear. His hands were shaking so hard, I was sure he'd drop the phone at any moment.

Davies' voice came from the other end. He was speaking in staccato fashion, anxiously calling out Thomas's name, asking if he could hear him.

Thomas just stared at the device numbly.

Davies mumbled something we couldn't hear, but Thomas's face went white, giving us a good indication of what his partner had just told him.

Katy leaned over to me to whisper. "You sure Davies is part of the racket, too?"

I didn't have an answer to that.

Not yet.

Thomas let his mobile fall to the carpet and stared out the window, seemingly forgetting we were in his living room.

I turned to his wife who was leaning against the counter.

"Did you know about your husband's lucrative side hustle?"

Nathalie's focus on her husband didn't waver. Her lips were curled in contempt and her eyes were flashing in anger.

"How could you?" she spat out. "How could you do this to us?"

Thomas spun around to her, his face a dark shade of purple.

"I gave you the life you never could have imagined. You think this house, your convertible, those clothes, are possible on a cop's salary?"

"I put up with all your shenanigans!" she screamed. "And now this?"

Thomas shouted back. "I did everything for you, but you're never happy!"

He pointed at the window.

"You know what they're trying to do to me? Push me out to the pasture with a reduced pension. That's what! They hate my guts. I put up with their BS for years. You never cared for me either. All you wanted was the money!"

His wife took a step back, her lips pulled back in a snarl.

The little girl had stopped crying and was watching the grown-ups.

She may not have understood the gravitas of the situation, but she had felt the dangerous energy. She kept glancing from Thomas to Nathalie, then back again, those huge, innocent eyes taking everything in.

Katy turned to the woman.

"Your husband's retirement plan is going up in smoke as we speak. You might want to think of calling a divorce attorney."

Nathalie's eyes flickered. The truth was sinking in, and she was looking for an escape.

"You don't seem too worried about Thomas going to jail," I said. "A loving spouse would be pleading for his innocence."

"I'm not falling to my knees for a cheating A-hole," she snarled.

"It was you, wasn't it?" said Katy, turning to Thomas. "You were having an affair with Jane Grayson."

Thomas didn't reply, but his face said everything.

A deep pink color rose from Nathalie's neck.

"You were sleeping with *Jane*?" she blurted, her arms waving in the air. "I thought it was that big fat slob of a Geena!"

Chapter Sixty-two

"I thought you were having a lark with that trailer trash prostitute, but Jane Grayson? *Jane Grayson?*"

Nathalie's anguished screech rose with every syllable.

"She was such a nasty bitch. I hated her! How could you!"

Her perfectly manicured fingernails grated on the kitchen's granite counter.

Thomas didn't speak.

The sound of static came from somewhere on the floor. Thomas's phone was lying by his feet where it fell.

Davies hadn't hung up. The faint background of shouting mixed with the crackle of fire told me he was still there, listening in.

"You had an affair with your own brother's wife," said Katy, shaking her head. "Then you viciously killed her and dressed it up as a suicide."

"Killed her?" Nathalie grabbed a stool by the counter to steady herself, her chest heaving.

Thomas swayed back and forth, his hands clenching and unclenching. His eyes flickered over to my gun, but he didn't make a move to fight back.

But I was on guard.

He had covered his tracks well and abused his position for years. He was also a cold-blooded murderer.

My head was clearing and the puzzle pieces were slowly coming together.

"Jane found out about your counterfeiting racket," I said. "Then she found out her daughter was still alive. You couldn't have any of that get out, could you? So, you murdered them both. But you did it in a way to stick it to Grayson as hard as you could."

I paused to think.

"I'd bet anything you stole those gold bars to hit Grayson where it hurt the most. That was all he had left to remember Lily. You didn't need that gold. You were printing money."

"You're a police officer," said Win, her voice hardening. "You took an oath. I hope your colleagues give you everything you deserve."

"How could you do this to your own family?" said Katy.

Thomas turned to us, fire in his eyes. "I hate that bastard!"

I leaned in. "What did Chris Grayson do that was so terrible you had to get back at your own brother?"

"He's not my brother!" Thomas's eyes flashed in furor.

"Your adopted sibling, I mean."

"He killed our parents!"

We stared at him in shock. Even Nathalie.

This was unexpected.

I could hear yelling and car doors slamming through the phone on the floor. I wondered what Davies' next steps would be.

"Your parents died in a car crash," I said, observing Thomas for signs of lying. "It was a hit-and-run."

"That's what everyone thought!" Thomas yelled, his spittle flying. "Chris said it was an accident. He hit their car and ran off, then came home a mess. Didn't even stop to make sure they were alive!"

He flung his arms around, agitated.

"He was scared. He thought they'd put him away for manslaughter."

For a minute, I wasn't sure if Thomas had become completely unhinged or was purposefully concocting a tale. But his outburst had been so forceful, he couldn't have been lying.

Or could he?

He pulled his head down and shook it violently, like he couldn't bear to re-live the story.

"We took the car to a junkyard and told them to crush it. I pretended to be his alibi. Me. A cop. I could get anyone to do what I wanted with the right words."

He turned to us, his face a picture of despair.

"I'm the loser in the family. My own parents rejected me for him. He was their golden boy, and I saved *him*!"

His breath was coming fast and shallow. His world was crumbling, and he couldn't stop it.

Thomas looked at his wife, tears welling in his eyes.

"Can you understand?"

Nathalie didn't answer, clutching on to that stool, like she was seconds away from fainting.

The puzzle pieces were clicking together.

"That was when you found out what was in the will," I said. "Your parents, whom Chris killed, left everything to him. The man you helped save got all of it. That would make anyone mad."

Thomas started convulsing. He turned his head back and forth, like a cornered animal.

I followed his eyes. He had to have his service weapon here somewhere.

My ears were alert to sounds of a car arriving, or to footsteps along the pier. If Davies was involved in this, he could run out of town. But he could also show up to back his partner.

"Thomas," I said, keeping my voice even. "Why don't you give yourself up? Save your wife and child the pain of seeing you get arrested. They've been through enough."

Thomas shot me a strange look.

"Never. They will never get me, you hear!"

His voice turned hard.

"If I'm going down, I'm taking my wife and that kid with me."

Nathalie's face turned white.

"Don't you dare," said Katy, taking a step forward.

"You people have created enough trouble!" he shouted, his blood-red eyes bulging like they were about to explode. "I should have killed you when I had the chance!"

He was turning.

"You didn't expect your brother to hire a private investigative service, did you?" I kept my voice calm, though my heart was pounding.

My only thought was how to come up with the best way to subdue this man before he hurt himself or others.

"That's why you sent your goons to snatch us from the airport."

He didn't answer. He spun around on the carpet, his eyes darting around the room like he was searching for something.

"I suggest you don't search for your weapon," I said. "I'm trained."

He spun around to give me a wild look. Then, without a warning, he stomped over to the kitchen, grabbed the toddler from the floor, and swung her up by her shoulders.

The kid shrieked in fear, her ear-splitting scream almost deafening us.

I stepped forward, aiming my gun at Thomas's head.

"Put her down. Now!"

He stepped backward, holding the squirming kid in front of his chest, one massive hand wrapped around her tiny neck. The toddler wiggled and howled, but he held on tight.

My heart pounded as I tried to find a good aim. I had never faced a man holding a child before. The magnitude of my next decision felt like a ton of lead wrapped around my right hand.

Thomas stepped backward, heading toward the open window.

The girl screeched and dropped her toy. The dirty cloth doll stumbled to the floor. It was the angel, the one I'd fished out of the water.

"Stop right there!" I hollered. "Stop or I shoot!"

I aimed at Thomas's knees. He let go of the kid's neck and dangled her by her arms, swinging her back and forth.

My heart skipped a beat.

I pulled my weapon up, trying not to shake. I was ten feet from him. If only that kid would stop moving.

Thomas pulled the girl up against his chest. The child kicked and cried.

Stop moving!

Suddenly, the front door crashed open, and the sounds of boots pounding on the floor came from behind me.

It was like an army had descended on the house.

Chapter Sixty-three

"Police!"

I swung around to see Davies rush in, followed by half a dozen uniformed officers, all armed.

"Put your weapon down!" he hollered, drawing his gun, aiming it at me.

"He's threatening to kill that kid!" I shouted. "You heard him on the phone."

"Thomas, what the hell's going on?" said Davies, swiveling around to his partner.

Thomas looked from his colleague to me and back. His face darkened.

"You guys get closer and I'm throwing this thing into the water." He took another step toward the window. "If I'm going down, I'm taking her with me."

Davies swung around and pointed his weapon at Thomas. "Put the kid down!"

Keeping his eyes on Davies as if to challenge him, Thomas squeezed the girl's throat.

The toddler screamed in pain and her face went red. She gasped for air and pulled furiously at his hands. He pressed tighter. The child's cries cut short, and she gurgled like she couldn't breathe anymore.

"Stop it!" cried Katy.

"What in goodness' name has got into you?" shouted Davies. "Let her go!"

I changed my aim from his head to his thighs, but Thomas was shaking, swaying, moving too unpredictably. The little girl was getting swung around like a puppet on strings.

"Don't do it," I said. "You're going to regret hurting a child."

Thomas scowled.

"I've done enough to regret for a lifetime. I would have gotten away with it if you interfering, worthless bitches hadn't come along."

"Thomas, please, listen to me," said Davies, putting a hand out to calm his partner. "Can we talk about this? We'll do anything you want. Just put that kid down."

Thomas turned to him. "So, you found the barge, huh?"

"Whatever happened there, we'll figure it out."

"What are you going to do? File a complaint with the damned police board?"

"For the love of everything, just put that kid down. You wouldn't do this to your own daughter."

A sneer came over Thomas's face.

I knew that look. It was the face of a killer.

A door in the back banged shut, and the sound of footsteps running came from the outdoor patio.

Who is that?

From the corner of my eyes, I could see the team of officers behind us, their weapons trained on Thomas now. But all the firepower in the world was useless in the face of a madman with an innocent child in his hands.

It was time to change tactic. I needed to distract Thomas, make him talk.

"Thomas," I said, looking him in the eye. "This child isn't your daughter, is she?"

He glared, but his focus was on me now.

"She's adopted," said a trembling female voice from a corner of the room.

"He went all the way to Romania to pick this girl," said Nathalie. "I didn't want children. Never wanted any. I went with it because he forced me to."

"Does it matter?" said Davies with an exasperated hiss. "Adopted or not, you don't want to hurt a child. What's got into you, for heaven's sake?"

"This girl wasn't adopted, though," I said, my eyes on Thomas. "She isn't from Romania, either, is she?"

That sneer came on Thomas's face again. The man was a psychopath.

But this was helping. His hand around the girl's neck loosened. The toddler's chest heaved as she gulped in big breaths of air.

"What a way to stick it to Chris Grayson again and again. You're a genius, Officer Thomas," I said, maintaining eye contact. "You stole Lily's baby and brought her here to raise her, right next to her rightful grandparents. And they never knew."

A shocked scream from Nathalie rang through the room. I turned my head to see an officer jump to catch her before she fell, but she fainted to the floor with a crash.

A loud splash made me spin around.

Thomas's hands were empty. He was staring out the window, a numbed look on his face.

Davies jumped on him in a split-second and slammed him to the ground.

I whipped around, dashed through the kitchen and burst through the back door.

Win was lying horizontally on the patio, desperately reaching for something in the water.

The kid!

I pulled off my jacket, threw my gun down, and plunged into the lake, headfirst.

I swam over to the child, put my arm around her little waist, and pulled her head above the water. She gasped for air, then punched and kicked hysterically. I turned my face away to not get hit, but maintained my hold, making sure her nose remained above the waterline.

"Here!" cried Katy's voice. "This way!"

I heaved my head up to see Katy and Win were lying on their stomachs on the patio closest to me, their arms reaching out. I propelled myself through the water toward them, struggling to hold on to the squirming child.

When I got close, I thrust the toddler toward them. They grabbed her and pulled her up.

I threw my weary arms on the dock, still in the water, my heart hammering, trying to catch my breath. It had happened so fast, my mind was a whir of emotions.

An ambulance siren sounded somewhere in the distance.

Katy and Win laid the child gently on the wooden patio. She had stopped flailing and crying, and was now completely still.

My heart skipped a beat.

Is she dead?

Two officers rushed over with a first-aid kit and pushed Katy and Win aside. We watched silently as they gave CPR to the child, praying, hoping against hope.

It felt like an eternity before the little girl coughed out water.

"She's breathing," called out one officer.

Win gave a subdued cheer. Katy collapsed on the patio, a hand over her heart. Relief flooded my body.

I hadn't realized I had been holding my own breath. Suddenly, I felt like my entire body was being pulled down by an unseen force. I was about to sink to the bottom of the lake. My exhaustion was overcoming me.

I reached out to pull myself out. Katy and Win seized me by my arms to help me out of the water and onto the patio. I sat with my friends, breathing hard, dripping wet.

More hollering and running footsteps.

Within seconds, the back patio of the navy-blue float home was swarming with paramedics. The police officers stepped aside to give them space.

We all watched as they put an oxygen mask on the girl and strapped her to a stretcher. She was so tiny, we could only see the mask jutting out once they were done.

Someone put a blanket around my shoulders.

I looked up. It was Katy.

"She'll be all right," she murmured, pulling me to my feet. "Her father and grandfather are still alive. She'll have someone to take care of her."

Win put an arm around my shoulder, ignoring my wet clothes. The three of us huddled together as we watched the paramedics carry the girl away on the stretcher.

Davies wobbled out the back door and wiped his sweat-soaked face with the back of his hand.

He stared at us for a moment, then gave us a brief nod, like he was at a loss for words, too shocked by the discoveries.

I nodded back. There was nothing more to say to him.

The person I wanted to talk to was Chris Grayson. I had to tell him everything, but I was too weary to speak.

I may not have prevented the deaths of Jane or Lily, but at least we had saved his granddaughter's life.

At that moment, that was all that mattered.

Back in New York

Chapter Sixty-four

"Remind me to never, ever travel with you," said Luc, glowering from behind the three-tiered birthday cake he was icing.

That jab was targeted at me.

I took a bite of the delicious black forest cupcake and tried not to make eye contact. When my chef got mad, it was best to let him vent and wait it out.

Luc hadn't forgiven me for not putting Win on the next flight home after she had been discharged from the hospital. My assertion that Win was a grown woman who made her own decisions fell on deaf ears.

As far as Luc was concerned, I was head investigator and had put my team, which included his wife, in the line of fire.

But this was temporary. He was going to come around when he needed help with a new recipe.

Win was sitting next to me, her entire focus on her laptop. She hadn't heard a word of the accusations Luc had been lobbing my way all morning.

The USB stick had divulged a lot more information on Thomas's operations than anyone had expected. While Win had relinquished the device to the police, she had secretly made a copy for herself and was poring through it, stopping every few minutes to announce yet another one of Thomas's nefarious schemes.

Even with an upset chef at my bakery, I was glad to be home.

It felt good to finally sleep in my own bed and get a much-needed hug and kiss from David. He had missed me too, but he knew better than to complain about my moonlighting work.

We were now all gathered around the kitchen counter at my bakery with an unexpected visitor.

Tetyana had taken two days of leave to join us in New York. Unlike the others, her intention was less to satisfy her curiosity and more to dress me down for being rash. She never gave up the chance to play big sister. But I knew she meant well.

"I can't believe I missed all this," she said, slamming her palm on the counter. "Why didn't you call me?"

"Hey!" Luc raised his head from behind his cake again, his glower turned on Tetyana. "None of that here. This is not some cop's mess hall."

Katy poured herself a cup of tea and turned to Tetyana. "We didn't want to bother you, hun. You have an important job now."

"What in damn hell...." Tetyana stopped and swallowed as Katy glared at her.

Little Chantelle was sitting by her mother, busy with a coloring book, but her impressionable mind was soaking everything in, I was sure.

"What I mean to say is you should have called me and given it to me straight," said Tetyana, lowering her voice and choosing her words more carefully. "Asha, your messages were cryptic and convoluted. A stolen limo license plate number? What was I supposed to do with that?"

I shrugged. "I didn't know the limo was stolen, and the plate was a fake."

"I know you girls can take care of yourself, but seriously?" Tetyana let out a frustrated hiss. "Next time, give it to me straight. And give me details. I will make the time to help you."

"You're FBI now," I said, waving my cupcake at her. "Why would you want to deal with small-time investigations anymore?"

Tetyana leaned back with a shocked expression on her face.

"A bank robbery, a corrupt cop, two murders, a kidnapping of a minor, and a major counterfeit operation are what you're calling small-time crime?"

She lifted her hand to slam it on the counter again. Luc raised his head. She let her hand fall and gave a resigned sigh instead.

"This entire investigation should have been dealt with by the FBI."

"But we solved it," said Katy, giving her a bright smile. "We saved the little girl's life. Chris Grayson brought Miles and his granddaughter into his home. All's well that—"

"Hey everyone!"

We turned toward the open kitchen doorway. Davis and Peace were entering in their white jujitsu uniforms.

Peace had only signed up to David's martial arts school next door after Katy complained his midriff was starting to bulge, but his healthy and happy face said he actually might be enjoying his weekly lessons.

"No, Max," said Luc, wagging a finger at the German Shepherd who had followed David and Peace here. "You know you're not allowed in the kitchen."

With a small whine and an exaggerated sigh, Max sat down at the threshold and put his head in between his massive paws.

"Aw, that face," said Tetyana, who had never fawned over anybody in her life before, but had taken a liking to our pup. "Let him in, will you?"

"And get shut down by a health inspector?" snapped Luc. "No, thanks."

"Any news on the dead rat?" said David, taking the stool next to me and circling his arms around my waist.

I shook my head.

"The police still think it's a juvenile delinquent, a street kid having fun. They took the rat to their lab for testing. I'm not sure what they will find, but I have a feeling it's low down in their list of priorities."

"You should tell them what you do for a living," said Tetyana, wiggling her brows. "Tell them about this case you solved. The entire local force will worship you then."

I smiled. "Tempting, but I promised Mary and Chris I wouldn't breathe a word about what happened to anyone. They have gone through so much as it is. They deserve their privacy."

"How are Mary and Oliver doing?" said David, a concerned expression on his face.

"Devastated but recovering," Katy sighed. "We visited them in Portland before flying over. I think she appreciated us sharing the news personally. They're planning a trip to Seattle to visit Chris and his new family this weekend."

"That little girl will save them," I said. "She'll perk everyone up, despite all that has happened."

"One life ends as another begins," murmured Luc from behind his cake.

"Did they round up all the gangsters in the end?" said Peace, reaching for the coffeemaker. "With all the evidence against them, that's one legal case I wouldn't touch with a hundred-foot pole."

"Thomas is persona non grata with the local cops," said Katy. "I don't even want to think of the treatment he's going to get in prison."

"I suspected Davies at the beginning, but he was just an arrogant jer..." I stopped as I caught Katy's eyes. "I mean a very rude person."

"How did they ever get into the bank?" said Peace with a frown. "That took a lot of guts and resources."

"Thomas had his hand in everything," said Win, looking up from her laptop. "I found a list of his accomplices in that USB stick. He had been wheeling and dealing with small business owners, security companies, bank managers, gang leaders, drug dealers, crooked politicians. You name it."

"So, the bank manager was in on this?"

"Thomas paid him cash to disable the alarm system that morning. He also paid the bank's security contractor to stay quiet about what happened."

"The two guards didn't know what hit them that night, then?" said David.

"Thomas wanted to make the robbery appear authentic." I shook my head. "I feel bad for the guards, but they will recover. They're young and have a future ahead of them. They'll have to find new jobs to pay for college, though, because their boss is now in jail."

"Didn't anyone realize Thomas was paying them off with fake money?"

"Davies and Lee said it was the best counterfeit they had ever seen," said Katy. "Probably fooled many people. Even a bank manager."

"Did you know Thomas got a local computer company to tap Chris Grayson's phone and install bugs in his house?" said Win. "Thomas even got into his computer and wrote creepy emails, and he stole Jane's diary. He royally messed with his brother's mind."

"How did he—" began Peace.

"He had an extra pair of keys to his brother's home and snuck in when he wasn't around," I said. "I can't blame poor Chris for being paranoid."

"What about Geena?" said David. "She sounds like quite the character."

I turned to him. "She was also having an affair with Thomas. They had been dating, if you can call it that, ever since they were teenagers. They kept it a secret from the family. He used her for small jobs and bought her that home to keep her compliant and happy."

"So, Geena knew all along?"

"Sadly, yes. She was also the only other person who knew what had happened to Thomas's parents, but she was too afraid to speak up."

Katy tsked. "Her loyalty to her lover, who took her out of her trailer home and gave her a better life, was far greater than doing the right thing."

"Will Chris Grayson go to jail for killing his parents?" said Luc, popping out from behind his cake again.

We had asked Davies and Lee that same question, but they had seemed reluctant to answer, not because of police business this time, but because they simply didn't know.

"It was an accident," I said. "I asked Grayson about it, and he said he will pay for what he did."

"His attorneys will need to check the statute of limitations," said Peace. "If it does get to court, the judge might grant some leniency."

"I just feel bad for Lily's girl," said Katy, caressing Chantelle's hair. "What a rough life that little one has had."

"She'll be all right," I said, more to make my good friend feel better than anything. "Chris wrote a new will, leaving everything to her. She will have the time and the resources to recover from the ordeal—"

The back door banged opened and in walked the rest of Luc's team from their break, giggling at some joke or the other.

Katy and I got up to give Sarah, Rosalie, and Bibi hugs and say hello.

The bakery phone rang, and Bibi leaped on it.

"Red Heeled Rebels bakery."

We fell silent. Bibi frowned as she listened to the caller.

"All right everybody," said Luc, straightening up. "We have cakes to bake and deliveries to make. Shoo."

Everyone picked up their half-eaten cupcakes, coffee cups, teacups, phones, and laptops and straggled out of the kitchen. Max stood up and wagged his tail furiously, realizing the party was shifting his way.

I slipped my arm around David's waist and walked out, hugging him close. It was good to be home.

Continue the adventure!

If you liked the Merciless series, you'll enjoy the brand new Tanya Stone FBI K9 mystery thriller series set in the west coast town of Black Rock.

FBI Special Agent Tanya Stone (Tetyana with a new name) goes undercover with her trusted German Shepherd K9 to hunt small-town monsters. But nothing in Black Rock is what it seems. The serial killer could be anyone. He could be standing right behind you...

Flip to the end of this book to read the first chapter of this spine-tingling new FBI mystery thriller.

Or, get HER COLD BLOOD, the first book in the new series, right now right here: www.TikiriHerath.com/Thrillers

Tick Tock. The clock is ticking. No one is safe in this seaside town.

Author's Note

D ear reader,

Did you enjoy this book?

My promise is to give you an exciting escape with every novel I write, and I sure hope I have done so.

If you have a minute, I'd much appreciate it if you would leave an honest review of this book on Amazon, Goodreads, or Bookbub. Just one sentence would do.

Honest reader reviews help my books get selected for international book promotions and I get to reach more readers.

Thank you so much.

One more thing.

If you'd like to learn the backstory of Tetyana, Asha, and Katy, flip to the end of this book to learn about the spin-off series that tells their stories.

The Red Heeled Rebels is an international crime series and is the origin story that shows how they all met. It spans four continents and features the back stories of everyone in this found family.

The Tanya Stone FBI K9 Thriller series features Tetyana as Special Agent Tanya Stone and her German Shepherd partner, Max, hunting a devious serial killer in a small seaside town on the West Coast.

Enjoy the reads!
My very best wishes,
Tikiri
Vancouver, Canada

PS: Join the VIP Red Heeled Rebels Club and receive your exclusive gift!

HER DEADLY END is a 250-page twisty thriller about an unusual murder-suicide case that Agent Tanya (Tetyana), Asha, and Katy accidentally stumble upon while vacationing in Paradise Cove. It's a pulse-pounding, nerve-shredding mystery of a devious serial criminal stalking a small seaside town in Washington State.

Click the link below to join the club and get your free book gift.

HER DEADLY END: A gripping thriller with a twisty end
https://books.tikiriherath.com/ts-b0-mmm-herdeadlyend

PPS/ If you didn't enjoy the story or spotted typos, would you drop a line and let me know? Or just write to say hello. I would love to hear from you and personally reply to every email I receive.

My address is: Tikiri@TikiriHerath.com

Her Cold Blood

Book One of the Tanya Stone FBI K9 Mystery Thriller Series

Chapter One - Escape to Death

His heavy footsteps thundered on the concrete floor.

Laura's blood chilled.

Her small naked feet propelled her forward like they had a life of their own. She didn't realize she was leaving trails of blood in her wake, like breadcrumbs for him to follow.

His footsteps got louder.

Terror coursed through her veins. Her heart beat so hard she was sure it would explode.

She wasn't going back to that dank basement, where she'd get strapped down like an animal to be butchered.

No!

Laura raced through the whitewashed corridors of the eerie underground maze. It smelled like a slaughterhouse in there. She passed the ominous red door, but didn't dare look that way.

Behind that door was where the nightmares began. Ones you could never escape from. Her mind spun like the head of an exorcist doll, mad memories exploding like fireworks.

Keep running.

The fluorescent light fixtures on the bare ceiling flickered and buzzed. It was like they were signaling her position to her captor.

Faster!

He was stomping down the stairs, calling her name. A second familiar voice hollered after him. Laura's heart sank.

Is she coming after me, too?

A loud plop sounded on the wall beside her. White plaster exploded into a thousand pieces and sprayed the corridor, stinging her bare arms and thighs.

She ducked and covered her head.

Another plop.

The wall plaster sprayed over her like gun shrapnel.

He's shooting at me!

She glanced back, her eyes wild with horror, expecting to spot him at the other end, but the corridor was empty.

He's shooting blindly. He doesn't know where I am.

She opened her right palm and looked at the crumpled paper she'd been clutching.

Quick.

She stuffed it into her mouth.

If they find me dead, they'll know who did it.

Laura spun around and rocketed through the corridor, trying hard not to make a sound.

Almost there.

She reached the door at the end of the tunnel, grabbed the handle, and turned it.

The force of the heavy basement door hurled her backward. Bright sunlight streamed through the narrow stairway, blinding her, but she didn't have a second to lose.

She raced up, her chest heaving, barely hearing the steel basement door clang shut behind her.

She halted on the top step and blinked, disoriented.

Rows of roses burst in colors next to a manicured cedar hedge. Tall, stately trees lined the perimeter, like giant sentinels shielding the house from the rest of the world.

From afar, she could hear waves crash against the shore below. She wasn't far from the Black Rock cliffs.

Her eyes darted back and forth, desperate for an escape. That was when she noticed the wall that ran along the property line.

Her heart sank.

She was trapped.

Again.

There was only one thing to do now.

She leaped toward the closest tree and grabbed the lowest branch. Holding on, she scrambled up the oak trunk like a monkey.

She clambered higher and higher on her wobbly legs, ignoring the rough bark scraping her bare skin, propelled by her will to live.

She was halfway up when the basement door banged open. She froze and squinted through the leafy foliage.

They're here!

She turned and peered over the wall.

Freedom.

The hiking trail was down below. The path she'd walked only a few days ago, before he seized her and....

Think! What do I do now?

The massive oak tree spread over the enclosure, giving shade to the trail outside. Clinging to a branch, she inched toward the wall.

"Laura! Come back right now!" came a furious male voice. "Get down or I'll punish you!"

But Laura wasn't listening to him anymore. She kept moving, clutching whatever she could. Her entire body was trembling so hard, she was scared her hands would slip.

"I'm warning you. Get down or I'll shoot to kill!"

He's lying.

He hated spilling even one ounce of precious blood. He needed her alive. That's why he had fired his weapon near her. Not at her.

She teetered over the wall, ignoring the furious shouting below.

The bough bowed dangerously. It was too thin at the end.

The branch snapped with a loud crack. Laura fell through the air, barely feeling her T-shirt rip against a sharp twig.

The cold air rushed against her face. Then she heard an ugly thump, followed by a searing pain that scorched through her frail body. Her head hammered like an army battalion had stormed inside and was firing machine guns.

She tried to open her eyes, but all she could see was a blur of blinking stars. She felt something crumbly next to her cheek.

Dirt.

A dog barked nearby.

Someone was shouting. She didn't recognize the voice.

Help. Please. Help me. Her cries were deafening inside her head, but her throat refused to work.

The barking was muffled, but so close.

Laura tried to raise her head, but she couldn't move.

Help me.

A dog barked again.

Wait.

It was an entire pack of dogs.

To be continued....

———◆———

Continue the adventure!

HER COLD BLOOD is the first book in the Agent Stone FBI Mystery Thriller series.

Agent Tanya Stone stumbles across a dying girl in a ditch by a lonely hiking trail. The girl's last words are chilling as they are disturbing.

A serial predator is terrorizing the idyllic west coast town of Black Rock. Agent Stone will have to fight her own past nightmares to unmask the psychopath hiding among the townsfolk.

Don't miss out on this fast-paced and spine-tingling murder mystery thriller featuring Special Agent Tanya Stone, Max the indomitable K9 German Shepherd, Chief Jack Bold, and the characters of this small seaside town, each of whom have their own dark secrets.

www.TikiriHerath.com/Thrillers

Available globally soon in e-book, paperback, and hardback editions on all Amazon stores. Also, soon to be available for free in libraries everywhere. Just ask your friendly local librarian to order a copy via Ingram Spark.

Debate this Dozen

Twelve Book Club Questions

1. Who was your favorite character?
2. Which characters did you dislike?
3. Which scene has stuck with you the most? Why?
4. What scenes surprised you?
5. What was your favorite part of the book?
6. What was your least favorite part?
7. Did any part of this book strike a particular emotion in you? Which part and what emotion did the book make you feel?
8. Did you know the author has written an underlying message in this story? What theme or life lesson do you think this story tells?
9. What did you think of the author's writing?
10. How would you adapt this book into a movie? Who would you cast in the leading roles?
11. On a scale of one to ten, how would you rate this story?
12. Would you read another book by this author?

The Reading List

The Red Heeled Rebels universe of mystery thrillers, featuring your favorite kick-ass female characters:

Tanya Stone FBI K9 Mystery Thrillers
www.TikiriHerath.com/Thrillers
NEW FBI thriller series starring Tetyana from the Red Heeled Rebels as Special Agent Tanya Stone, and Max, as her loyal German Shepherd. These are serial killer thrillers set in Black Rock, a small upscale resort town on the coast of Washington state.
Her Deadly End
Her Cold Blood
Her Last Lie
Her Secret Crime
Her Dead Girl
Her Perfect Murder
Her Grisly Grave
Coming soon!

Asha Kade Private Detective Murder Mysteries
www.TikiriHerath.com/Mysteries
Each book is a standalone murder mystery thriller, featuring the Red Heeled Rebels, Asha Kade and Katy McCafferty. Asha and Katy receive one million dollars for their favorite children's charity from a secret benefactor's estate every time they solve a cold case.

Merciless Legacy
Merciless Games
Merciless Crimes
Merciless Lies
Merciless Past
Merciless Deaths
One more to come.

Red Heeled Rebels International Mystery & Crime - The Origin Story
www.TikiriHerath.com/RedHeeledRebels
The award-winning origin story of the Red Heeled Rebels characters. Learn how a rag-tag group of trafficked orphans from different places united to fight for their freedom and their lives, and became a found family.

The Girl Who Crossed the Line
The Girl Who Ran Away
The Girl Who Made Them Pay
The Girl Who Fought to Kill
The Girl Who Broke Free
The Girl Who Knew Their Names
The Girl Who Never Forgot
This series is now complete.

The Accidental Traveler

www.TikiriHerath.com

An anthology of personal short stories based on the author's sojourns around the world.

The Rebel Diva Nonfiction Series

www.TikiriHerath.com/Nonfiction

Your Rebel Dreams: 6 simple steps to take back control of your life in uncertain times.

Your Rebel Plans: 4 simple steps to getting unstuck and making progress today.

Your Rebel Life: Easy habit hacks to enhance happiness in the 10 key areas of your life.

Bust Your Fears: 3 simple tools to crush your anxieties and squash your stress.

Collaborations

The Boss Chick's Bodacious Destiny Nonfiction Bundle
Dark Shadows 2: Voodoo and Black Magic of New Orleans

Tikiri's novels are available around the world, on all Amazon stores everywhere. The nonfiction books are available on Apple, Kobo, Barnes & Noble, Indigo Chapters, and all good bookstores around the world.

All these books are also available in libraries everywhere. Just ask your friendly local librarian or your local bookstore to order a copy via Ingram Spark.

Happy reading.

Tanya Stone FBI K9 Mystery Thrillers

How far would you go to avenge your family's brutal murder?

<u>Tanya Stone FBI K9 Serial Killer Thrillers</u>

Her Deadly End

Her Cold Blood

Her Last Lie

Her Secret Crime

Her Dead Girl

Her Perfect Murder

Her Grisly Grave

To come!

A brand-new FBI K9 serial killer thriller series for a pulse-pounding, bone-chilling adventure from the comfort and warmth of your favorite reading chair at home.

Can you find the killer before Agent Tanya Stone?

www.TikiriHerath.com/thrillers

Some small-town secrets will haunt your nightmares. Escape if you can...

FBI Special Agent Tanya Stone has a new assignment. Hunt down the serial killers prowling the idyllic West Coast resort towns.

An unspeakable and bone-chilling darkness seethes underneath these picturesque seaside suburbs. A string of violent abductions and gruesome murders wreak hysteria among the perfect lives of the towns' families.

But nothing is what it seems. The monsters wear masks and mingle with the townsfolk, spreading vicious lies.

With her K9 German Shepherd, Agent Stone goes on the warpath. She will fight her own demons as a trafficked survivor to make the perverted psychopaths pay.

But now, they're after her.

Small towns have dark deceptions and sealed lips. If they know you know the truth, they'll never let you leave...

Each book is a standalone murder mystery thriller, featuring Tetyana from the Red Heeled Rebels as Agent Tanya Stone, and Max, her loyal German Shepherd. Red Heeled Rebels Asha Kade and Katy McCafferty and their found family make guest appearances when Tanya needs help.

There is no graphic violence, heavy cursing, or explicit sex in these books.

The dogs featured in this series are never harmed, but the villains are.

To learn more about this exciting new series and download the FREE novel—HER DEADLY END—as a gift, go to www.TikiriHerath.com/thrillers

Asha Kade Private Detective Murder Mysteries

How far would you go for a million-dollar payout?

The Merciless Murder Mysteries

Merciless Legacy

Merciless Games

Merciless Crimes

Merciless Lies

Merciless Past

Merciless Deaths

More to come!

———

Each book is a standalone murder mystery thriller featuring the Red Heeled Rebel, Asha Kade, and her best friend Katy

McCafferty, as private detectives on the hunt for serial killers in small towns USA.

There is no graphic violence, heavy cursing, or explicit sex in these books. What you will find are a series of suspicious deaths, a closed circle of suspects, twists and turns, fast-paced action, and nail-biting suspense.

www.TikiriHerath.com/mysteries

A newly minted private investigator, Asha Kade, gets a million dollars from an eccentric client's estate every time she solves a cold case. Asha Kade accepts this bizarre challenge, but what she doesn't bargain for is to be drawn into the dark underworld of her past again.

The only thing that propels her forward now is a burning desire for justice.

What readers are saying on Amazon and Goodreads:

"My new favorite series!"

"Thrilling twists, unputdownable!"

"I was hooked right from the start!"

"A twisted whodunnit! Edge of your seat thriller that kept me up late, to finish it, unputdownable!! More, please!"

"Buckle up for a roller coaster of a ride. This one will keep you on the edge of your seat."

"A must read! A macabre start to an excellent book. It had me totally gripped from the start and just got better!"

"A great whodunit with a lot of twists and turns along the way. The story was amazing!"

"I could not stop reading it. It was as if I was there witnessing the murders myself. The characters had depth and personality and backgrounds that were explained nicely. It was awesome!"

"Nothing is more terrifying than the fear of the unknown. Do you have any nails left? Another NAIL-BITING story from a very talented master storyteller!"

———⊱⊰———

A brand-new murder mystery series for a pulse-pounding, bone-chilling adventure from the comfort and warmth of your favorite reading chair at home.

Can you find the killer before Asha Kade does?

———⊱⊰———

To learn more about this exciting series and download the FREE novel—HER DEADLY END—as a gift, go to www.TikiriHerath.com/mysteries.

Sign up to Tikiri's VIP reader club to get the chance to win personalized paperback books, chat with the author and more.

———⊱⊰———

Available globally in e-book, paperback, and hardback editions on all Amazon stores. Print books are available for free in libraries everywhere. Just ask your friendly local librarian or your local bookstore to order a copy via Ingram Spark.

The Red Heeled Rebels International Mystery & Crime

The Origin Story

Would you like to know the origin story of your favorite characters in the Tanya Stone FBI K9 mystery thrillers and the Asha Kade Merciless murder mysteries?

In the award-winning Red Heeled Rebels international mystery & crime series—the origin story—you'll find out how Asha, Katy, and Tetyana (Tanya) banded together in their troubled youths to fight for freedom against all odds.

<u>The complete Red Heeled Rebels international crime collection:</u>
Prequel Novella: The Girl Who Crossed the Line
Book One: The Girl Who Ran Away
Book Two: The Girl Who Made Them Pay

Book Three: The Girl Who Fought to Kill
Book Four: The Girl Who Broke Free
Book Five: The Girl Who Knew Their Names
Book Six: The Girl Who Never Forgot
The series is now complete!

———⋈———

An epic, pulse-pounding, international crime thriller series that spans four continents featuring a group of spunky, sassy young misfits who have only each other for family.

A multiple-award-winning series which would be best read in order. There is no graphic violence, heavy cursing, or explicit sex in these books. **www.TikiriHerath.com/RedHeeledRebels**

———⋈———

In a world where justice no longer prevails, six iron-willed young women rally to seek vengeance on those who stole their humanity.

If you like gripping thrillers with flawed but strong female leads, vigilante action in exotic locales and twists that leave you at the edge of your seat, you'll love these books by multiple award-winning Canadian novelist, Tikiri Herath.

Go on a heart-pounding international adventure without having to get a passport or even buy an airline ticket!

———⋈———

What readers are saying on Amazon and Goodreads:
"Fast-paced and exciting!"
"An exciting and thought-provoking book."
"A wonderful story! I didn't want to leave the characters."
"I couldn't put down this exciting road trip adventure with a powerful message."

"Another award-worthy adventure novel that keeps you on the edge of your seat."

"A heart-stopping adventure. I just couldn't put the book down till I finished reading it."

"Kept me mesmerized and captivated with the rich descriptions which made me feel like I was actually inside the story."

"This is a fantastic read that will have you traveling the globe. I absolutely loved this book. You won't be able to put it down!"

"A real page-turner and international thriller. Reminds me of why I've always loved to read. Because I can visit worlds and places, I wouldn't ordinarily get to see."

Literary Awards & Praise for The Red Heeled Rebels books:

- Grand Prize Award Finalist - 2019 Eric Hoffer Award, USA

- First Horizon Award Finalist - 2019 Eric Hoffer Award, USA

- Honorable Mention General Fiction - 2019 Eric Hoffer Award, USA

- Winner First-In-Category - 2019 Chanticleer Somerset Award, USA

- Semi-Finalist - 2020 Chanticleer Somerset Award, USA

- Winner in 2019 Readers' Favorite Book Awards, USA

- Winner of 2019 Silver Medal - Excellence E-Lit Award, USA

- Winner in Suspense Category - 2018 New York Big Book Award, USA

- Finalist in Suspense Category - 2018 & 2019 Silver Falchion Awards, USA

- Honorable Mention - 2018-19 Reader Views Literary Classics Award, USA

- Publisher's Weekly Booklife Prize - 2018, USA

———※———

To learn more about this addictive series, go to **www.TikiriHerath.com/RedHeeledRebels** and receive the prequel novella - **The Girl Who Crossed The Line** - as a gift.

Sign up to Tikiri's VIP reader club and get short stories, exotic recipes, the chance to win paperbacks, chat with the author and more.

———※———

Available globally in e-book, paperback, and hardback editions on all Amazon stores. Print books are available for free in libraries everywhere. Just ask your friendly local librarian or your local bookstore to order a copy via Ingram Spark.

Inspiration

Note: These external links are shared for interest and fun and their active status cannot be guaranteed.

Seattle's Floating Homes

https://www.seattleafloat.com

https://houseboatsofseattle.com

Floating Home Lists for $2.8 million

https://www.mansionglobal.com/articles/floating-home-on-seattles-lake-union-lists-for-2-85-million-01629323358

Abandoned Historic Bank Vault

https://www.youtube.com/watch?v=8t1L6I-r5j8

Toddler Locked in Bank Vault

https://www.nbcnews.com/id/wbna41794596

Biggest Bank Robberies of All Time

https://moneywise.com/life/entertainment/the-biggest-bank-robberies-of-all-time

Counterfeit Money

https://losspreventionmedia.com/8-ways-to-spot-counterfeit-money

Acknowledgments

To my amazing, talented, superstar editor, Stephanie Parent, thank you, as always, for coming on this literary journey with me and for helping make these books the best they can be.

To my international team of beta readers who gave me their frank feedback, thank you. I truly value your thoughts.

In alphabetical order of first name:

Kristen Harnish, United States of America

Laura Edwards, United States of America

Michele Kapugi, United States of America

To all the kind and generous readers who take the time to review my novels and share their frank feedback, thank you so much. Your support is invaluable.

I'm immensely grateful to you all for your kind and generous support, and would love to invite you for a glass of British Columbian wine or a cup of Ceylon tea with chocolates when you come to Vancouver next!

About the Author

Tikiri Herath is the multiple-award-winning author of international thriller and mystery novels and the Rebel Diva books.

———※———

Tikiri worked in risk management in the intelligence and defense sectors, including in the Canadian Federal Government and at NATO. She has a bachelor's degree from the University of Victoria, British Columbia, and a master's degree from the Solvay Business School in Brussels.

Born in Sri Lanka, Tikiri grew up in East Africa and has studied, worked, and lived in Europe, Southeast Asia, and North America throughout her adult life. An international nomad and fifth-culture kid, she now calls Canada home.

She's an adrenaline junkie who has rock climbed, bungee jumped, rode on the back of a motorcycle across Quebec, flown in an acrobatic airplane upside down, and parachuted solo.

When she's not plotting another thriller scene or planning another adrenaline-filled trip, you'll find her baking in her kitchen with a glass of red Shiraz in hand and vintage jazz playing in the background.

To say hello and get travel stories from around the world, go to
www.TikiriHerath.com